Unholy Birth

I0573710

ANDREW NEIDERMAN

POCKET STAR BOOKS

New York   London   Toronto   Sydney

If you purchased this book without a cover you should be aware that this book is stolen property. It was reported as "unsold and destroyed" to the publisher and neither the author nor the publisher has received any payment for this "stripped book."

Pocket Star Books
A Division of Simon & Schuster, Inc.
1230 Avenue of the Americas
New York, NY 10020

This book is a work of fiction. Names, characters, places, and incidents either are products of the author's imagination or are used fictitiously. Any resemblance to actual events or locales or persons living or dead is entirely coincidental.

Copyright © 2007 by Andrew Neiderman

All rights reserved, including the right to reproduce this book or portions thereof in any form whatsoever. For information address Pocket Books Subsidiary Rights Department, 1230 Avenue of the Americas, New York, NY 10020

First Pocket Star Books paperback edition August 2007

POCKET STAR BOOKS and colophon are registered trademarks of Simon & Schuster, Inc.

For information about special discounts for bulk purchases, please contact Simon & Schuster Special Sales at 1-800-456-6798 or business@simonandschuster.com.

Cover design by John Vairo Jr.; Baby carriage © Adrianna Williams; Mountainside © Paul Mason/Photonica/Getty Zefa/Corbis Images

10 9 8 7 6 5 4 3 2 1

ISBN 978-1-4516-3188-3

Also by Andrew Neiderman

Finding Satan

The Hunted

Deficiency

The Baby Squad

Under Abduction

Dead Time

Amnesia

Curse

Neighborhood Watch

In Double Jeopardy

The Dark

Duplicates

Angel of Mercy

The Solomon Organization

After Life

Sister, Sister

The Need

The Immortals

The Devil's Advocate

Bloodchild

Perfect Little Angels

Surrogate Child

Sight Unseen

Reflection

Playmates

The Maddening

Teacher's Pet

Night Howl

Love Child

Imp

Child's Play

Tender, Loving Care

Someone's Watching

Pin

Brainchild

Sisters

THE EVIL WITHIN

I almost fell into a deep sleep, but the phone rang. It's probably Willy checking up to see if I was okay, I thought, and smiled to myself as I said hello.

"Get an abortion," I heard.

"What?"

"Before it's too late. Get an abortion."

Even though I heard the caller hang up, I shouted, "Who the hell is this?"

And then I felt it again.

A stirring in my abdomen as if there really was a fetus developing within me and it had heard the threat and woke with terror inside my womb.

Publishers Weekly praises Andrew Neiderman's

THE BABY SQUAD:
"[A] nightmarish novel . . . fast-moving . . . intriguing."

. . . and *DEFICIENCY:*
"Neiderman unleashes a remorseless monster . . . in this fast-paced medical mystery."

For our children, Melissa and Erik,
who will always be HOLY BIRTHS to us.

Unholy Birth

Prologue

THE DREAM DREW ME up from the depths of a sleep so deep I thought I had been in a coma.

My stomach felt as sore as the stomach of a woman who had just suffered severe labor contractions.

My feet actually were pulled in, my knees up, my legs spread.

"What the hell are you doing?" Willy asked me.

She looked back at me over her shoulder, her body on pause, waiting for my answer. She wore an expression of confusion and from the way she gripped the blanket and from the way her body was poised, I thought she might just jump out of the bed to get away from me. Her light-brown untrimmed eyebrows arched, the right side just a little higher as usual. Strands of her recently cut hair curled at the base of her skull.

Morning sunlight filtered through the curtains threw a sheet of gauze over our king-size four-poster oak bed and the café au lait walls of our bedroom. The ceiling fan set on low looked like it was struggling to push the air. I had kicked the blanket away from myself, and a small part of my portion bundled about the size of a baby beside me.

My dream was so vivid, I was still too stunned to speak. I didn't move, didn't lower my legs, didn't lift my arms. Because of the way I was holding my head, I felt my neck muscles straining, the dull ache seeping into my shoulders.

"Huh?" Willy followed, starting to turn now.

"A dream," I said.

"What the hell kind of dream is this?" she asked, nodding at my knees, which were still up, and my legs, which were still spread.

"I dreamed I gave birth. It was the baby's cry that woke me," I said.

She slapped my right leg sharply and I dropped both my legs to the bed.

"You're driving me crazy," she said, and turned over again, tightly wrapping the blanket around herself.

"I'm getting up," I told her.

She grunted a "Whatever."

I went to the bathroom and stood by the cream and brown granite counter covered with my beauty aids and stared at myself in the large oval mirror. My face looked sunburned, red blotches over my cheeks and my forehead. There were even some on my neck. I was cold from sweating. I pulled my nightshirt over my head, surprised at how damp it was from my perspiration. I dropped it into the hamper and then stepped into the shower stall.

The warm water streamed between my breasts,

cascading down over my slightly bulging belly and then along the insides of my thighs. It felt so much like blood that I gazed at the drain expecting to see the red stained water spiraling down through the sewer pipes and into oblivion.

Leaning up into the flow of the shower, I enjoyed the pummeling over my face and my chest. My breasts ached. A quick review of dates told me it was too soon for a period, and I had always been clock-work regular. Willy was the erratic one. Her whole life, even her bodily functions, was characterized more by spontaneity than was mine. We were not two peas in a pod, but it was precisely the differences between us that brought us together. I believed we each harbored a secret desire to be more like the other, but neither of us would admit to it. There were times when anyone listening to us speak about each other would think we detested each other, not loved each other.

When I came out of the bathroom, wrapped in a large terry cloth towel with a smaller towel twisted around my hair like a Sikh turban, I found Willy sitting up in bed, her hands behind her head, lean-ing against the headboard, waiting. The blanket had fallen to her waist. Her perky firm breasts called to me the way they did most mornings. Her nipples were darker, slightly larger than mine, and seemingly always erect.

She dropped the corners of her mouth, draw-ing her full upper lip down and over her lower. The dimple in her chin deepened. Her eyes were soaking in suspicion.

"What are you going to tell me this dream means, Kate?" she asked before I could offer any explanation.

I shrugged. I didn't have to say it; I had said it many times, more frequently over the last few months.

She looked away, took a deep breath and looked back at me.

"Everything about us, our lives, our style, our pleasures will change. It drives friends away, too. They don't trust you anymore because you become totally different."

"Oh, that's silly, Willy. Why should our being a bigger family drive anyone away?"

"The whole country is twisted, hemorrhaging over questions like gay marriage, abortion, stem-cell research, and you want us to raise a child, bring a child into this . . ." She held her arms out and bounced them in the air as she panned our bedroom, "this mess?"

"I don't think it's such a mess, Willy. We make good money. We're better equipped to raise a child than most heterosexual couples."

"If there is anything you and I know, Kate, it's that money doesn't guarantee a good family life."

"It's one of the major things to consider. Besides, we're more stable than most people we know, aren't we?"

She looked away and then she lowered herself under the blanket again.

"It's Sunday, Kate. Our day off. From everything, including obsessions," she muttered, closed her eyes, slipped down under the cover and turned her back to me.

"Something bigger than us is telling us to do this," I said.

"Not telling us. Telling you. You're out of your mind. Go to the shrink your parents tried to arrange and pay for when you moved in with me."

"Stop it, Willy."

She was silent. We didn't push arguments anywhere near the point of no return. One or the other would simply clam up and leave the room.

I went out to the kitchen and turned on the coffee maker. While it began perking, I stood there pouting. If I were willing to undergo a pregnancy, why wouldn't she agree? Why shouldn't we have something more than ourselves? It was not an admission of failure to want a child in our lives. On the contrary, it was a statement illustrating the strength of our relationship because we were willing to sacrifice and cooperate and work together for greater things. How could I make her see that?

Maybe I couldn't.

Maybe Willy was too selfish to share anything. How could I go on living and loving someone like that?

On the other hand, I couldn't envision living without her.

The conflict put me into a depression.

She sensed it, of course, and came out. We had ESP when it involved each other's feelings and moods. She stood in the kitchen doorway, naked, her arms folded under her breasts, just glaring at me. Her neck muscles were taut, her jaw line distinct. Her whole body was clenched like a fist.

"What?"

"Just because you're having such vivid dreams about it, doesn't mean it's right for us, Kate. It's a decision not being made on rational grounds."

"Who's to say what's rational and what's not anymore?"

"Oh brother," she said. She nodded at me. "You're willing to go all the way, suffer through it, be a mother?"

"Hopefully, not alone," I said.

"Thanks for the invitation."

"It will make us stronger."

She shook her head.

"You're the one who believes in omens, in that sixth sense crap, but I'll tell you this," she said. "It frightens me on a primeval level."

"Primeval? Why?"

"I don't know why and I'll never mention it again. Consider yourself forewarned and I'll consider my responsibility to do that completed. Now you do what you want."

"Do what I want? What does that mean, Willy? What are you telling me?"

"I spoke my piece and that's all. Now go get pregnant," she said, and returned to the bedroom.

"Go get pregnant?"

I stood there, excited and yet a little terrified.

Already like a pregnant woman, I thought the combination was wonderful.

I.

THE FIRST QUESTION someone like me obviously has to ask herself is how are you going to do it? Making love with a man, even if it were done as impersonally as a medical exam, was abhorrent to me. I could count on the fingers of one hand how many men I had kissed on the lips, much less permitted to touch me anywhere intimate. It was always difficult for me even to imagine a relationship with a man. It never took me long to discover who I was. I never had to go in and out of any closet. It was my parents who kept themselves shut up, and still did. I hated to think of the excuses, the rationale they used to explain my lifestyle. They chose to live in some illusion. I supposed I should be grateful. They could have considered me dead and gone the way some of the parents of gay people I knew considered them.

Of course I realized that there were women who got married just to have children. The years were nicking away at them and they panicked to the point where they considered themselves sufficiently in love with a man to marry him. Afterward, after the children were born, these women lived what were practically separate lives. Their husbands were just a different sort of deliveryman.

But even that was clearly not for me.

What's more, there was the matter of inherited genes, resemblances. Whenever I looked at our child, would I always see the man I had employed, reminding me of what I had done? I could end up resenting my own child.

Employed was the kindest word I could use to explain it. It would make me feel like a john, not a prostitute. I'd be paying a man to have intercourse with me. If I didn't spend actual money, I would spend my self-respect.

Nevertheless, I realized it might be interesting to consider whom of the men we knew we would choose. He certainly wouldn't be anyone we had worked with or who worked for us. Would we choose on the basis of his personality or his looks? Money wasn't a concern.

Willy and I ran a successful catering business in Palm Springs, California. We had both begun our lives here as waitresses. Her first restaurant went out of business just before the end of the tourist season, and my first restaurant was set on fire either by the owner or by someone who hated him. It was definitely an unsolved arson.

Nevertheless, both Willy and I wanted to remain in the desert. It had become a comfortable place for the gay community. There were gay people involved in the local government and more and more gay entrepreneurs were opening their own restaurants, clothing stores, bars. There was even a small supermarket owned by two gay men right in the downtown area.

I didn't meet Willy in any gay watering hole. We both were hired by the manager of a new restaurant chain that was already known nationally to be a restaurant catering to gay people. The manager himself was not gay, but he did make an effort to staff it with as many gay people as he could find qualified. It was ironic because any restaurant not hiring someone because he or she was gay would be subject to a lawsuit.

Willy was not quite sure about me when we first met. There was never anything butch about me or anything else that would immediately give away my sexual identity. I wasn't particularly good at any sport. I had enjoyed acting in high school and during my first two years of college, but I dropped out after that, mainly because I had a disastrous love affair with another girl in my dorm. I liked gourmet cooking, and I was admittedly obsessed about my appearance, chasing a variety of skin products that claimed Fountain of Youth capabilities. I paid a lot of attention to my hair and wore it long, or at least what was considered long, which by now was merely down to the nape of my neck. I was also a clothes junkie, reading fashion magazines as obsessively as some members of the religious right read the Bible.

In short, I was what is called a femme, a feminine

woman who is attracted to masculine women or butches. I was really a high femme, a femme who dresses very femininely, high heels, skirts, makeup, the whole enchilada.

Whenever we sat around talking about ourselves, Willy enjoyed practicing amateur psychology and accused me of battling myself.

"You're still in denial about your sexual identity," she insisted. I knew she was just trying to bait me, but I couldn't resist arguing.

"I am not. That's ridiculous, especially in light of my personal history, where I am and whom I'm with, Willy."

"Not really. You're still carrying more baggage than I am or ever was. You came from a far, far more conservative world than I did. No matter how independent we claim to be, we still mourn the loss of parental approval. Your brother doesn't even talk to you anymore, Kate. You told me yourself that he and his wife are too embarrassed to admit you're related. Don't sit there and claim none of that wears on you."

"I'm not."

"It's all right. We both have our own demons. Just don't go any deeper into denial. You're still struggling with this heterosexual, good-girl thing," she insisted.

I knew she liked to tease me about it, but I think she was at least half serious when she suggested my sexual confusion was also a major motivation for my wanting to have a child.

"Nothing makes you more of a heterosexual woman than motherhood," she said. "Don't give me that word *parent*. You don't want to simply be some generic parent, Kate. You want to feel like a heterosexual woman inside as well as outside, and nothing will do that for you as well as pregnancy and birth. Otherwise, you would be talking about adoption. You don't even mention the concept."

I suspected that part of the reason why she brought these things up in discussion, whether she did it in a teasing manner or not, was to get me to develop a tougher skin. She wanted me to be more prepared to handle those demons she saw circling our wagons.

"Face up to this," she insisted, "otherwise, you'll spend your life in one form of denial or another and never be happy or comfortable. Believe me, I've seen it. It can destroy you."

She was always working at getting me to commit fully to our relationship, which ironically was one of my prime motivations for wanting the child in our lives in the first place. Why couldn't she see that as clearly as I could?

At times I thought I was so distasteful to her, I wondered why she remained with me. Because of her commitment to me despite my inner conflicts, I felt more assured about her love for me and I loved her more because of it. Although she could be as cold and as cruel to me as she was to anyone else, she wouldn't permit any other person to come close to saying these negative and nasty things to me.

She was butch.

She walked with a prizefighter's swagger. Her body was as tight and firm and muscular as any gymnast's body, and as a matter of fact, she had been one in high school and had won awards. At times I thought she could metamorphose into a steel arrow and shoot herself into an argument. I was probably the only soft, feminine thing she had ever permitted in her life. She often took a lot of heat because of me, but she never minded it or complained. In fact, there were occasions when I thought she looked for the arguments, the fights. She could just put on that sort of angry mood the way someone would put on a blouse.

After we had been together a while, I confessed to having been afraid of her when we first met. I told her she entered the restaurant like a gunslinger searching for a duel in the street and looked at me with some disdain.

"I thought you disapproved of everything about me, detested me, and made fun of me behind my back."

"I should have," she said.

Willy wasn't exactly the romantic type. Squeezing affectionate words out of her was as difficult as squeezing juice out of a dried, old orange, but when it came, it was sincere, so sincere, it took my breath away and made all the frustration and waiting worth it.

About six months into working at the restaurant,

we had been with each other long enough to consider moving in together. Once she saw how well I cooked and how our friends raved about my gourmet meals, she came up with the idea of our starting our own catering business. We didn't have enough money saved, but one of our still-in-the-closet bisexual friends, the wife of an attorney in town, convinced her husband to capitalize us so we could rent a small warehouse, equip it with stoves, walk-in refrigerators, dishware, etc., and rent a delivery vehicle and we were off and running.

We advertised a little, but it was truly word of mouth that built our business until we had to take on some help. Our service area expanded, and we even began to prepare dishes secretly for a Palm Springs restaurant. A number of magazine write-ups, some television exposure, and a few celebrity testimonies made it necessary to find a bigger warehouse and hire more employees.

Soon after, we bought a home in the Indian canyons of Palm Springs for over a million dollars. We could now service the mortgage. It had a drop-dead view of the mountains that boxed in the canyon, and at night we could see the light of the Palm Springs Tramway nearly 11,000 feet high. With a sizeable income, valuable property, and continually expanding business, I found myself thinking more and more about having the child.

Willy was right about my feelings concerning adoption. I never seriously considered the option even though most other gay couples we knew who had children had adopted. Our child had to be part of me. Maybe she was right in saying that was the heterosexual longing in me talking.

Willy was certainly right about the aftermath for these gay couples with children. They had so many new interests and demands that they moved away from our circle of friends. But I couldn't think of a friend with whom we were so close or upon whom we were so dependent that I wasn't willing to risk that friendship in the name of our own child.

However, up until relatively recently, I wasn't fully convinced gay people should have children. There were so many arguments against it. There wasn't a father figure, or in the case of gay men, there wasn't a mother figure. The children could suffer later when they went to school and other children found out who their parents were. They could grow up with all sorts of deep psychological issues. If they weren't gay themselves, they might feel they were betraying their parents or deeply criticizing them. Because gay marriage wasn't recognized as legitimate, they'd feel even weirder. On and on, the arguments rained down around me in books, on television, in news columns, as well as out of the mouths of other gay couples who vowed they would never adopt or have a child.

And after all, considering how my parents had reacted to my sexual identity, I was living through most of this myself. Willy loved to remind me about it.

But I was driven more and more toward having a child until I began to think Willy was right in saying my high femme stuff was just a psychological security blanket. Maybe I was trying to be more of a heterosexual female than I would care to admit. In the end I concluded that none of it mattered, however. I should do, we should do, whatever makes us feel more complete as people, not as gays or women or whatever we were. We should give something back to the world that was being so good to us, although whenever I said that aloud, people would look at me with eyes that said, "Please, stuff the bullshit."

Later that day, after she had risen, had her breakfast, and come out to the living room where I was watching a show on modern new house design, Willy plopped on the sofa, drew her legs up, and asked the question I was asking myself.

"So how are you going to do it, Kate? You going to get laid or what?"

"I don't know. I think it's a decision we should make together," I said.

"I already said I don't want to do this."

"You also just said do it. What I do, you do. Remember? You're the one who came up with that."

She smirked.

"Look," she continued, sitting up straight now, "I will admit I'm not going to be happy if you're not happy. The bottom line is if you feel incomplete, I'll feel incomplete, so yes, I said do it. If I had my druthers, I would rather you hated kids, period, but I'm not going to turn away from you, and besides, sometimes you're right," she added, which brought a smile to both our faces. "Rarely, but sometimes," she added quickly.

"Well, I suppose we could make a list of men we know who we'd both approve."

"That's going to be a short list. The last man I approved of was my father and that was only until I was five," she said.

"Would it bother you if I did it that way?"

She was silent, thinking.

"Maybe," she admitted.

"You're afraid I might enjoy it?"

"If you did, I'd kill you," she replied. "And him," she added.

I smiled and turned off the television. Finally, we were going to have a substantive conversation about this.

"The only reason I can think of doing it with a man we know is there is something we definitely think he adds positively."

"Maybe. It's just as much of a crap shoot the other way, isn't it?"

"I don't know, Willy. I haven't really gotten into this yet."

"Well, then why don't you do that before you work me up about it, stupid. Do some research."

She rose and then paused in the doorway.

"I'm going for a hike with some friends. I know

you don't want to get any calluses on your precious feet, so I won't bother asking you to go along."

"Who's going?"

"Paula, Arlene, and maybe Janet."

"Janet has a thing for you," I said.

"Just like you to say something dumb like that. You want me to curl up on that sofa with you all day and comfort you and soothe your worried mind about this baby thing instead of getting some fresh air and exercise, which you, a prospective mother, should have anyway?"

I shrugged.

"I know what I know. Janet drools when you walk into a room."

"Maybe she's coming down with rabies, Kate. I wouldn't do her with your dick," she added, and went to get ready for her hike.

She shouted her goodbye twenty minutes later. I was still on the sofa, soaking in the muck of my own thoughts. I shouted back and then I rose and went to the computer. If I really was going to do this, I had better do what she said. I had better get all the information I could about it so we could make a sensible discussion.

Otherwise, as Willy would say, I was just mentally masturbating.

In minutes I knew about the various sperm banks that existed and were approved in California. I saw that there even were banks that specialized in inseminating gay people, the sperm donated by gay men. I also found sites formed by individual men who were advertising their sperm and were willing to send it to a recipient at no cost. They all claimed to be motivated by the urge to do something good for other people, but I thought they were driven by swollen egos because every one of the sites by individual sperm donors I viewed described a man who was a genius if not near genius, wonderfully athletic, healthy with a perfectly balanced temperament and excellent family history. All claimed they would produce the necessary medical screening and tests for the sperm delivered.

I printed it all and organized the information for Willy to peruse when she returned from her hike, but as I sat there reading the material, I heard the "You've got mail" signal on the computer and returned to the monitor.

How odd, I thought, one of the sperm banks had contacted me, but I hadn't asked any questions or left any messages. I opened the e-mail and read.

Dear Prospective Mother,

Thank you for contacting Genitor. Genitor is licensed as a Tissue Bank by the State Department of Health in California. These are the strictest standards in the nation. We are eager to provide for your needs and invite you to interview the manager of our company, Dr. Lois Matthews. Dr. Matthews will come to you for the interview and will explain in detail how we screen donors. Please call 555-440-0001 and go to extension 100.

I recoiled in my chair and stared at the monitor. It was one thing to begin to investigate the idea, but another to have someone out there, someone other than Willy, aware of my intentions. I actually felt myself tremble with the shock of how easily someone on the outside could enter the sphere of your most intimate thoughts and actions.

My second reaction was indignation, anger. How dare whoever this was think he or she could contact me? I wasn't inquiring about furniture, clothes, a vacation. It was truly as if there were invisible antennae out there just waiting for you to move in one direction or another or even think aloud. Instantly, they picked it up and you were exposed. The walls of our homes were rapidly turning into glass, and it wasn't a deterrent to stop other people from throwing stones either. All your actions, your blood, your very DNA, your essence was easily on display. Technology and purveyors of Patriot Acts were battering privacy into some ancient memory. The word would soon disappear entirely from our vocabulary.

When I calmed my reflexive indignation, I reread the invitation. Wasn't this what I was really seeking after all? This particular company was just more aggressive than others, more entrepreneurial. In many ways Willy and I followed the same path to develop our catering business. We pursued prospective clients, leaping on every indication one might do business with us.

My annoyance gave way to curiosity. How did they manage this instant pursuit? Should Willy and I be using their techniques and doing something as obviously productive with our business, too? I was still sitting there thinking about it when she returned, hot and sweaty but invigorated. Before I could say a word, she was raving about the hike, the pack of coyotes they had seen, a hawk with a wingspan that was nearly as wide as a car, the cool breezes at the top of the hill, and the way she had left the others panting behind her.

"I thought I was climbing into the sky," she said.

I was jealous of Mother Nature. Nothing I could do with Willy or say to her would bring such ecstasy to her. She truly fed off her physical stamina and her health, sucked on the energy around her to feed her hunger for life. It was insatiable. Would our having a child in our midst add or detract from it? Was I about to destroy or build our relationship?

"What about Janet?" I asked.

"She might have died on the mountain. She was moaning and groaning, struggling to breathe like some beached whale. I didn't wait around to see."

"You just left them?"

"Hey. They knew from the start I wouldn't slow

myself down to let them keep up with me. It wasn't exactly a social tea."

"I don't know how you keep any friends."

"I'm taking a shower," she said. "And I'm starving so think of lunch."

"I have some of that information to show you," I called to her. She was already on her way to the bathroom. "And something very interesting happened!" I added.

I waited.

She returned to the doorway.

"Okay, what?"

I described what I had done and nodded at the monitor. The e-mail was still on the screen. She approached slowly and read it herself.

"You did nothing but go to their Web site?"

"I didn't even go to it. I did a simple search of sperm banks and a list came up of which this was one. Almost instantly, the e-mail came from this one called Genitor."

She thought a moment and then shrugged.

"Hey," she said, "you knocked on a door and someone answered. What's the big deal? Forget it."

"I don't want to forget it. First, I was indignant, but now I'm impressed. This company is on the ball."

"So call the doctor at that extension and make an appointment," she said slowly. "Do they bring it in vibrators or what?"

"Stop it," I said, laughing.

"Hey, it's not as farfetched as you might think. Remember when girls thought they could get pregnant sitting on dirty toilet seats?"

"No."

"I do. They thought they'd have to tell the kid his or her father was a Kohler or something."

"Go take your shower," I said. "You're about as much help as a toilet."

She nodded at the computer.

"Too bad you can't just do it all over the phone. Then you could tell him or her his or her father was Alexander Graham Bell. Or if it were done over the computer, you could tell the kid his father was a Pentium."

"Any other brilliant comments?"

"Naw. I think I used up today's quota. Let's think about lunch," she said. "Unlike children, you make it, eat it, and forget it," she added, and walked off.

At least she was being humorous and relaxed about it, I thought. I looked at the e-mail. The invitation seemed innocuous enough. There were no demands for down payments or anything to be signed. It simply said, "Hey, you want to find out more about this? We'll be glad to tell you."

I wished I could be like Willy about it, I thought. Once Willy made up her mind about anything, she put all the tension and the anxiety outside and forgot it, but something was lingering under my heart, some small, instinctive alarm.

It was too easy to shut it off or consider it just simple nerves.

I understood that I wouldn't know if that was a good or bad thing for some time, and by then, it would surely be too late to matter anyway. It was a lifetime commitment. You just don't give a child away the way you could give away a puppy or a kitten.

Could you?

I made the call.

2.

As was true for most of America in 2005, the real estate boom in the California desert communities was still well under way. The promise of overnight wealth had shifted from dot com companies to housing investments and that included developments, more gated communities, and expansion of existing ones. Palm Springs was the most famous desert community in the Coachella Valley. It wasn't the one developing with as much of a frenzy as the other communities farther east, but it was well into an economic growing pattern that included development of its famous Main Street. With its variety of restaurants and music, it began to resemble the French Quarter of New Orleans before the hurricane.

During the height of the season, the weekends were jammed with tourists walking the streets, eating on the outdoor patios, dancing, and enjoying the perfect weather, especially the clear and sharp night sky with stars and a moon that truly looked closer. It was romantic and exciting, injected with a joie de vivre that turned it into more than the simple water oasis the Indians had first discovered and settled. Now it was an oasis of pleasure in a desert of turmoil driven by the winds of war, terrorism, and corruption. For twenty-four to forty-eight hours, visitors could step into an adult Disneyland in which the sun seemed to always shine and the rains of turmoil and trouble were prohibited from entering. More than once, I heard people remark about how when they came east from Los Angeles toward Palm Springs, they could literally see the sky clear as if God had wiped his hand across the blue and declared this to be the safe haven.

Would it be that for us, always? If we permitted ourselves any fantasies, that was surely one. Where else would we go to enjoy this sense of well-being and protection? Willy would say we're with our own kind here. We don't have to be afraid of the eyes that turn to us. We could hold hands in the street, kiss, embrace, be ourselves.

And yet somehow the openly gay segment of the community didn't drive away the *straight* people from the resort. Willy hated the word straight more than I did. I admit it bothered me, but it enraged her to hear heterosexuals called straight.

"What does that mean, we're crooked, off-kilter, twisted? What?"

Even gay people referred to the heterosexuals as straight.

"You know what that's like?" Willy told them. "That's like black people using the word *nigger* to refer to their own kind. They accept the term. When you accept the term, you generate all the negative imagery about you that follows," she lectured. "You contribute toward it!"

Some agreed. Some just chalked her remarks up to the perennial chip on her shoulder.

"Relax. Forget it," she was advised. "Who cares what they think about us?"

"It's what we think about ourselves!" she would shout back over the chatter and music.

It most always came close to blows. Something had to redirect the conversation.

"I'm warning you," she told me at work the following day, "don't ever use or let anyone use the term *straight* in reference to our having a child. It's not a straight thing. It's our thing or else don't do it," she said.

"Okay," I said.

"If that Dr. Matthews uses that word when she comes to see us, we call the interview to an immediate end and ask her to get her ass out. Agreed?"

"I'll sign a paper so stating and have it notarized," I said.

She relaxed and we didn't discuss it any further. Dr. Matthews was coming on Wednesday night. According to its web site, Genitor was located just outside of Irvine, California. If she avoided the usual rush hours, she would be in Palm Springs in about an hour and a half. The fact that she would come that distance and spend so much time with us encouraged me about the company, but Willy was her usual skeptical and suspicious self.

"They might be desperate for business," she said. "Maybe because they're not that good."

I had a different view.

"Maybe, knowing our community, she thinks if she gets us, we'll tell others and she'll get more gay clients. Ever think of that? If any two people should know the value of word of mouth, Willy, it's you and I."

She grunted a reluctant "It's possible" but reserved her judgments for our interview and meeting. Of course, I kept anticipating her changing her mind about going forward. All day and all night until the hour of the meeting, I expected her to tell me she had made a mistake. We were making a mistake. We were rushing into it. Cancel the meeting until we had more time to think about it. Our business needs made it impossible at this time.

A few times I think she was about to do that. I caught her starting to say something, look at me, and then shake her head and keep silent. She concentrated more on our work, too, as if she didn't want to have to think about what we were contemplating. She went to sleep early and generally avoided me as much as she could. I saw it all, but I didn't challenge her for fear that if I brought it up, she would pounce and end it all.

"You look like you're about to give birth now," Willy told me the night we waited for Dr. Matthews to arrive.

I had been too nervous to eat much of a dinner.

Her ravenous appetite actually annoyed me. When I muttered something about it, she laughed.

"What am I supposed to do, Kate, act like an expectant father?"

Actually, what made me nervous was her being herself. She could be so intimidating that this Dr. Matthews would stammer some excuse and run out of the house.

"Be nice," I said when the doorbell sounded.

"Yes, Mommy," she replied. She sat back in our living room and flipped through the most recent issue of *Food Concepts*.

I took a deep breath and went to the front door.

It is amazing how the title of Doctor colors your view of people and triggers preconceptions. We're all comfortable with stereotypes. It's so much more difficult to have to make judgments about individuals. I know Willy was anticipating the same sort of person I was: intellectual-looking, not at all feminine, a combination of a female medical person and a businesswoman.

The woman who stood in our doorway was so different from that image, I wondered if she were someone else. She looked like a former Miss America, six feet tall if not a bit taller, with radiantly raven black hair in a classic Lana Turner style reminiscent of the Forties. In the patio lights, her almond-shaped ebony eyes were dazzling and full of warmth, even more highlighted because of her rich, peach complexion.

Her face was angular with classic high cheekbones, her features diminutive, her lips perfectly shaped and full.

She wore a turquoise cotton blouse that fit like another layer of skin and clearly outlined her shapely bosom. The ankle-length skirt of darker blue had an intricate pattern of red lines that looked hand-embroidered. Her feet were in a pair of thongs and she had a gold ankle bracelet on her right ankle.

I was immediately self-conscious about the way I had perused her body and clothing. I could see it amused her.

"Hi, I'm Lois Matthews," she said, leaving off her doctor title, which was obviously an attempt to get into an informal situation as quickly as possible. "Are you Kate Dobson?" she followed when I didn't automatically respond.

"Oh, yes. Please come in," I said stepping back.

She entered and looked around.

"What a beautiful home and what a view you have. It impressed me as soon as I drove up."

"Thank you."

"How long have you lived here?"

"We're in a little more than a year," I replied.

"What is it, about five, six thousand square feet?" she asked, looking at the house.

"Closer to six," I said.

"Lots of space. That's good when you're contemplating having children," she said lowering her voice.

It wasn't until that moment that it occurred to me

this could be an interview of us as much as it was to be an interview of her and her company.

"Please, come in," I said, leading her down the corridor to our living room where Willy sat, still pretending greater interest in the food magazine. She looked up, but held on to the magazine. I nearly laughed at the look of surprise on her face, too.

"This is my life partner, Wilma Radcliff," I said. "We all call her Willy."

"Please to meet you, Willy," Dr. Matthews said crossing the room. "Lois Matthews."

Willy rose and offered her hand, but said nothing.

"Please, have a seat," I said indicating the sofa. Dr. Matthews sat and placed her briefcase on the glass-top coffee table I had cleared in anticipation.

"We were wondering how you people work out that Internet contact," Willy began with a little more of an aggressive tone than I would have liked. "Kate said she didn't leave her name or e-mail address or anything. She merely began to do research for us."

"Yes, well, it's not unlike the way the phone system can work. You can reverse the incoming and see who's made the phone call. We have developed or had developed for us, I should say, the system that alerts us as to inquiries and then we follow up. If people wish to respond, we're happy to do what we can."

She turned to me. Her smile reminded me of the aluminum sheets some people put on the windows of their mountain houses to deflect the direct sunlight.

"We're grateful you took the time to drive here," I said, eyeing Willy. She had that impish smirk.

"How long have you been in business?" she asked Dr. Matthews.

"We're into our tenth year. How long have you two been together?" she countered.

"We're into our fifth year," Willy replied.

"Well, that shows some longevity, commitment on your part," Dr. Matthews said, nodding at me, too.

"As does your ten years," Willy replied. She loved verbal ping-pong. I felt like stamping my foot. "How did you get into this business or service, whatever you call it?"

"It's both. I didn't set out specifically to be in this enterprise. I decided to specialize in andrology."

"Which is?"

"The science of diseases of the male sex, especially those related to the male sex organs."

"How many sex organs do they have?"

"Willy!"

"Just kidding. Go on, Doctor," Willy said, looking sincerely interested now.

"I suppose I was moved to do this work when I learned that nearly ninety percent of impotence has a physical or physiological cause. A good deal of it is blamed on the female partner who gets labeled unfairly as frigid."

"Ah, so you're really doing this for women?" Willy said, jumping in like an attorney in a cross-examination.

Dr. Matthews smiled again.

"In every sense, Willy. Most females in a sexual relationship want their men to, shall we say, function properly? You would be surprised how many women are too embarrassed to push their husbands or partners into exploring the reasons for their failure to perform. Some leave the relationship and some . . ." She paused.

"What?" Willy asked, refusing to fill in any words for her.

"Find alternative means of satisfaction."

"Vibrators," Willy said, looking at me. "See?"

"Stop it," I mouthed.

"Among other things. After I was practicing for about three years, I was offered the position at Genitor, a position that turned into a full partnership. I'm working with some very good people," Dr. Matthews said, opening her briefcase and taking out a brochure she held up. The cover had pictures of three good-looking and distinguished-looking people. "Dr. McKinny is a certified urologist and a national authority now on sperm banking. Dr. Lasman is a board-certified pathologist and a recognized authority on semen storage. As you will see, we also employ a well-respected psychologist, Morgan Patterson, who has practiced family counseling in particular for over twenty-five years."

"What does a psychologist do with sperm?"

"He interviews prospective donors in particular," Dr. Matthews replied, ignoring Willy's sarcasm.

"There are some things you can't determine through lab testing and family history alone. Our clients are impressed with the service. I don't know many sperm banks that do it. There are many out there who only do the minimum required screening before sending out its donor package."

"Does it come in the mail?" Willy asked dryly.

"No," Dr. Matthews said smiling. "It's frozen. Cryopreserved sperm is frozen in liquid nitrogen at a temperature of minus 192 degrees Celsius. The sperm cells are held in a state of suspended animation, and all cellular activity is halted until thawing. It will be hand delivered. I might deliver it myself," she added and looked at me. "I know Kate contacted us, but which one of you is . . . ?"

"She's Mommy Dearest. I'm Dad," Willy said.

Dr. Matthews held her smile. Now it was more of a soft, almost angelic smile, possessed by someone who was truly at peace with herself. I longed for that smile.

"I don't mean to sound as if I'm prying, but our benefactors insist that we provide sperm donations only to truly qualified recipients."

"What does that mean?" Willy asked, her voice now bulging with resentment and aggression.

"Nothing whatsoever to do with rejecting gay couples. A majority of our business comes from the gay community lately," she said.

"Is that right?" I asked.

"We've not made a significant number of deliveries

to this area yet, but we have done quite a bit of work in the L.A. basin."

"Oh, is that so?" I practically sang, throwing a look of self-satisfaction at Willy. It looked like I was right about the motivation for Dr. Matthews making the trip.

Willy smirked, but sat back, relaxed.

"Okay," she said. "How do you define well-qualified recipients?"

"Obviously, we're concerned about the recipient's own health, age, sexual history. I'll get into further detail as we move along."

"Yes, we should move along," Willy said. "Give us the whole story."

Dr. Matthews laughed.

"It's a story, I suppose. Let me begin with the willing-to-be-known donors. Most prospective parents today believe that their children should be able to know their lineage to help them understand their identity. This does not mean the donors develop any sort of relationship with the children," she quickly added. "They are not required to meet them. The children simply have the right to know who they are and as much about them as you, the parents know. Where they take it from there is their own affair. We at Genitor do not release this information to the children until they've requested it after they have reached the age of eighteen. There are some sperm banks doing it earlier, but we're not one."

"Do we have to meet the donor?" Willy asked.

"Absolutely not."

"Oh, I'm sorry, Dr. Matthews, I didn't offer you anything to drink," I said.

"Please. Call me Lois."

"Lois. What would you like?"

"Just cold water would be fine," she said.

"Willy?"

"Get me a beer," she said as macholike as she could just to annoy and tease me.

Dr. Matthews did not lose her smile.

"What do you two do?" she asked as I rose to get the drinks.

"We own and operate a catering company. Kate designs the gourmet dishes and runs the business end and I manage the physical operation. Currently we employ six people, including two delivery personnel. We're well off enough to afford children," she added, raising her voice as I reached the door.

I hurried to get the drinks, terrified about leaving Dr. Matthews alone with Willy, but when I returned, they were both laughing.

"What's so funny?" I asked handing the glass of cold water to Dr. Matthews and then Willy her beer. I had poured myself a glass of pinot noir.

"What do you know, Kate. The good doctor here has just confessed to being bisexual," Willy told me.

"Confessed? I'll bet. How did you manage to get her to tell you that?"

Willy raised her hand to be sworn to tell the truth.

"She volunteered the information. I didn't fish or prod, did I, Lois?"

Once again she was being impish, suggesting that perhaps Dr. Matthews had made a pass at her.

"Oh?" I said. "That is interesting."

"And being bisexual is good for her work," Willy said, sipping her beer.

"Why is that, Willy?"

"This way she can get both perspectives on the sex act. Speaking of which, how the hell does she do it, Lois? Does she stand on her head while I pour it in or what?"

Dr. Matthews sipped some water and laughed.

"It's not complicated, but it has to be done correctly." She looked from Willy to me. "It's not part of our normal service, but I can assist," she said.

Willy nearly spilled her beer.

"My goodness," she said. "You really do love your work."

Dr. Matthews laughed again.

"Let's just say, Willy, that it's in our mutual interests for this to succeed. You get a child and our percentage of success goes up."

Willy looked at me, her eyes widened and that impish smile forming around her mouth.

Touché, we were both thinking.

"Well, Lois, it does sound like you guys got this down to a science. It's actually a lot more fascinating that I had anticipated," she said, suddenly sounding more interested in the whole thing than I had been.

Dr. Matthews smiled.

There was a pregnant pause as they held each other's gaze. I felt my heart skip a beat.

That was the first warning, the first note in the song of regret that I was destined to sing.

That we were both going to sing.

3.

"I know your biggest concerns will be about the sperm donation itself," Dr. Matthews continued.

Willy had finished her beer and had gotten another. She also talked Dr. Matthews into a glass of my pinot noir. When she went out to get that, she returned with a platter of goat cheese and multigrain crackers, a small bowl of olives, and some dried apricots. I couldn't remember when she was as cordial to a stranger in our home. Usually, the hospitality fell to me.

"Yes, of course. We're very concerned about that," I said, trying to be more businesslike.

"There has to be no evidence of HIV, hepatitis B or hepatitis C, human T-cell lymphotropic virus-1, and of course, syphilis. We screen our donors in accordance with the parameters recommended by the FDA, the American Society for Reproductive Medicine, the American Association of Tissue Banks, and the Center for Disease Control and Prevention."

"You forgot *Good Housekeeping*," Willy quipped. Dr. Matthews laughed.

"I know that sounds like overkill, but we believe it's better to err on the side of paranoia."

"Good name for the baby, huh Kate? Paranoia. Say, we haven't decided on the name," Willy remarked. She was nearly finished with her second beer. "Will it be Dobson or Radcliff?"

"I can offer no input on that matter," Dr. Matthews said quickly.

"Well, we do have at least nine months to figure it out," Willy said.

"I wouldn't wait until the last moment. Those sort of decisions should be well thought out beforehand."

"We always think out those sort of decisions beforehand," Willy said. "Our work has taught us the importance of proper preparations."

"That's good," Dr. Matthews said nodding.

I was beginning to feel like I wasn't in the discussion.

"Go on about the screening please, Dr. Matthews," I said sharply.

"Yes, of course. We use only cryopreserved semen, and all sperm are quarantined for a minimum of six months before they are released."

"Must be horny little devils by then, huh Kate? Makes them more anxious when they're set loose, I suppose, huh, Doc?"

Dr. Matthews laughed and sipped her wine. She had beautifully shaped legs, I thought. I followed the line of them under the exposed portion of her thigh, down to her calf and on to her foot. I liked the shade of light turquoise she had chosen for her toenails.

Willy caught the little journey my eyes had taken.

She tightened her lips and put her beer bottle down on the side table a little harder than necessary.

"I never thought of it that way. I'll mention it to Dr. McKinny. To continue," Dr. Matthews said, nodding my way, "the clinical evaluation includes one complete semen analysis, at least five sperm counts and post-thaw evaluations. Morgan Patterson conducts a personal history interview supported by a four-generation medical-genetic history. Included is an HIV risk assessment based on sexual activity and drug use."

"Jeez. Why would anyone want to be a donor?" Willy asked. "His whole life exposed. What secrets are left?"

"Some do it for the money, but most want to see their family line continued. We have husbands whose wives are not interested in having any children or any more children or who can't have children and don't want to adopt, and we have single men who are worried they'll never have children. Reasons vary.

"Of course we screen for a variety of diseases and the donor is given a complete physical. A sperm count is performed on every sample to be sure it meets our standards."

"What are the standards for sperm count these days?" Willy quipped, and finished her second beer.

"For us it's a minimum of twenty million motile sperm per cc."

"Sounds crowded. So?" Willy asked, turning to me. "You like what you're hearing, Kate?"

"There are post-evaluations of a donor after he has donated as well," Dr. Matthews added, and finished her wine.

"Kate, you should be asking more questions," Willy urged. "It's your womb, not mine."

I gave her a scowl, which brought a smile to her face. Then I turned to Dr. Matthews.

"How do we decide or how do we know who . . . ?"

"Oh, I'm going to provide you with donor profiles." Dr. Matthews took out a packet of papers. "There are well over fifteen hundred here."

"Fifteen hundred!" Willy exclaimed. "That's one helluva singles bar."

"Yes, there are lots of choice, but you'll narrow it down rapidly. Each profile includes age, education, current occupation, physical characteristics, ethnicity of course, religion, family medical history, the lab results, and personal comments about himself, such as his view of his exceptional abilities, skills, hobbies. We then include Morgan Patterson's personality evaluations, and," she said turning to Willy, "you'll be happy to know we include his answer to the question, why do you want to be a sperm donor?"

"Sounds exhausting," Willy said.

"It's meant to be. Actually, it's meant to make a prospective mother more confident about how her child will turn out than she would be with the man she met and married. Too many women get married too quickly these days and find themselves still discovering things about their husbands a year later, things they are not happy to discover. We eliminate that risk."

Willy nodded. I had never seen her look so impressed with anything or anyone.

"I'm sold," she said. She turned to me. "Kate?"

"How soon do I have to make a decision?"

"Oh, take your time. It's a life decision. And don't hesitate to call on me with every question that you have. Of course, we advise you to have a full physical yourself, and we like to see the results. I should say, we insist on it. If you like, we'll recommend a physician somewhat familiar with our work."

"Here?" Willy asked.

"Well, you would have to travel to our area, but you could be confidant the doctor is doing all the right things. Again," she said, smiling and turning more to Willy, "we're taking a risk, too, with our reputation. I'm sure you understand."

"Completely," Willy said. "Failure to conceive, miscarriages, reflect badly on your company. Kate, don't you have any other questions?" she asked me. I knew she was enjoying this now and also teasing me.

"Dr. Matthews has made a complete presentation. I think I know enough for now."

"Really? I don't," she said,which surprised me.

Dr. Matthews held that smile.

"How can I help?"

"You haven't explained the method, the one you volunteered to assist with," Willy said.

"We haven't gotten to that point yet," I said.

"It has to impact on your thinking, Kate. Dr. Matthews?"

"Yes, I agree."

She reached into her briefcase and produced another set of papers. Without speaking, she handed them to me.

"What is it?" Willy asked.

I held it up.

" 'How to Inseminate at Home,' " I announced.

"You mean, we can't do it in the rear seat of a Ford?" Willy joked.

"I suppose you can do it anywhere."

"I know," Willy said. "We'll have an insemination party, sort of a pagan ritual of sorts. We'll sacrifice a virgin goat in the backyard."

"Very fucking funny," I said, getting more pissed. She laughed.

"Good choice of words."

"Why don't I leave you two with it all to discuss?" Dr. Matthews said, closing her briefcase. She rose, smiling. "As I said, don't hesitate to call me about anything."

"Thank you," I said, rising. Willy remained sitting and then thought about it and rose, too.

We walked her to the front door. She paused and looked around.

"I really do like your home. It's airy and has a nice energy about it. Any child would be happy living here."

"A house does not a home make," Willy muttered.

"Of course not, but, it's nice to have one like this as a starting point. You two look like you could handle bringing up baby," Dr. Matthews added. "Thanks for refreshments and the wine."

"We give you wine. You're giving us a whiner," Willy muttered with a laugh.

Dr. Matthews held that soft smile and left.

"You're such an idiot, Willy," I said, still standing in the doorway. I watched Dr. Matthews go down our walk and around to the driveway and her car.

"If you can't have fun, why do it? She was pretty impressive, I'll admit. The whole thing sounds pretty impressive."

"Yes, I thought so, too," I said, holding my breath. Did she mean it or was she setting me up for another burst of sarcasm? "Let me see that Inseminate at Home stuff," she asked, reaching for the papers. She took them and returned to the living room.

Our front door was still open so I stepped out. Dr. Matthews was just backing out of our driveway. As she drove off, the lights from the neighbor's house threw a wedge of illumination into Dr. Matthews's car and when it moved deeper into the light, another figure took shape. I was pretty sure I saw a man sitting beside her. He looked shorter and heavy in the shoulders. The car moved out of the light and into the darkness, the silhouetted figures lost in the shadows. The car turned and headed away.

I stepped back inside, closed the door and headed back into the living room.

"This is wild shit," Willy said, looking up from the papers. "Did you see this part where it's recommended you have an orgasm? This is going to make me feel like a father for sure," she said, smiling. She stopped when she saw the expression on my face. "What?"

"Strangest thing. I stepped out just as Dr. Matthews was leaving and I swear I saw a man sitting in the car."

"A man?"

"Why would she leave someone sitting out there all that time?"

Willy thought, sat back, looked at the papers and then up at me.

"Probably because she thought it would have inhibited us to have some man sitting in on this conversation. Maybe it was her husband."

"Did she say she was married?"

"I don't remember. No. As I said, she admitted to being bisexual so that could have been her boyfriend, husband, whatever."

"Why bring him along?"

"Maybe they're going somewhere together now, Kate. Jeez, what's the big fucking deal here? He's an understanding son of a bitch who probably thinks it's well worth sitting out there in the dark in a car to wait for what he thinks is the fuck of the century. Do you have to do this all the time, read some voodoo meaning into everything?"

"You're right. I'm sorry."

I sat on the sofa. A long moment of silence passed between us while Willy stared at me.

"So what are you going to do now, Kate, contact a new sperm bank company because there was a man sitting in a car out there?"

"I didn't say I'd do that."

"I'm not going through this again," she warned. "Besides, I liked her. She was . . . efficient and kind of hip, if I can use that old-fashioned term. Don't you think so?"

"Yes, yes."

"You know you can drive someone crazy. You have been eating and breathing this thing for weeks, if not months, having dreams, virtual births, reading every parenting book you could find, and convincing me and now you sit there with that far-off look you inherited from your superstitious grandmother."

"I'm okay with it," I insisted. "I was just making a comment about an odd thing, but you've explained it and I'm fine."

"Okay. Then all that's left is for you and I to review the donor list. I'm not so sure I was kidding about the insemination party though. That might be fun."

"Like hell. Willy!"

"Don't be so damn serious about this. You'll squeeze all the fun out of it. I'll make it a small party."

"Absolutely not."

She shrugged and reached for the donor list.

"You know," she said perusing it, "it's times like

this you wish cloning was a real option. Well, what do you prefer, Scandinavian, Western European, Asian, English-Irish, Native American? There's one that might make sense. We're surrounded by Indians here. You could go African-American. Wait a minute. Look at this. They actually have an Eskimo donor."

"Are you going to be serious about it?"

"I am serious. Here," she said, dividing up the pages, "you take these and I'll take these. Circle the ones you favor on your sheets and I'll circle mine. Then we'll compare our lists, discuss our reasons and narrow it down. How's that for serious?"

I took the pages.

"Better," I said. I rose. "I'm going off to be alone."

"Fine."

I took the tray, empty glasses and beer bottles to the kitchen and then went out to the patio and the pool after I turned on the outside lighting. There were stars just peeking above the top of the mountain. The pinhead size light of the tram car descended into the darkness. There was barely a breeze, but it was comfortable, cool. Some bats circled the pool, dove and then flapped into the vampire night. I could hear a pack of coyotes making their way east along the wash, yelping with excitement as they chased some desperate creature that could be someone's stray dog or cat. Nature was at once beautiful and cruel.

I curled up in a lounge and began to go through the donor list, while Willy the wise ass turned on the CD and put the music through the outside sound system after she had located Eddie Fisher singing "Oh! My Pa-Pa."

I couldn't help but laugh. It made me feel better, but I couldn't relax completely.

There was something about that male figure silhouetted in Dr. Matthews's car that wouldn't let me relax. I put the papers aside for a moment and thought about it, resurrecting the image.

Maybe it wasn't a man. It could have been a little heavier-set woman. Maybe I was assuming too much. So what? She had admitted to being bisexual.

What bothered me?

Just the way that figure appeared, I thought. He or she seemed to materialize, fade in like a shot in a movie and then fade out, a silent figure, waiting patiently out there the whole time.

It was just so odd. It had to mean something. But what? What?

You and your omens and dreams, I could hear Willy saying. If I brought this up again, she would surely change her mind about the whole thing.

So shut up, I told myself and returned to the donor list.

4·

DESPITE THE SIZE OF the list, it didn't take us that long to cut it to five names between us, three for me and two for her. Without comparing notes, we were on the same wavelength. We wanted a child who would resemble us as closely as possible or as Willy joked, "As near to a clone as we could get."

Because of all the information about donor lineages we read, we considered our own. Over the years, we had talked at great length about our genealogies, intrigued with the possibility we would learn more about each other this way. Both our great-grandparents came from England and Ireland on our father's side. My mother's people had some German and Polish origins, and Willy's mother's people had Dutch and French. I wondered if we should concentrate on someone with a similar genealogy or look for variety to make a more interesting personality? I stayed safe and went for someone with similar genealogy and so did Willy.

Next, we went for donors who had higher levels of education and were professionals. Willy said it was the snob in us. Of course, we screened out as many of those who had family with even a suggestion of any serious illness experiences and we then went for men who were close to us in age.

Three days after we had met with Dr. Matthews, we drew out our short list and sat in the living room to discuss each and every one in detail. For a while I thought it might actually boil down to height and weight. Willy naturally favored the one who had the best athletic background.

"He's not as financially successful perhaps, or hasn't the doctorate two of your final candidates have, but to me he's more well rounded, and according the psychologist, he's an aggressive personality. We need to balance out your temperament, interests with someone like this. You're too meek and we don't want to raise a sissy."

"I doubt that we'd raise a sissy with you in this house. You'll probably have the baby doing sit-ups in the crib."

I looked at the profile of the donor she was suggesting. Choosing someone Willy wanted was probably a good political move for our relationship and for her assuming half the responsibility for our child. If I did it all, made the choice, got pregnant, delivered, and took on most of the mother role, Willy would feel estranged.

"I think you're right," I said. I tapped the paper with the name she had chosen as her top candidate. "This donor is Daddy-O."

She smiled.

"I decided I definitely want to be part of the home

insemination process. In the old days, people used to call it intercourse," she said and we both laughed. "I think we're making a mistake not making something of that day or night. It's a momentous occasion. How often to we permit sperm loose in this house?"

"Stop it, Willy."

"Not even an insemination dinner with a dozen or so of our friends?"

"No. This is highly personal and private, only for us."

She sat back and thought and then smiled.

"Okay," she said, "I'll come up with something highly personal. I have just the idea."

I didn't like the way she said that. What had I unleashed?

"What?"

"No comment yet. I have to crystalize my thinking a little more about it, but I promise to make it an enjoyable, erotic experience."

"Willy, I don't like the sound of this," I warned.

"Relax. I promise you will enjoy it as much as I do. Call the good doctor. Tell her we have chosen our sperm."

The following night, Lois Matthews returned to our house. This time, when she drove up, I stepped out to look at her car to see if there was someone waiting for her again. There wasn't.

"Thanks for coming so quickly," I told her when she extended her hand.

She was wearing a silky, gold-laced, flesh-tinted camisole with a built-in shelf bra under her white suit jacket. Her pants were form-fitted. I thought she looked smart, but even more beautiful.

"No problem. I'm glad you two called so soon. I enjoy this trip and love Palm Springs. It's more pleasure than work for me, believe me," she said.

I saw she carried a bottle of wine.

"You brought us wine?"

"To celebrate and toast your decision," she said, handing it to me.

"Thank you. Come in," I said.

Willy emerged from the kitchen carrying a silver tray with three wineglasses and a plate of cheese and crackers.

"Hey, Doc," she said.

"How did you know we'd need the glasses?" I asked, smiling with surprise.

"Lois told me she was bringing a top pinot noir from Napa," Willy said.

"Told you? When?"

"Will you stop the Inquisition. As the other half of this, I have a right to talk to our sperm pusher. Shall we?" she added, nodding at the living room.

Dr. Matthews and I followed her. This time Willy sat beside her on the sofa. She looked at the wine when I handed it to her and nodded, impressed.

"See what she brought?" she asked, turning the label to me. We knew the vineyard and knew it was expensive.

"I see what it is, Willy. Thank you, Lois."

Willy began to uncork it.

"Now then," Dr. Matthews said. "Before we start, let me congratulate you on your choice of donor. I always like to try to guess about whom my clients will choose after I meet them."

"Don't tell us you choose him, too," Willy said.

"No, not him specifically, but he was one of my top three choices."

"We're that predictable," I said, not completely disguising my note of annoyance.

"It's not a matter of being predictable. It's a matter of intelligent evaluation, and the two of you looked like you were capable of that."

"Hey, Lois," Willy said, pouring the wine, "you don't have to stroke us anymore. We're in, ready to sign, ready to get impregnated."

Dr. Matthews laughed.

"That was a sincere compliment," she said, "absent of any ulterior motive."

"Willy always says every compliment has an ulterior motive," I said. "Even if it's just to win a compliment for yourself. Don't you, Willy?"

"Do you mean that as a compliment or a criticism?" Willy asked, and she and Dr. Matthews laughed.

"Let's get to our toast," Dr. Matthews said, raising her glass.

"Kate?" Willy said, holding out mine. "I assume you want to be part of this since you're making a small poached egg contribution."

"Very funny." I took the glass.

"To a wise decision and a successful pregnancy and birth," Dr. Matthews said.

We all drank.

She then opened her briefcase and spread the papers on the coffee table.

"These are for you to read and sign. They include all the fees involved and what is involved in your physical," she explained.

I looked at it.

"We have a doctor of our own," I said.

"He's just a regular practicing family physician, Kate," Willy said. "Why not use their specialist?"

"It won't cost you any more than it would with your physician, I'm sure," Dr. Matthews said.

"I'm not worried about the cost."

"So?" Willy said.

"All right, perhaps," I said.

"Good. Now, let's talk about your menstrual cycle."

"A most interesting topic," Willy said. "Fortunately, our Kate here is as regular as a Swiss timepiece."

"That's terrific," Dr. Matthews said. "Morgan Patterson believes that is a good indication of a contented woman, someone who doesn't suffer too much stress in her life."

Willy smiled as if she were solely the reason. Dr. Matthews picked up on it instantly.

"At the risk of being accused of delivering another compliment, might I say you two are one of the most compatible and satisfied of the couples I have met, and I have met quite a few."

"Thank you," Willy said. "Kate?"

"You haven't known us that long. How did you come to that conclusion so quickly?"

"I have a built-in people meter. Am I wrong?"

"Yes, Kate, is she wrong?"

"No. I guess what you say about us is true. Thank you. Let me continue looking over the paperwork," I added, reaching for the rest of the documents.

"Please don't consider this in any way condescending, but I do like to explain the basics about fertility and success."

"Oh, do enlighten us, Lois," Willy said. "Not being a heterosexual couple, we haven't been overly concerned about it."

I stared at her and felt the heat in my own eyes.

"What?" she cried.

"Stop," I merely said.

Lois watched us and then sipped some more of her wine before putting the glass down to continue.

"You might have had some of this in basic biology or high school health courses, but . . ."

"It's all right," I said. "I'm not arrogant enough to think I know it all."

"Actually, most heterosexual couples even with a well-planned intercourse have only a twenty to twenty-five percent chance of getting pregnant in any given cycle."

"What's your success rate at Genitor?" I asked.

"One in twelve, about eight percent for vaginal insemination."

"This can get pretty expensive then," I said, glancing at the fee schedule.

"You already said money is no object," Willy said quickly, and poured herself and Dr. Matthews more of the pinot noir. "Besides, let's be more optimistic considering Kate's regularity."

"That is a plus as is her age, being under thirty. We'll work on her fertility awareness, too."

"We? Aren't you proposing to do a lot more for us than you usually do?" I asked. I had, unbeknown to Willy, made inquiries of other sperm banks and their procedures. Few gave the personal attention Dr. Matthews was giving us.

"We intend to become the number one sperm bank in the country," Dr. Matthews said. "Doing a little more is what will get us there."

"Well said," Willy cried, and tapped her glass to Dr. Matthews's glass.

The way they were smiling at each other was beginning to make me uncomfortable. They were like conspirators and I was on the outside. Willy was being too carefree. After all, we were still talking about my body. There goes our perfect, stressless relationship, I thought.

"As you know, a woman's peak fertility occurs right before ovulation. Her egg lives for only six to twenty-four hours after ovulation. Frozen sperm makes the timing even more crucial."

"Why?" I asked.

"While fresh sperm can live three to five days within a woman's body, thawed sperm lives for twenty-four hours at most."

"Fresh sperm lives inside a woman three to five days?" Willy asked.

Lois nodded.

"I knew there was a good reason to avoid men. Creepy crawler for three to five days."

"I'm sure women don't feel anything, Willy," I said.

She shrugged.

"Since ovulation occurs twelve to sixteen days before the first day of the next period, we have more of a crapshoot," Lois continued, ignoring us the way a teacher might ignore two annoying students in her class.

"Shouldn't that be 'sperm shoot'?" Willy asked.

"More of a deposit than a shoot," Dr. Matthews told her.

"Touché," Willy said, and they clinked glasses.

Was it the wine or was Willy just being a horse's ass to irritate me? Glaring at her didn't matter.

"We'll watch your fertile cervical mucus," Dr. Matthews continued, returning to her formal and professional demeanor, "chart your basic body temperature, and use an OPK, Ovulation Predictor Kit, in which a simple urine test measures the presence of LH, luteinizing hormone, the catalyst for ovulation. We do recommend inseminating two days in a row at twelve-hour intervals."

"Well, that sounds like we're hedging our bet a bit, doesn't it, Kate?"

"Yes."

"So, are you signing those papers or not?" Willy asked, nodding at the table. I had the pen poised but had not signed anything.

We had finally come down to it. The moment of truth.

"We have some more wine to drink," she added, and again, Dr. Matthews and she smiled as if they were old friends.

"Before I sign, are you sure you want this as much as I do, Willy?"

"After some deep introspection, and the fear that if my arm is twisted anymore it will simply come apart, I believe I do," she said.

I signed the papers.

Dr. Matthews quickly put her copies into her briefcase, giving me the impression she was afraid we might change our minds.

"Well, then," she said, sipping her wine and sitting back on the sofa, "From the way you two talk about your periods, Kate, I think we could attempt it just before your next ovulation."

"But isn't that's a serious departure from normal procedure? I read that most sperm banks recommend following a client's cycle for three months prior."

"Well, it's true that most sperm banks recommend that and in general we do as well, but if you are as regular as you say you are, I don't . . ."

"You are as regular as we say you are, aren't you, Kate?" Willy interjected. Of course, she knew.

"I suppose so."

"So? Don't you want to get this started sooner than later?" Willy pursued.

"Yes, of course."

"So?"

Willy was more interested in my being pregnant than I was and I found it annoying. It was irrational of me. I had been working so long at getting her to agree and to want it at least as much as I did and now that she was enthusiastic, very enthusiastic, I was bothered. It made no sense.

"Okay," I said. "Let me look at the calendar."

"I can tell you right now," Willy said. "You're nine days away from your next ovulation." She turned to Dr. Matthews. "Please don't ask me how I know that with such certainty, Lois," she said. "You'll make me blush."

They both laughed. I sat back and reviewed dates and time. Willy was right.

"All right, then," Dr. Matthews said. "We should get you to see the doctor ASAP. How about tomorrow afternoon, say about three?"

"How do you know the doctor is available?"

"I know her schedule," she said. "We have other clients in the pipeline, don't forget."

"She?"

"Yes. Dr. Esther Aaron. If all goes well, we could begin in seven days. Let's be optimistic. I'll put the date down right now," she said, reaching into her briefcase for her PDA. "I'll return here with the donor sperm about eight P.M. We would inseminate again at 8 A.M. How's that sound?"

"You would have to drive back and forth and leave pretty early for the second insemination," Willy commented.

"It's not a problem for me."

"So you're definitely going to personally deliver it and supervise the insemination?" I asked.

"If you don't mind. Only if you don't mind," she emphasized.

"Why would she mind, Lois?"

"It's a pretty personal event, Willy," Dr. Matthews said.

"Exactly," I added.

The two of them looked at me, both looking surprised at my vehemence.

"I would think you'd want to do anything, have anything to ensure success, Kate," Willy said. "Besides, Dr. Matthews is a professional. She's seen it before, I imagine," she added, suddenly referring to Lois as Dr. Matthews.

"Oh, a few times," Dr. Matthews said, smiling. "But don't feel pressured. That would be detrimental. You need to be rested, relaxed, comfortable."

"Well, we have a few days. We'll discuss it," Willy said, looking at me.

"Of course. I just need some heads up to plan the

delivery should I not be bringing it," Dr. Matthews said.

Willy and she stared at each other a moment.

"Would you excuse us a moment, Lois?" Willy said, rising. She jerked her head toward the doorway.

I rose and followed her out. We went into the kitchen. Willy leaned against the counter and folded her arms under her breasts tightly.

"What's the bug up your ass?"

"Since when did you get so cozy with her?"

"I'm not cozy. Why do you say that?"

"You called her and didn't tell me you did."

"Yes, I called to ask some questions on my own, and she said she was very excited for us and wanted to bring the wine."

"Maybe she's not so bisexual."

Willy shook her head.

"First you complain about Janet's drooling over me and now this. You're behaving like a woman in the throes of some kind of pregnancy depression. What's going to happen when you look pregnant and lose your precious figure?"

I felt the tears coming to my eyes and turned away.

"Thanks."

"Look, Kate. I'm not trying to upset you. You don't want her to do anything more? I'll tell her thank you. Please just send the sperm airmail."

"I didn't say that. It's just . . ."

"What? Happening so fast? Jesus, Kate, you're like

one of those people who are warned they should be careful what they wish for; they're liable to get what they wish for."

I took a deep breath.

"You're right. I'm sorry. I'm getting too emotional."

"You are. As I said, you're behaving like a woman who's already pregnant? Sure you're not?"

"What?"

"Maybe this whole thing is a cover-up," she teased.

"You know what you can do with that idea, Willy?"

"I used to do that. Got bored with it. If you're sure now, we'll go back and let her know. Are you sure?"

"Yes, I'm sure. I don't know what the hell I'm saying."

"Could have fooled me," Willy said.

She smiled and then stepped forward to kiss me.

"I just want to see you happy," she whispered. "Then I'm happy, so it's a selfish thing. You know, like Do unto others as you would have them do unto you. It all comes out of what you want for yourself."

"You're such an idiot," I said, laughing. "But that's what I like about you."

"Funny, that's what I like about you."

Dr. Matthews was sitting back coolly, sipping her wine when we returned to the living room. She looked up at us, anxious, her eyes scrutinizing our faces.

"It's settled," Willy said. "We've decided we would

appreciate your being a part of the home insemina-tion."

"No problem. Glad to do it." She set her wineglass down. "Now how about a tour of your house? I haven't gotten any farther than this room."

"What? Sure," Willy said. "Kate?"

"Yes, of course. Please. Let us show you the den, the kitchen, the bedrooms. We have two guest bedrooms, and Willy has her own gym."

"Sounds wonderful. I admire the view from the rear, too. I been looking through the windows here," she said.

"We'll show you the pool, too," Willy said, and we began our tour.

When we arrived at our bedroom, Willy asked her how she liked the laboratory. Of course, she laughed.

"All laboratories should be this comfortable. Be-lieve me, it beats some aseptic, impersonal, cold room in a clinic. I think there's a lot to say for home insemination."

"I know what you mean," Willy said, winking at me. "Most of the nicest things that happen to you, happen to you in your own bed."

Dr. Matthews laughed again. It seemed nothing Willy could say would be unamusing.

"Well, I had better get going," she said.

We returned to the living room so she could get her things. As we were about to say goodbye the phone rang. It was for Willy. She waved goodbye to Dr. Matthews and I escorted her to the front door.

"This is going to go just fine for you, Kate. I have no worries about your physical, and I know you'll be getting ideal sperm. You're going to have a beautiful child."

"We are, Willy and me," I emphasized.

"Of course. That's what I meant."

She opened the door.

My heart was pounding, but I had to say it.

"The last time you were here, I thought I saw someone in the car with you. Someone had been waiting for you all that time?"

"My car? No. There was no one," she said. "It was probably just the shadows and the light playing tricks. Besides, why would I leave someone in the car all that time?"

"That was what made me curious."

"Well, there was nothing about which to be curious. Have a good night. I'll call in the morning to confirm your doctor's appointment. Good night," she said, and walked to her car.

This time when she pulled out, there was no question she was alone.

But I didn't believe her.

Someone had been in that car with her the last time.

Why would she lie?

5.

"AS A MATTER OF FACT," Willy said, when I told her what Dr. Matthews had just said. "I already asked her about that."

"Why didn't you tell me?"

"I thought it would only spook you. I'm sure what you saw was just a play of light and shadows, Kate."

I stared at her. Those were almost the exact words Dr. Matthews had used.

"You should have told me you had asked her. You should have told me what she said," I said and walked away.

This wasn't like her. We didn't hide things from each other for any reason. Small deceptions chip away at relationships, I thought. They're like cancer cells spreading, growing, destroying, little mouths gobbling up the goodness.

I went outside again and sat on a lounge chair. The lights of a commercial jet making its way into Los Angeles slipped through the stars, the sound of its engines so far behind it that it seemed there was another jet right above us. I watched the light until it was gone. It was fantastic to think of people inside those lights, all of them preparing themselves for the impending landing, excited about their arrival and being greeted by family, loved ones, friends. Time and distance fell behind them with the plane's exhaust. Those sitting at the windows and looking down probably had similar thoughts about the world below. It was just as fantastic to think of people within those tiny lights, families with their separate dramas. Maybe they were looking back at our house. What passenger in his or her wildest imaginings could come with our play on our stage?

"This is exactly what I was trying to avoid," Willy said, coming up softly behind me. "You're in one of those depressing moods."

"Trust is more important than worrying about moods, Willy. What have I kept from you lately?"

"All right, I'm sorry," she said.

She sat on the lounge, keeping her back to me.

"This whole thing has brought more tension to this house than I can tolerate," she said.

"Tension? You seemed to be aboard every step of the way now. What tension?"

She turned to me.

"I know you're nervous about it all. I would be and I can feel your anxiety, so don't try to pretend it's not there. Ironically, you're now blaming me for not ignoring you, for being concerned and sensitive and trying to make things easier for you."

She fixed her eyes on mine. I couldn't help being drawn to the strength in her face. She made me feel safe. Maybe, that was always more important than actual love. With Willy beside me, part of my life, I did feel invulnerable, protected.

"Okay, I'm sorry I was such a femme," I said, and she smiled.

We kissed softly. Her hands moved along my ribs and over my breasts. I moaned and sunk lower on the lounge. While she undressed me, I kept my eyes closed like some child told to do so in preparation for a surprise. Our sex was always a surprise and never tired or repetitious. Every kiss, every touch seemed different, new. It was as if we each discovered something previously unexplored, whether it be a tender spot under a breast or just below a navel.

"Too bad we don't have semen tonight," she whispered when I moaned with pleasure at her touch, at the way her lips drew a sensual line over my stomach, against my inner thighs. She leaned back to undress and then our two naked bodies entwined in passionate embraces, our lips bringing on orgasms that made us both gasp and cling to each other as if we were falling, only not down but up toward those stars, toward those planes and those people who looking out their windows saw the two of us floating by like two angels who had discovered how to transcend their own bodies and visit their very souls.

There are often times when making love to the one you love is infected with some dishonesty. It doesn't matter if you are a lesbian, gay, or heterosexual. Sometime during that act of lovemaking, you will drift off or be suddenly driven by other images and thoughts. In my case and I suspected in Willy's this particular night, this particular time, we both, even if just for a few fleeting seconds, conjured Dr. Matthews, thought of her lips, her eyes, her breasts, and especially those shapely legs. We used her to enjoy each other even more and the enjoyment we brought to each other made it possible to forgive each other for the distraction, the mental infidelity.

I saw this in the way Willy shifted her eyes guiltily away from mine and felt it in the way I turned from her as well. Neither of us said anything about it. It wasn't necessary. It was as obvious as the stars that witnessed our passion and winked at each other. They knew. The heavens knew it all.

Laughing at ourselves afterward, we both leaped into the pool. It was just a little too cool, but we didn't complain. Later, exhausted, we lay in bed talking until both our voices drifted away like smoke and our eyes closed. Sleep rolled over us with the lightness of fog until we were engulfed in our own dreams and finally let go of each other's hands, both feeling as safe as possible.

Dr. Matthews called in the morning to confirm my appointment with Dr. Esther Aaron.

"She can see you today at three. Will that work?"

"Yes," I said.

"Here's the address," she said, dictating it to me. "She's a wonderful person besides being an excellent physician. Don't worry about a thing. You're in good hands now, Kate."

"Thank you," I said.

I told Willy and she decided she would come along.

"You sure?"

"I want to be part of this every step of the way," she said. "When I commit to something, I commit."

We went over to our warehouse to be sure the day's work was going well and there would be no problems while we were away. I couldn't help being distracted. I watched Willy closely and admired how focused she could be. She could compartmentalize her life much more efficiently than I could. Occasionally, she would look my way and smile.

"Relax, Kate," she said when we left the plant and started toward Irvine. "I know enough about all this to know that if you are tense, it could have a negative effect."

"I'm relaxed."

"Yeah, like a coiled rattler," she quipped.

All the way to the doctor's office, we talked about our baby as if he or she was already school age. Willy was adamant about enrolling our child in a private school. She was very down on public education.

"It's hit and miss. Who the hell wants to go into teaching these days? You get the bottom five percent of the graduating classes and no one can blame them, considering what's demanded of them and what they get paid for it."

I knew she was reciting Janet Madison's litany of complaints about her grade school teaching job.

"My public school education wasn't that bad," I dared say.

"Look where the hell you lived, the community, the wealth. They didn't need a private school there. They paid teachers the best salaries around. You told me so yourself."

"Yes, that's true," I admitted.

"It's never too soon to think about these things," she continued.

I couldn't believe this conversation we were having. This was my partner, the one who had been fighting me about having a child and becoming parents?

"Are you the same person who slept with me a week ago," I asked, "and thought my talk about having a baby was the babbling of an insane person?"

"Very funny. I told you, Kate, if I agree to do something, I agree all the way. With me it's a solid yes or no, no maybe crap. We know too many people who have difficulty making up their minds about bowel movements, much less important life choice decisions."

"How do you know about their bowel movements?"

"I know what I know," she said.

She looked firm in the driver's seat, her hands clenching the steering wheel as if she was about to jerk us off the road any moment if I dared disagree with a single syllable.

"Okay, let's pick out the kid's college tonight," I said.

She looked at me and finally smiled.

"You're a wiseass for a high femme," she said. "I must be rubbing off on you."

I laughed. Maybe she was. Maybe, we were truly becoming each other, although I couldn't see all that much of me in her yet.

The doctor's office was a surprise. Instead of it being in a medical office building, it was in the doctor's house, a bilevel style. We'd soon discover that the lower floor had been converted into a small lobby, offices, and examination rooms. I thought we had made a mistake when we turned into the driveway and the parking lot.

"No mistake," Willy said. "GPS navigator brought us to the address. What's the big deal? Lawyers are doing the same thing these days, converting houses into offices. It makes them feel more at home or something, gives it some personality. Don't you think?"

"Yes, I like it. I was just surprised, that's all."

We parked and got out. There was nothing different from other residences about the front door. I was again surprised that it was locked, however. We had to press the doorbell button. A voice asked us who we were and I identified myself. We heard the buzz and Willy opened the door.

"What is it, a bank, a jewelry store, or a doctor's office?"

"Can't be too careful these days, I guess. Doctor's offices have drugs," Willy said with a shrug. "Besides, people usually don't have to get in quickly. They don't go to their doctor's offices in an emergency anymore. They go directly to the hospital or some immediate care center."

We walked through what was a short entryway with its coat hanger rack, its limestone tiled floor, an antique bench and a small chandelier. The lobby was relatively small and looked as if it had been converted out of a small sitting room. There was just one simple painting above a tan leather sofa, a picture of what looked like an apple orchard and an inexpensive print at that. In front of the sofa was a table and on the floor, a dark gray oval rug. The floor itself looked like the original floor boards, a light oak. Another sofa faced this one.

On the far wall there was a glass window half open behind which sat the receptionist, a pleasant looking older woman with stark white, but neatly cut and styled hair. Her eyes looked as if they belonged in the head of a woman years younger because they were a vibrant blue, clear and full of energy. Except for some shallow web feet at the corners of those eyes, her face was soft, smooth. It made me think that perhaps her hair had turned prematurely gray. Why didn't she have it colored back to her natural shade? I wondered. I could give her some good suggestions, I thought, and that included some improvements in her makeup as well.

"Good afternoon," she said, handing out the usual form for new patients asking that the squares next to a slew of questions about previous illness, family history, allergies and the like be answered by checking yes or no.

"Thank you," I said, and took it. I sat on the soft tan leather sofa below the one picture. Willy picked up a magazine and began to thumb through it even before she sat across from me.

I glanced up at the receptionist, who was staring at me with the most unusual smile of excitement and happiness. She made me feel as if I were some sort of celebrity at whom she couldn't stop staring. I flashed a smile back, expecting her to turn back to whatever work she had, but she continued to gaze that way at me. I cleared my throat and shifted my eyes to Willy, signaling she should look at the receptionist, too. She did and then smiled and looked at her magazine again.

When you know someone is watching you so closely, it's very difficult to simply ignore it. I tried, but I couldn't help looking up at her once in a while. She hadn't moved a muscle in her face. It was beginning to disturb me.

"Is something wrong?" I asked.

Willy looked up sharply.

"Oh no, dear. I was simply admiring your earrings and your outfit. Very smart."

"Thank you," I said. "I have a great little boutique in Palm Springs. If you're ever there, you should definitely stop in," I said, stressing definitely and indirectly implying she needed to update her fashion.

Willy scowled at me.

I completed the form and gave it to the receptionist. She glanced at it and nodded as if she were the
one who had to stamp approval.

"It'll will only be a little while longer," she said. "Dr.
Aaron is just finishing up with another patient."

I returned to the sofa.

"Relax," Willy whispered. "You're beginning to really make me nervous."

I shook my head at her and picked up a magazine.
Just as I opened it, the door to the examination
rooms opened and a girl who looked no more than
sixteen at most came out, followed by a woman
who was obviously her mother. There were enough
resemblances. Both were strawberry blondes with
prominent jawbones and similarly shaped mouths.
Both had necks that were just long enough to attract
attention to them.

The girl was obviously in the final trimester of her
pregnancy and had been crying. She was just sucking
in her tears when they stepped out. The look on her
mother's face told me this was not a happy doctor's
visit. The girl glanced at me and then hurried toward
the front door. Her mother kept her head up, her eyes
fixed on her.

"Not too difficult to figure out that story," Willy
quipped. "Probably a right-to-life family."

The receptionist had moved from her desk to the
still-opened door and stood there looking out at me,
that smile still stuck on her face. She was shorter than
I had realized, with wide hips and rather short, rolling

pin arms. I thought there was something dwarfish about her. It was as if her body had run out of growth hormone just as it had begun to form her appendages.

"The doctor will see you now," she said.

Willy and I rose and walked through the door. The receptionist led us to the first examination room on the right and turned, her smile finally gone. "There's a gown inside hanging on the door. Please take off all your clothes," she said, suddenly all business.

Willy glanced at me and we entered the room. The receptionist closed the door. The room was bare bones: an examination table, a chair, a small desk, an X-ray light and a cabinet for medical implements, bandages, and some antiseptic creams. The floor was the same oak as the floor in the lobby. There were no windows and nothing on the walls. Willy took the seat. She had brought her magazines with her and continued to read an article while I undressed and put on the gown.

"This is a pretty stark doctor's office," I said, "compared to the medical offices in Palm Springs."

"You're not in Palm Springs," Willy said dryly.

"Looks thrown together to me."

"We'll recommend a decorator," she said. "It's not the doctor's office that counts. It's the doctor."

"Right, but that receptionist is weird," I said, slipping my arms into the sleeves of the gown.

"Don't invite her to the insemination party," Willy said, again not raising her eyes from the magazine.

"Very funny."

The door opened, and Dr. Aaron entered with my form in hand and looked from Willy to me as if she was still unclear as to whom the patient was, even with me in the gown. She fixed her eyes on me for a moment before giving me a quick, perfunctory smile.

She was as pretty as Dr. Matthews, with a hairstyle so similar I wondered if I had missed the latest new fashion. Her complexion was rosy, a blush in her cheeks, and her lips were slightly orange. Her eyebrows were styled without any mascara. She was tall, too, with the slimness of her figure obvious even under her doctor's gown.

"Good afternoon. I'm Dr. Aaron," she said. "You're Kate Dobson, and you're Willy Radcliff," she added, nodding at us both as though she had just assigned us parts in a play. "Dr. Matthews speaks very highly of your both."

"She's a quick study," Willy said. "We're terrific."

Dr. Aaron smiled and turned to me. "Well, I see from this that you have an excellent health history, and I like the fact that you have no known allergies. So many of the women we see these days have developed allergies to this or that. It's a wonder they can live outside of a plastic bubble."

"That's where we thought we were living," Willy said.

Again, Dr. Aaron smiled at her. Then she looked at me more intently.

"I can see you're somewhat nervous, Kate. Don't

be. We're not going to put you through anything unusual. We'll get your vital statistics, take some urine to determine your LH level, some blood for some routine screening and do a basic vaginal inspection."

"Inspection?" Willy quipped.

"Examination," Dr. Aaron corrected. She looked at me and tilted her head toward Willy. "Did you have to bring her along?"

I laughed and Willy's mouth dropped open.

"Just kidding," Dr. Aaron said, and began by taking my blood pressure. As she worked, she talked. "I think it's wonderful that you two have decided to do this. If I may be frank . . ."

"Be anyone you like," Willy said.

"Will you shut up?" I told her.

"As I was saying," Dr. Aaron continued, "if I may be frank, the only criticism I have about gay couples is that they're too into themselves. Nothing like a child to diminish that," she said, glancing at Willy.

"That's exactly what I told her, Doc," Willy said. "If anyone needs to have her narcissism diminished, it's Kate here."

"You son of a . . ."

"Now, now," Willy said. "Not in front of the doctor. She just told us how she heard we were perfect together."

Dr. Aaron laughed. We were all suddenly like old friends.

"Something tells me you two are," she said. "You're perfect for what we are about to do."

"We?" I said.

"See," Willy pounced. "Narcissism uncovered!"

Dr. Aaron looked at me as if she believed what Willy was saying.

She smiled.

"What of it?" she said. "This modesty thing can be carried too far. Churches impose it on us to keep us subservient. A good dose of self-love helps build confidence.

"Besides," she continued, smiling at me, "We high femmes enjoy vanity too much to think of it as a sin. Isn't that right, Kate?"

I looked at Willy. Her jaw had come unhinged again.

She looked from Dr. Aaron to me.

High Femmes? We?

Finally, I thought, someone took her breath away.

And I don't think I ever enjoyed that more.

6.

"You passed every test with flying colors," Dr. Matthews told me when she phoned the following morning. "And your LH is elevating. You're right on schedule, Kate, which means I should be as well with the insemination process. We're a go for 8 P.M. six days from today as we planned. Okay?"

"Yes," I said, and then thinking about the tests I added, "That was quick."

"Not really. Anyway, we have a little pull with the lab we use. Did you like Dr. Aaron?"

"Very much," I said. "She has a great sense of humor."

"Yes, that's why we recommend her to our clients. Many of them then decide to have her function as their OB/GYN as well. You can check her out on our Web site where we have testimonies from previous patients. I don't know anyone who wasn't satisfied with her."

"Really?"

"It's not too early to think of all this, Kate. You want someone like Dr. Aaron to manage your pregnancy, your labor, and your puerperium."

"My what?"

"The time period directly following childbirth. It's important. All this is very important. Stories about people's great-grandmothers giving birth in the field and returning immediately to their farmwork are more urban legend than you think."

"I never heard that story from my grandmother about her mother. I think we go back to Adam and Eve and we were all born in a hospital, even then."

She laughed.

"Well, check her out. I don't imagine you've been hanging about with women who discuss pregnancies and their OB/GYNs and can steer you in the right direction."

"No I haven't. I'll check her out," I said. "Thanks."

"No problem. Give my best to Willy."

"Yes," I said, and hung up. I don't know why it bothered me to hear her say "Give my best to Willy," but it did. I guess I was far more jealous and possessive than I had thought. Willy was obviously right about me. I knew pregnant women were more than likely to become a little paranoid. I was getting off to a good start even before I even started to lose my figure.

"Who was that?" Willy asked as soon as she stepped into the kitchen. I had been first up this morning even though I had a miserable night, waking practically every half hour because of one nightmare after another, one in particular having to do with a maternity ward in which all the home-inseminated babies had faces like toads. I thought I would wake her with my tossing and turning and groaning, but she was practically comatose. I envied her and finally just rose to make myself a cup of coffee and surrender to whatever demon shut sleep for me outside our bedroom door.

"Dr. Matthews. The examination went well. All tests are good and my LH is elevating."

"That was quick."

"I said the same thing. She told me they have pull with the lab they use."

"Makes sense. They probably pipe in a lot of business. Palms grease palms," she said pouring herself a cup of coffee. "You all right?"

"I didn't sleep well."

"I told you that you're too anxious. We might see about something to help you relax. I know Dr. Malisoff isn't happy about prescribing anything that could turn someone into a dependency, especially when we make an appointment to talk to him about your getting pregnant, but . . ."

"Dr. Matthews suggested we consider Dr. Aaron as my OB/GYN."

"Really?" She sipped her coffee, thought and nodded. "Well, Malisoff delivers babies but he's just a GP, right? That does make sense."

"I don't know. I'll think about it," I said. "I've always been comfortable with Dr. Malisoff."

"You're not worried about her because her offices weren't up to Palm Springs standards, are you?"

I didn't respond.

"Didn't you like her?"

"Yes, I did. I just said I'd think about it, didn't I?"

She pulled her head back as if I had taken a swipe at her.

"A little testy already? You haven't even begun conception."

"I'm not testy. I'm just giving everything some thought, Willy. We do have a lot longer trip to go see her. It was one thing for these tests; it's another for regular checkups and delivery. Dr. Matthews told me to check her out on their Web site. That's all I'm saying."

"Whatever. I'm for anything that makes you comfortable." She stared at me a moment.

"What?"

"Are you having real second thoughts about having this baby, Kate, because if you are. . ."

"No. God. Can't I think about anything without it being considered doubt?"

"Okay, okay. Calm down. I need my head today. We've got a lot to do at the plant," she said. "We picked up four more accounts yesterday. I think we have to consider hiring more help."

"Four more accounts? Really? That's good news."

"It's all good news, Kate, and good news stimulates my appetite, all my appetites. I'm very hungry this morning," she said, and started to make some scrambled eggs. "How about you? Got to keep up your strength and health, you know."

"I'll have a little," I said.

"So everything is on schedule then?" she asked as she broke some eggs into a mixing bowl. "She'll be here in six days?"

"Yes."

She nodded and then turned to smile at me.

"I'm not handing out cigars. That's where I draw the line," she said, and finally, we both laughed.

After breakfast, we rode together to the plant. The warehouse was about two miles from downtown Palm Springs, out toward the airport. The delivery-man could get onto the 10 Freeway rather quickly and service communities from Cathedral City to Indio.

After we arrived, I tried to lose myself in the work as much as Willy did. I was never as intense about it as she was, but today, I wanted to be. I wanted to share in her excitement and enthusiasm. After all, this business was our first creation, truly the first offspring of our union.

During the day, we picked up another account. We had a sizeable client list as it was, but suddenly it seemed we were being discovered by a whole new area of our desert community. I wouldn't dare use the word *straight,* but I thought it. None of these new clients had any ties to the gay community.

"This is an amazing coincidence," Willy said, coming into the office where I was working on our accounts. She hated any form of bookkeeping and I was much better with our business software on the computer than she was or even cared to be. We had state-of-the-art-computer equipment, broadband service, copy machines, fax, everything we could possible need or want. I kept it all very neat and organized, too. I could retrieve a document in seconds, if need be. The only thing Willy knew about in our office was it housed the coffee machine.

"What is?"

"This morning I was talking about the need to hire an additional employee and I just received a call on my cell phone from Dr. Matthews asking if we had any need for another chef. She has a cousin who just lost her job in Anaheim and wants to move to the desert. She was working as the morning head chef in a restaurant that went belly-up and she's tired of moving from one restaurant to another. Lois mentioned us to her and she was very interested. She sounds like a perfect candidate. She attended a prestigious culinary arts school in San Francisco after attending a two-year business college. She's an unattached twenty-eight-year-old. I told her to tell her to come in for an interview. If she's acceptable, she might even be able to take over some of your bookkeeping duties toward the final stages of your pregnancy and after. Her name is Eve Stoner."

"Why didn't she call the office?"

"What?"

"Dr. Matthews. Why didn't she call the office? Why did she call you on your cell phone? And how did she get that number?"

Willy shook her head, poured herself a cup of coffee and flopped into a chair.

"I don't know, Kate," she said. "I think we really should think twice about all this. You might not have the temperament for it."

"Oh, bullshit, Willy. Don't start again. Those are legitimate questions."

"First, I left my cell phone number with her answering service the first time I called her. She knows we're at work so she wouldn't call the house and I didn't give her the work number. The cellular was probably just the most convenient number for her to call. Second, she probably didn't want to bother you with business calls, and now, because she was being considerate, you pull the cord on your paranoia engine and start it purring away."

She sipped her coffee and looked at me. I did feel stupid coming at her like that. What she said made sense.

"Okay, okay," I said. "You're right."

"Something's eating at you, Kate. It's not just nerves bickering around this home insemination event either, right?"

I shook my head and looked at the computer monitor.

"Since when don't we tell each other what we're really thinking, Kate?"

I turned back to her. She was right again. Why was I acting like this?

"I think Dr. Matthews really is coming on to you," I said. "It's not just a flirtation."

She smiled.

"So do I."

"You do?"

"Yeah, so what?"

She leaned forward, her face a map of anger, the lines around her mouth deepening, her eyes blazing.

"So what?"

"Yes, so what? You think she's the first one out there to come on to me while we've been together? You already pointed out Janet the other day. I'm not being immodest here. It happens once in a while, but I've done nothing to encourage anyone, including Dr. Matthews. I would think you would have a little more faith and confidence in me and in our relationship," she said.

She sat back, now looking sincerely wounded.

"I know. I'm sorry. I just don't want to lose you now or after we start building a family together."

"And I'm telling you that you have nothing to worry about on that score. Can we put an end to it or what? I'll write it in blood."

"Okay, okay. I'm sorry," I said.

"I want you to remember something, Kate. Every time you have the slightest doubt here involving Dr. Matthews or anyone attached to her or this, what should I call it, adventure? Every time, remember you were the one who started it. I'm on board and with you all the way, but you're the one who came up with the idea."

"You make it sound like we're headed for a disaster and you want to cover your rear in case of blame."

"There's no disaster unless we bring it on ourselves," Willy said.

"Since when did you get so wise?"

"Well, I can't remember the exact date, but two weeks ago, I woke up. . ."

"Shut up, you idiot."

"That's better. Now I feel more at home," she said, standing. "I'll handle the interview if you like."

"No, it's okay. I'd like to meet her, too. She does sound perfect, too perfect, especially because of the timing."

"Sometimes, we just get lucky, Kate. People do win lotteries."

I nodded and turned back to the monitor. She came over and put her arms around me, burying her face in my hair.

"You smell good," she said. "I should pull the shades and lock the door and have a matinee."

I turned and we kissed. Then she drew back.

"What happened to the matinee?"

"I've got to oversee the packaging of our horse's ovaries for the Hamilton party tonight."

"You better not let them hear you call their hors d'oeuvres ovaries, horse's or otherwise," I warned. "You know how finicky those two are."

"Worry not," she said, walking to the door. "Or worry only about your own ovaries," she added laughing.

"Get out of here," I said and tossed some crumpled paper at her.

I hated myself for the things I had said to her and vowed to swallow back any and all jealous thoughts. Of course, I knew that was easier said than done, but I was determined not to be obvious about it.

Later that afternoon, I went to the Genitor Web site and saw the links to Dr. Aaron. I read her professional history and then some of the testimonies. They made her sound like God's gift to pregnant women. I made the decision to use her as my OB/GYN and I called her office to see about it.

"Oh yes, dear," her receptionist said the moment I gave her my name. "I was hoping you would call the doctor and ask her to be your OB/GYN."

"How do you know that's what I'm calling to ask?"

"Oh, it's usually the case. She delivered my child, you know."

"No, I didn't know."

How would I know she had a child or was even married? I couldn't imagine her with anyone or with a child.

"Well, she did and thank heaven, too. I had a few complications, but for Dr. Aaron, they were nothing. One moment. I see the doctor is free now," she said, and connected me with Dr. Aaron.

"I'd be delighted to assist you, Kate," she said when she heard the reason for my call.

"Assist?"

She laughed.

"Yes, that's the way I see an OB/GYN's role when it comes to pregnancy and delivery. Nature is really in command. We just listen to Her orders and follow them obediently. You do most of the work here. I would expect you to have a pretty routine pregnancy. Piece of cake," she added.

"Thank you. I'll call you after I go through the procedure. I understand it could take a number of attempts."

"I have no doubt it will happen and the first time," she said confidently, so confidently that it gave me pause. What was really her experience with this process? The way her receptionist had leaped to conclusions still irked me.

"How many of Dr. Matthews's clients do you have as patients, if I may ask?"

"Sure you can. I'm not ashamed of it," she said, laughing. "As I understand it, Kate, I have most of them."

"Really?"

"Adding you to the list, I might actually have them all," she said.

Why such a vote of confidence in her should disturb me, I did not know, but her answer took me by surprise.

"All?"

She laughed.

"See you soon in the capacity as your OB/GYN," she said.

I still couldn't understand how could she be so sure about that. From what I had read on the Internet and in magazine articles, and from what Dr. Matthews had told us about the percentages of success using frozen sperm, I knew such certainty was anything but usual. When I described the conversation to Willy later, she just shrugged.

"I'm sure she's doing what she can to build your confidence, Kate. It's what a good doctor should do, don't you think?"

"I suppose."

"Still looking for spiderwebs in every corner?"

"No."

"Good." She checked her watch. "Surprise of surprises. Our new candidate is due to arrive here in ten minutes."

"So soon?"

"She drove up in anticipation she could see us this afternoon. She was able to change some things and wondered if she could pop in. That shows good enthusiasm. There's a lull so I thought it would actually be better, but if you'd rather skip it and put her off until . . ."

"I said I'm aboard. Why put her off if she went to the trouble of driving here?"

"Okay. I'll bring her in. I'm sure you and she will talk about our business software anyway. As you know, it's Greek to me."

A little more than a half hour later, I heard laughter and looked out the office window to see Willy with a young woman dressed in jeans and a white tank top. She had short, dark brown hair, but not as short as Willy's hair. As she drew closer, I saw she was quite dumpy with a small bosom and wide hips. However, she had a sweet, almost childish face with big eyes and a smile that seemed to ripple around her jaws and engulf her features like a mask.

Willy opened the office door and had her step in first.

"Kate, this is Eve Stoner. Eve, my partner, Kate."

"Hi," she said extending her hand. It was small with stubby fingers.

"Hi," I said shaking her hand.

There was something oddly familiar about her.

"I love your setup here," she said. "Impressive office, too," she added, nodding at everything as she panned the room.

I guess I was staring and thinking too hard. Willy gave me a look.

"Kate?"

"Oh, yes," I said. "Please, have a seat." I nodded at the chair across from me and she sat.

She saw how I was staring at her.

"Sorry," I said, "but for a moment you reminded me of someone."

I looked up at Willy, who squinted and pressed the lines of her forehead into a fold of confusion.

"Perhaps it's someone you just met," Eve suggested, and then laughed.

"Oh? And who would that be?" I asked.

"Probably Dr. Aaron's receptionist," she said. "She's my older sister."

7.

ALTHOUGH HEARING THIS DISTURBED ME, I certainly couldn't complain about Eve Stoner's credentials. She was not only familiar with the foods we prepared, but knew some interesting variations on our recipes. When I questioned her about our business software and her experience with bookkeeping procedures, I arrived at the same conclusion. She knew everything I did and made a suggestion that would streamline some of my work. Willy sat back during most of this with a look of self-satisfaction on her face as if she had personally brought this candidate to our company.

"Well?" Willy asked as soon as the interview was finished. Eve had left and we told her we would call her. She was going to hang out in Palm Springs for another day or two. Willy had her cell phone number.

"Did you know she was Dr. Aaron's receptionist's sister?"

"No. How would I know that? What difference does it make anyway?"

"Difference? That means the receptionist is Dr. Matthews's cousin, too."

"Yes, and soooooo?"

"Nobody mentioned any of that."

"Kate, why should they? What are you getting at here? Is this girl perfect or what?"

"She's perfect," I admitted.

"Good. That's all I care about. She could be related to the plumber we used last week for all I care. People talk to people they know and ideas, possibilities, opportunities come up. What's the mystery here?"

"Okay," I said.

"It's not incest."

"Of course it isn't."

"Relatives try to help relatives. It goes on all the time."

"All right. You made your point. Leave something for the vultures."

"You're such a dorky broad sometimes."

"I knew you liked something about me."

She laughed.

"I have an idea," she said. "Just hear me out," she added quickly.

"What?"

"Why not let Eve use our casita?"

"Our casita? It's just a bathroom and a bedroom. Why wouldn't she want her own apartment?"

"I read between the lines. She's not in good financial shape. For a while at least, this would help her get over the hump. I think it's worth it to get a decent, responsible, and talented employee. You know the flakes we've had come by and some we've had to let go."

I was silent, thinking.

"Why all this hesitation, Kate? You certainly can't see her as any sexual or love threat," Willy added. "She's shaped like a pear. Which I know is soon to be your shape."

"Screw you, you know."

She laughed.

"So?"

"Okay. Make her a card-carrying member of our family if it pleases you."

"It should please us both to add someone worthwhile to the picture here." She slapped her knees and stood up. "Let's celebrate our new business, new employee, and your good physical tonight. Dinner at The Meadow. I'll even get dressed up," she added.

"In what? Your new athletic suit?"

"No. The pants and blouse you bought me for my birthday last month."

"I wondered if you'd ever wear it."

"Well, now you know. I'll wrap things up out there, call Eve, and tell her to come by tomorrow, and we'll go home. Be happy, Kate. We're on a good luck streak," she said, and left the office.

Maybe we were on a good luck streak. Maybe I was just a spoiled, ungrateful bitch.

Goodness knows, we were familiar enough with the type and half the females in my family, especially the cousins to my darling snob sister-in-law, fit the bill.

Perhaps I was infected with the same selfishness. If so, I had full confidence in Willy to provide the antidote. She loved to pick on self-centered people, egotistical people, and could do so with sarcasm so biting, it might just bring on a case of rabies.

I would never admit it, but I was experiencing some second thoughts and that made me nervous and irritable. I didn't want to think them or give them any time and attention. Despite the face I put on for Willy, knowing well that if I did show even the slightest hesitation, she might bolt, I still had these nagging questions.

Was the process so weird, so artificial so as to make the whole thing feel unnatural and would that feeling carry over to the baby?

I thought about my parents, everyone's parents, who, except for those who married after the woman became pregnant or because the woman became pregnant, created their children in an act of loving commitment, creating their destiny. Could it be that the lovemaking for them carried something more than physical pleasure, that something spiritual and mystical happened between them and as a result of that the child was formed? Would I be missing this? More important, would our child?

All sorts of horror-movie scenarios played on the screen in my imagination. A child born of such an insemination procedure would be without soul. It wasn't enough for him or her to be in my genetic stream. Deep inside himself or herself, he would know he came from a procedure and not from love. His daddy was delivered in a frozen container.

These ideas were so off the wall I didn't dare even suggest them to Willy, but that didn't mean they weren't in my head. My hope was I would overcome them. Beyond a doubt, I would see that our child was too beautiful to be anything but perfect. Everything appeared to be working our way, too. Maybe my questions about Dr. Matthews, Dr. Aaron's receptionist, Eve, all of it simply came from my own unvoiced hesitation. I had to get over it so I wouldn't be so paranoid.

Actually, I was glad Willy suggested going out to dinner. I needed company, noise, friends, music, chatter, wine, and good food. It was a good idea to put all this aside for a while anyway. For too long it had dominated my every thought. Lately, every night I went to sleep thinking about it and it greeted me with the sunlight every morning as if it had been in the middle of a sentence when I fell asleep.

I knew Willy was being patient with me. I was being heavy and no fun. She was afraid that if we brought a child into our home and lives, we would lose the carefree world in which we worked and frolicked, and here I was sinking into that muck and mire already. We would become like our own parents and play the heavies who always saw the negatives, the dangers, the waste and somehow forgot the joy of living. I had to do my best to dissuade her of that. I would lose nothing. We would lose nothing. We would only gain.

As soon as we were home, I rushed to dress, to

spruce up my hair and my face and look like the high femme she was proud to escort and show off, especially in a place like The Meadow. It was a restaurant in Rancho Mirage, off Frank Sinatra Drive. Once it had been a hot jazz club frequented by all the old Hollywood celebrities who had originally put Palm Springs on the map as the playground of the rich and famous. Some of the old photographs remained on the walls, even though the establishment had been redesigned with bright colors, leather seats, a brass bar, and gilded mirrors. It was ostentatious, flashy, and reeking of the glitzy well-to-do gay community, although the food was so good and so well priced, it was frequented by heterosexuals as well. Willy had me terrified of even thinking the word *straight*, much less saying it.

It turned out to be one of those spontaneous evenings when many of our friends had the same idea and just showed up. By the time we arrived, the bar truly resembled a watering hole. All forms of creatures, large and small, hovered over it, jabbering, laughing, drinking, and flirting. There was so much heat and excitement, I thought the air would fill with static electricity and jolt those dining in the room to the right and even in the enclosed garden patio.

Marlee Peters, a tall, thin dyke with light brown hair, pretended to be the owner. No one challenged her even though just about everyone in our world knew she was fronting for a wormy accountant who worked his ownership through some Nevada corporation to keep it, along with some other valuable assets, out of his wife's reach. California was a community property state, and there were too many divorces. Fewer and fewer had the patience, the tolerance for conflict. It was easier to get a divorce attorney. The joke was he or she took the first steps to divorce today: He or she got married. Confidence in a lifetime relationship was at an all-time low, even in the so-called Bible belt states.

"Well, look who's here," Marlee cried from the corner of the bar when she saw us enter. "Jack and Jill."

"Hello Marlee," Willy said. "What you do, advertise free pussy tonight?"

Marlee shrugged.

"I won't charge you," she said.

She had been flirting with Willy for as long as I knew both of them, but Willy didn't consider her homosexual. She considered her asexual. She told me Marlee reminded her of a praying mantis. "She was born of some insect."

"Thanks. I'll keep it in mind next time I'm desperate, without hope, and a few seconds from committing suicide," Willy told her. Those who heard roared. A space at the bar was instantly created for Willy, which meant for me as well. Willy was always clearing a way for me.

Despite the little verbal duel between Marlee and Willy, they, along with everyone else, quickly got into the ebb and flow of usual banter, discussing political issues, music, the newest vacation destinations for gays, even clothes and medical topics. These people were highly successful in their businesses and their professions. At that bar were doctors, dentists, lawyers, and teachers. For the most part, most were well read and well educated. None of them felt they were somehow denied the benefits of life in the mainstream.

Just like everyone else, I was soon having a good time. I put on a little buzz with the wine and looked forward to a great dinner. I was more vulnerable, I guess, so when Janet slipped beside me to congratulate me, I smiled with confusion, but without any fear or anxiety.

"For what?" I asked.

"On deciding to have a baby, to have the responsibility of bringing up a child. I think that's terrific. For you. Not for me," she added with a smile. "But I do have to admire your guts. Who wants to bring up children today? And bottles and diapers? Ugh."

I simply stared at her.

And then, recouping, I smiled and said, "I suppose your parents asked themselves that hundreds of times after you were born."

"You know, fuck you, Kate. I was just trying to be nice."

"Keep trying. You have a ways to go," I said, and she turned and shouldered her way out of the crowd.

Willy, always watching after me, caught it and stepped over.

"What was that about?"

For a moment I was unable to speak. Then I turned on her.

"You went and told people?"

"What?"

"About my deciding to get pregnant, about our deciding to have a child. You told? I would have thought you would wait until I actually became pregnant, Willy. What if it doesn't work? What if . . ."

"I haven't told anyone anything," she said. "I don't know what you're talking about, Kate."

"Yeah, right. How the hell would Janet Madison know? You should have heard her half-ass congratulations. Her little digs. Thanks."

"I told you I didn't tell anyone," Willy said.

Paula Benson was nudging her to listen to her new joke. I glared at her and then walked out of the restaurant. I didn't even realize I had taken the glass of wine with me. I went to our car and stood beside it, fuming. Every time the restaurant's door opened, the laughter, chatter and music flowed out like smoke. An elderly couple went by, both looking at me oddly because I was standing there with a glass of wine in the parking lot. I could see from the way they walked faster to their car that I unnerved or frightened them. The slightest thing out of the ordinary rang alarms these days. I couldn't fault them. I was just as neurotic and I was probably half their age if that.

"First," I heard Willy say, "I don't know why it would bother you so much. You're not going to be doing this in secret. You didn't intend to leave the area for nine months, did you?"

"That's not the point, Willy," I said, turning to her and leaning against the car. "This is our business. Our is the operative word here. We decide when everyone else finds out about this."

"I told you. I didn't tell anyone anything," she said with her jaw taut. "I just grabbed Janet by the scruff of her neck and pulled her aside. She heard it from Tommy Ryan at the plant."

"Tommy Ryan?"

"He's in there," she said, nodding toward the restaurant. "Didn't you see him on the other end of the bar?"

"No. But how would Tommy know?"

"Eve," she said. "When he was showing her the kitchen equipment, they got into a discussion about how she found out about us, et cetera, and she told him how you had gone to the doctor her sister works for and why. I'm sure it was just an innocent thing on her part. She probably had no idea you'd want it kept secret.

"Besides, you know how difficult it is to keep anything secret in this town. People feed on gossip like vampires feed on blood. Now, you've gone and made Janet think you wanted it to be secret and she'll come up with all sorts of reasons that will make it look even more peculiar."

"She better not."

"I warned her. Don't worry, but that won't stop it

from happening behind our backs. What I suggest we do is turn around, go back in there, and announce it to as many people as we can. Put the fire out before it starts."

"Now?"

"Events have a way of choosing their own births and deaths."

"I don't know."

"Why wouldn't you?" She stepped closer, studying my face. "I ask you again, Kate, are you having serious second thoughts?"

"No, it's not that. It just isn't exactly how I had hoped we would tell people . . . blab it over a bar."

She shrugged.

"Good a place as any. Half of them won't remember what we said. Well?"

"This new employee better understand we don't gossip about our private lives, Willy, especially if you're going to permit her to live in our casita for a while."

"I'll talk to her. As I said, I'm sure it was all done innocently. Don't you agree?"

"I suppose."

"Good. Committing yourself, us, to this is important now, Kate. Going in there and telling some of our friends is just another way to seal it. Ready or not?"

"Okay," I said. "Okay."

"I hope I'm not twisting your arm the way you twisted mine for the last half a year."

"Okay, Willy. I get it," I said.

Although I made it seem ridiculous, I had the strangest sensation that now I was the one being talked into everything. What was it Willy had said, "Be careful what you wish for? You might get it?"

We returned to the bar. A number of people had picked up on the tension and were waiting to see what we would do. Janet had returned, too, and was at the opposite end next to Tommy. She looked like she was in a sulk. If there was one person I knew she didn't want disliking her, it was Willy.

"Everything all right?" Paula asked us. That gave Willy an opening.

"Yes, we're just a little jittery these days."

"You are? Why?"

"We've made a major decision, a major commitment," she replied, and looked at me.

"What decision?"

"I'm going to have a baby," I offered.

"Have a baby? You mean, like in I'm pregnant?"

"It's about the way I'd put it, yes," I said, and glanced at Willy, who was smiling.

Paula, however, suddenly looked at me strangely.

"What?"

"Are you pregnant now?" she asked, and both Willy and I immediately knew where she was going.

"No," I said. "And don't you dare say that I am. I've never been bisexual, Paula."

She looked skeptical.

"Even as a teenager? I was," she said before I could reply. "It's just natural to experiment."

"I didn't need to. I knew who I was," I said, just as much for Willy as for her.

"Good for you. So, if you're not pregnant, when and how will you be?"

"Soon," I said.

"Is it going to be one of those lab things? They take one of your eggs and . . ."

"No. It's a home insemination. Just with the sperm," I followed with emphasis.

She laughed. I never thought of Paula as being very intelligent. She got by on her charm and enthusiasm. She worked as a dental hygienist and, from what I heard, was best with children.

"Do they give the sperm a name these days?" she asked, looking to Willy and hoping she would be as lighthearted as she was.

"Yes," Willy said. "They do."

"And what would that be, Willy?"

"Dick," Willy said.

Paula's loud peal of laughter stopped conversations behind and around us.

"I'm hungry," I told Willy.

"Me too. Shall we to the table go?"

She scooped her arm through mine, nodded at Paula, who was holding that silly smile, and walked us into the dining room. We sat and watched how the news spread around the bar. Faces turned our way. Willy nodded and smiled back at some.

"That's it," she said between her teeth as she smiled. "There's no turning back now."

She picked up her wineglass to tap against mine.

"To the three of us," she said. "Whoever he or she might be."

"To the three of us."

I shivered with expectations. I saw how many of our friends were looking at us and whispering.

This change we would bring about in our lives had actually begun.

8.

Eve moved in the following afternoon. From what she brought with her, I concluded Willy was probably right about her not being all that well fixed financially. She had three cartons of clothing, four garment bags, two suitcases, a carton of books, and a box of her personal toiletries. Everything fit easily in the back of her SUV. It took us less than five minutes to carry it all into the casita, which wasn't big enough to take much more anyway.

She couldn't stop thanking us for our generosity, and made promise after promise to be a loyal, efficient employee.

"And you know," she added after she was settled in, "I don't mind helping out with the baby."

"Pardon?" I said.

"For a while I took care of my brother's baby."

"Your brother's baby?" I looked at Willy. Something told me she knew all this. "Why couldn't his wife take care of the baby?"

"She died in childbirth. It's so unusual these days, I know," Eve said quickly.

"Dr. Aaron wasn't her doctor, was she?" I asked.

"Oh no. My brother and his wife lived in New York. Not in the city. A small town upstate."

"How long ago was this?"

"Two years ago," she said. "It was very, very sad."

Something else occurred to me.

"Was your sister-in-law inseminated?"

She looked at Willy. The expressions on their faces provided the answer.

"She was? By Genitor?"

"No, it was a company on the East coast, but . . ."

"Who is helping your brother now?" I asked.

"Oh, he remarried. I hung around for a while, but I didn't want to get in the way and I had to get back to my own work and career. That was when I came out to California."

I nodded. Willy was just staring at me, making me feel bad for asking so many personal questions. I didn't want to know anymore anyway.

"Okay," I said. "If there is anything else you need, let me or Willy know."

"I'm fine. Thanks again, you two," she said. "I'm heading over to the plant. I want to get as familiar with everything as quickly as possible."

"Good idea," I said. "I'll be there soon myself. I have some work to complete on the books."

I walked out and returned to the main house, leaving her and Willy behind. The casita was just off to the right of the pool. We had intended to use it as a guest house, but had not yet invited anyone.

Once again, I found myself feeling strange, even

trembling a little inside, and not knowing why exactly. I poured myself a glass of energy water and stood in the kitchen leaning against the counter and thinking.

"Well, how about that?" Willy asked, entering and going to the refrigerator. "We might have a built-in babysitter, too."

"I'm beginning to think we did win the lottery."

"Yeah, I know what you mean," Willy said, pouring herself a glass of orange juice. "What's that expression? Don't look a gift horse in the mouth?"

"You knew none of this? You didn't know her sister-in-law went through an insemination process and died in childbirth?"

"How would I know any of that? I met her when you did and spent the same time with her you did."

"Dr. Matthews didn't mention it to you?" I asked suspiciously. "She didn't describe Eve's experience taking care of an infant?"

I wondered if she was already thinking of ways for us to pawn off our child with some nanny.

"No. Why should she? How could she volunteer her cousin for anything like that anyway?"

I was silent.

"Kate?"

"Just curious. I never won anything in my life, especially not a lottery."

Willy laughed.

"Sometimes," she said, stepping closer, "you're so like a child, a beautiful child." She touched my cheek and then kissed me softly. "Good things are coming our way. Get used to it," she whispered.

"Okay," I said, wishing I had her confidence in our destiny.

"I have to pick up some things at the market. I'll meet you at the plant," she said.

"Right."

She left and I looked at the telephone. There was a call I had been putting off, but suddenly, I wanted to hear my mother's voice even if that voice would, I know, be full of shock and surprise. It would also be comforting just to hear her.

"You and Willy are having a child?" she repeated as would someone who had to confirm she was hearing correctly after I had told her.

"Yes, Mom."

She was silent.

"You're adopting a child?"

"No, Mom. I'm having a baby. We're having a baby."

I could envision the way her face moved: her lips rotated counterclockwise, her eyes went up and then down, and then she pulled her mouth back and deepened all the wrinkles around them and into her chin. My father wasn't home or else she would be repeating it all for him. For some reason they never liked to pick up two phones so they could listen in and talk simultaneously. The concept of a conference call was beyond them. Even though they were not terribly old people, they shook their heads at every technological advancement as if it were part of some black magic. Unlike most of their senior citizen friends who circulated jokes on e-mails, often sending the same ones twice, they did not have a computer and still thought of the Internet the way some primitive African tribe thought of the telephone or electricity.

"And how are you having this baby? Willy didn't have some sort of sex change, did she?"

"No, Mom," I said, finally feeling light enough to laugh. "I'm undergoing home insemination."

"It's an injection?"

"Sort of," I said.

"Into . . . you know where?"

"That's it, Mom. In a nutshell."

"Does it hurt?"

"No, of course not. It's not guaranteed to work the first time and maybe not the second or even the third, but I'm starting in a few days. Willy and I have discussed it and decided we'd like to have a child, be more of a family."

"I don't know what I'm going to tell people," she said. It was more of one of her thoughts she hadn't kept contained.

"You'll tell them you have another grandchild and it will be the truth."

"I don't know anything about this insemination."

"I'm learning about it myself as I go along," I said.

"It's not important for you to learn, Mom. I just didn't want you to be surprised if I called you next month and told you I was pregnant."

"I would have been surprised. That's for sure."

"That's why I'm calling you and Dad now."

"I don't know how to explain it to him."

"Just tell it to him the way I told it to you. If he wants to call me later, tell him to call. I'll be home after work."

"Home insemination. I'm living too long," she said. It was one of her favorite expressions because it drew sympathy from whomever heard it. "This world has gone nuts."

"Maybe, but it's the only one we have at the moment. I'll keep you up on things," I added. "I have to go now."

"Yes, keep me up," she said. She didn't say goodbye. She just hung up and, I was sure, stood there shaking her head to see if what she had just heard would fall out of an ear.

I couldn't help wondering how my brother would react to the news. I knew my mother would be on the phone with him within the hour. It would do nothing to bring us back together. In fact, it might even drive us further apart, if that were possible. Maybe I was desperate to develop a new family to replace that part of my own I had lost.

I left for work.

There was a great deal of excitement at the plant

when I returned. The entire crew was around Willy, jabbering away, and from the laughter and smiles, I knew it was something very good.

"Don't tell me someone really did win the lottery," I said soon after I entered.

"We did win a lottery," Willy replied. "We were just informed that we got the White Party at the convention center. They're anticipating 35,000 people."

"Are you serious?"

"She is," Eve said. "What a way to start a new job!"

Everyone laughed.

"How did we win that? I wasn't aware you even bid on it," I said.

"I didn't."

"Didn't? Then . . ."

"You know that Glen Isler has been doing that party for the last five years."

"Right. So?"

"He had a heart attack yesterday while he was driving and crashed into an oncoming beer delivery truck. He was the heart and soul of his company. They're in total disarray."

"How horrid!"

"Someone's bad luck is someone else's good luck, Kate. It's how the world works."

"But can we do it?"

"We will even if we can't," Willy said.

"I forgot when the White Party is."

"Six weeks. Plenty of time to work up a menu and

get what we need to get done. And, it will keep your mind off you know what."

She followed me into the office.

"A job like this is quite a bonus for the year, Kate."

"I know. I just can't help wishing we got it a different way. What a terrible way for Isler to go!"

"You want me to turn it down?"

"No, no. Of course not, but thirty-five thousand people?"

"And climbing. We've got a lot of planning to do."

"How can we do it? Even contemplate doing it?"

"We will work it out. There are many ways. Eve worked a few big venues and has some good suggestions. I've already made some calls for temporary servers, and Eve and I are looking into the assembly line, what needs to be upgraded, etc. From her previous employment, Eve has some good connections concerning machinery. We'll have a meeting later," she said, and went out to talk equipment and process with Eve and the others.

I watched them through the window and saw how their excitement lit their faces and animated them. Eve, although new to our plant and to these people, appeared to be right in the thick of it. She wasn't shy, but that was probably because she knew what she was doing and saying, I thought. That's good. It would give the others confidence. We were generous with our employees and they all knew that with such a big job would come well-earned bonuses. That would bring extra tender loving care to all we produced.

They moved like one animal already, going from stoves to tables to dishware. Willy and Eve were holding court, their excitement so vivid that I thought the machinery would start to dance around them. I couldn't help but smile. I loved her for her energy and the power with which she seemed able to address anything and anyone in our lives.

All this good fortune didn't overwhelm me, however. I certainly hadn't come up from a difficult and misfortunate background. My family had always been well-off. My father had been a very successful business attorney and through his work had invested in a number of projects that made him wealthy quickly. My brother followed in his footsteps and was moving even faster up the economic ladder. My frustrations and disappointments were minor in contrast with most people's. There wasn't anything I wanted that we couldn't afford.

But when you join your life with someone else, it no longer mattered how fortunate you had been or even who you were. You were now a different person, part of a combination that created a new you. The old expression been there, done that didn't apply. Everything was new because everything was now done as a couple. Willy's pleasures and disappointments were mine as well. It was truly like being reborn.

Preparing for this huge undertaking did take our mind off the impending home insemination. Our days and nights were one continuous planning session. Willy and Eve were everywhere acquiring people, machinery, serving equipment. They made frequent trips to the convention center to plan out our logistics and they met with the White party committee twice within the week to seek some direction and get approval for all the suggested hors d'oeuvres and entrees, as well as drinks, for we learned they had also given us the bar concession. This was huge in terms of potential profits.

"If I were really a superstitious person," I told Willy, "I would conclude we're getting all this good luck because we decided we would have the baby, be bigger and better together, and give of ourselves."

"Okay," she replied smiling. "I'll sign on to that theory."

It was practically the only time we even mentioned the baby during the week. Just about every night, she was at the plant until after I had given up waiting and had gone to bed. By the time she arrived, she was exhausted and I didn't want to bother her with talk or even making love. She was the first up, too, and out of the house before I had even finished dressing.

The work for me increased considerably as well. All the ordering and money we were committing made me nervous, but Willy continually came into the office to reassure me we were going to be fine.

"It's all going smoothly," she said. "We're a hit, and they just love Eve. Every time there's a small or even a big glitch, she seems to have the answer based on previous experience."

"When did she have all this experience?" I asked. "She was tied up caring for her brother's baby so long she couldn't have worked that many years before she came here."

"It wasn't the length of the time; it was the quality of the jobs, the experiences, Kate. I don't care how long she's been at it. She's coming up with solutions almost as fast as the problems arise. She's something to behold."

I nodded and stopped questioning about her. I didn't want Willy to see just how jealous I was. I knew how much she admired hands-on, take-control people, people with a strong sense of themselves, people with confidence and even a bit of arrogance when it was necessary. It made me wonder some-times if she didn't see me as she would some kind of pet, the dependent one she needed around her to reinforce her own sense of control and power over destiny.

Finally, the day before the home insemination, Dr. Matthews called and my getting pregnant moved back to the forefront of our thinking.

"How are you?" she asked immediately. She called me at home just after I had arrived from work and was about to prepare some dinner for Willy, Eve, and myself. Despite Eve's culinary skills, I didn't shy away from making the things Willy and I loved and that she loved me to make for her. I was not going to be intimidated, and didn't care whether she was just being gracious to me or not when she complimented my food.

"I'm fine," I said. "Excited and nervous."

"Yes, I'm sure. I heard how busy you two have become. That's good as long as you take care of yourself," she said adding the warning. "Your body has to be receptive to what we're about to do." She laughed. "I like to compare my prospective mothers to well-fertilized and nurtured fields, prime for planting the seeds."

"I understand," I said.

"Is our plan for the insemination to occur at 8 P.M. still okay?"

"It's okay with me," I said. "I'll tell Willy when she gets here. I'm expecting her any moment with Dr. Aaron's receptionist's sister, who I understand is your cousin?"

"Oh, yes, Eve Stoner. I was told she was staying with you."

"Not with us exactly. She's living in our casita for a while."

"I met her only a few times, but when I recalled what she did for a living, I thought she might be of some help to you and Willy in your business. She seemed to be a very nice young lady."

"She told us about her brother's wife dying in childbirth."

"A horrible thing. Yes, I know, but I don't know

much more about her brother. My extended family is just that, extended. I'm afraid I've been too dedicated to my work and have lost touch with many of my relatives. Isn't that true for you?"

"Yes, but not for the same reasons."

She laughed.

"Well, a baby has a way of bringing people to-gether."

"That's not my purpose, but I suppose it's not something I would reject."

"Exactly. Anyway, it appears then that Eve is working out for you at a perfect time, is she not?"

"She is," I said, and with some reluctance added, "She's terrific."

"I'm glad. Like anyone else, I'm always shy about making recommendations. If they don't work out, people blame you and not the person you recommended."

"I can't see her not working out," I admitted. "Don't worry about it."

"Good. It's wise to reduce your burdens during this period of time."

"Apparently, she can help afterward as well," I said. "She's even had experience caring for a newborn, but I suppose you knew about that?"

"Oh, yes, that's right. I had forgotten she was there for her brother. Well, considering how busy you two are, it's nice to have some additional options."

"Yes," I said. I heard Willy and Eve enter the house. "Willy's back. I'll remind her of the time."

"If it's all right, I'll be there at seven. There's preparation."

"Sure. Why don't you come for dinner?" I asked as Willy entered the kitchen. She stopped and waited, a puzzled smile on her face. Eve was right beside her.

"Oh, I don't . . ."

"It's not problem. As you know, I have an assistant cook at home, too," I said, eyeing Eve. "See you at seven."

"At seven," she said and I hung up.

"Dr. Matthews?" Willy asked, remembering.

"Herself. Tomorrow at eight. D-day. She'll be here at seven for preparations so I invited her to dinner."

"Oh, this is so exciting," Eve said.

"It could be," Willy said, winking at me.

At dinner the conversation centered entirely around the White party at the convention center. I tried to be interested, to ask questions and listen, but my mind continually wandered. Every once in a while, Willy glanced at me and smiled.

"Let's let our little mother relax," she said after we had eaten. "Eve and I will take care of the cleanup. You go outside and rest, Kate."

"I'm fine," I said.

"And that's how we want you to be tomorrow night, too. Go on before we shove you out," she said.

"I'm not going to be one of those pampered pregnant women," I insisted.

They both laughed.

"I'm not!"

"Fine. You're not. For now, pamper and humor me. Go relax," Willy said. Eve started to clear the table.

I stood there a few moments and then I turned and went out to the lounge at the pool. The moon was almost full and was sliding toward the west. It was just over the house now, casting the mountains in an amber tint and capturing the incredible turns, twists, and dives of bats in and around the wash, a huge canal built by the army engineers to prevent flash flooding. A long thin wisp of clouds spread wider as the wind carried it east, thinning out the ghostlike blanket even more. Stars flickered and threatened to go out like dying embers. They brought to mind dozens of candle wicks lit but endangered in a breeze.

I could hear the music and Eve and Willy's laughter behind me. Everything seemed to be making me melancholy tonight, sad and alone. I wanted Willy out here with me, holding my hand or cuddled up beside me, speaking softly, watching the night perform. I wanted to fall asleep in her arms, to feel comforted and safe, unafraid of our decision, my decision.

Suddenly, I resented our good financial fortune. Why couldn't the big job and the bonuses come afterward? I didn't want to be distracted. I didn't want to put anything in the back of my mind. I didn't want to think of it as something to fear or make me nervous. It bothered me that it would be considered in that light.

We should be talking about it all night. It should have been the main topic at dinner.

I heard another peal of laughter and then a door close. Moments later, there were footsteps and I relaxed. Finally, I thought, Willy was coming out to me.

But it wasn't Willy. It was Eve. She stopped at my side.

"What a beautiful night," she said.

"Yes, it is."

"You're not worrying about tomorrow, are you?"

"No, why should I be?"

"Exactly," she said.

"What do you know about it?" I asked, a little more petulantly than I intended.

"Oh, not really very much, but what could it be? There's no pain involved, I'm sure. Well, I didn't realize how tired I was," she added. "It just hit me that we've been going ever since six this morning and nonstop, too."

"Hmm," I said, not showing any interest or sympathy.

"I'm going to sleep. Have a good night," she added, and walked toward the casita.

Just as the wispy blanket of clouds touched the face of the moon, Eve crossed to the opposite side of the pool. She was silhouetted in the filtered glow.

I sat up quickly.

"What's wrong?" I heard Willy ask. I hadn't heard her come up behind me.

I swallowed hard and shook my head.

I wouldn't dare say it.

No telling how she would react to such a thought.

How could I say it?

How could I tell her Eve reminded me of the figure sitting beside Dr. Matthews in her car that first night?

9.

I DIDN'T HAVE A RESTFUL SLEEP and it annoyed me that Willy did. Every time I sighed or moaned, turned or sat up, she remained still, her body relaxed, her breathing soft and regular. She looked like a contented baby. At one point I rose and went out to get some milk. I stood by the patio door and looked out at the night sky. The later it was in the desert, the more stars appeared and they always appeared bigger, brighter. Willy thought it had something to do with the thinness of the air.

The moon had gone below the San Jacinto Mountains, but the sky was still ablaze with its diamond eyes. There was enough light to see the pool, the patio, and lounges clearly. My gaze went to the casita and I was surprised to see what looked like a candle flickering in a window.

Why would Eve be burning a candle this late at night? Was there something wrong with the electricity? If she had to get up to go to the bathroom, why wouldn't she just turn on a light? A candle wouldn't burn all night so she couldn't have it lit because she liked a little light when she slept.

Suddenly, an oval-shaped shadow about six feet

tall moved to the window. It swept past it and then was lost in the darkness, but when it was gone, the candle had gone out. I stared at the dark window for a while and then returned to bed.

Willy groaned.

"What?" she muttered, vaguely aware now of my moving about and returning.

"I couldn't sleep so I got some milk. When I looked out, I saw a candle lit in Eve's casita window."

She didn't respond.

"Did you hear what I said?" I asked.

She had fallen back to sleep. I lay there a while and then turned over and swam through a sea of paranoia to settle finally in the darkness of my own comalike sleep.

Willy was up ahead of me in the morning. I was so groggy my eyelids were defiant. Shards of sunlight felt more like knives. I wanted to put the pillow over my head.

"I would have thought you would be up before me today," I heard Willy say.

I peeked out through the narrowest possible slits in my eyelids. She was standing there with a steaming cup of coffee for me.

"I don't think I slept two hours," I told her and sat. "Thanks."

She stood there, sipping her own coffee and staring at me.

"What?"

"You should have taken something to relax you. Dr. Matthews was right about that."

"When did she tell you that?"

"I don't know. During one conversation or another she mentioned it. Eve's up and gone already," she said. "Going to be a big day at the plant. We're getting a shrink wrapper to package some of the foodstuff and we have to hook it in to our conveyor. Don't worry about dinner tonight. Eve's going to come home earlier and prepare chicken Kiev, one of your favorites."

"What about Dr. Matthews? Maybe she isn't fond of it."

"She is. We checked," Willy said.

"Checked? When?"

"A half hour ago, Eve called her. Doctors get up early, you know."

"She's not that kind of doctor."

"Whatever. She gets up early. I'm taking off. I'll grab something at the plant. Take your time. You should really take the day off anyway."

"Why?"

"To get yourself mentally prepared."

"I don't need to mentally prepare. And I don't intend to be one of those chronic complainers when I do get pregnant. If I do get pregnant," I corrected.

"You will," she said. She kissed me on the cheek and started out.

"Hey."

"Yeah?"

"Do you remember me telling you about a candle lit in Eve's window last night?"

She shook her head.

"No. When did you tell me that?"

"It was late. I thought you were awake, but I guess you were talking in your sleep," I said.

"Candle?"

"I thought so."

"She has no candles. Why would she light candles anyway? There's nothing wrong with the lights in the casita. You probably saw the reflection of a star in the glass."

I thought about it and nodded. It made sense.

"Yeah, probably."

"Don't start getting hokey on me today," she warned, then smiled and left.

I sat there sipping coffee until I felt my body gradually waking up all over. Then I rose, showered, and dressed. I didn't eat much for breakfast. My stomach felt like it had been turned into a beehive. Before I left, I stood by the patio door and gazed at the casita. Impulsively, I walked out, marched across the pool patio, and went to the casita door. I was surprised that it was locked. I didn't even remember our having a key for it. Shading my eyes, I peered through the window. It was so neat inside. It looked like no one had been in it. I didn't see any of Eve's things about either. The bed was made and the pillow looked untouched, no evidence that she had lowered her head to it, not a crease in the blanket.

When I stepped back, I noticed what looked like a spot on the inside of the glass. It suggested the residue of a candle flame, the sort of waxy glaze it might deposit flickering so close to it. It looked like a cross upside down. Was it just an ordinary smudge? Probably, I concluded. Get out of this, I told myself. This is not the day for it; this is not the time. I should be focused on one thing only, and if Willy suspected I wasn't, she would surely be very upset. I needed her, needed her support and her love more than ever.

Immediately after I arrived at our plant, I realized she didn't have much time for any of my emotional problems anyway. There were electricians, plumbers, and a carpenter all working feverishly to adjust our equipment, add equipment, and get the plant redesigned for a much bigger operation.

"Hey," Willy shouted to me when she saw me enter. "There's a new pile of invoices and we've had four orders this morning from our regulars. You have to get on the horn with that pain-in-the-ass manager at Breckman's Produce, too. He's moaning and groaning about the schedule of delivery we've requested. Use your feminine charm," she added.

"I thought you wanted me to take the day off."

"That was before I realized I was only one person. Besides, it will keep you from worrying and being nervous. And imagining things," she added.

"Thanks," I said, and she laughed. She returned to work and I went into the office.

She was right, of course, for the most part the work

did keep me from thinking about what we would be doing tonight. But every time I took a breather, those concerns came rushing back to the forefront. The questions were like little creatures waiting in the corners of my mind for an opportunity to pounce.

How did most heterosexual couples decide it was time to have a child? I wondered. Was the man usually the insistent one or the woman? I knew plenty of women who would snap back with, "You're not the one who's going to be losing her figure, carrying the baby, going through the labor."

On the other hand, there were women I had met who claimed they had felt at their best when they were pregnant. They raved about the wonder of having a life inside them and having that child come out of them. Would that all be true for me?

Then there were those women who repeatedly failed, even with fertility drugs. I heard stories about that, about how difficult it was for them to go anywhere and see a pregnant woman. They were always wondering what it was about them that made it so difficult. It had to hurt their sense of themselves, their egos. Their very identity was in doubt. Could that happen to me if we failed the first and second and even third time? How many times would I try before giving up and what would it do to my relationship with Willy? I had no doubt she would deal with it fine. After all, this was still my idea originally. But would my sadness, my depression effect us, effect how she saw me?

We weren't bound by any in-sickness-and-in-health oaths, not that those who took those oaths seemed to feel so bound by them anyway these days. No, we were married in a different way, through the oaths we had taken with our eyes and our lips, our bodies and our very being. Whatever mysterious power drew people together went to work on us. Neither of us ever doubted it. Would we still feel that way in the coming months? How could I help but not be nervous?

I dove back into my work, now actually grateful for the phone calls, the arguments, the pile of paper to transfer to our computer software, and the faxes of invoices and orders I had to process. All this added business didn't really occur to me until I was almost finished. A quick calculation told me we were heading toward some very big numbers. Wasn't our accountant going to be surprised? In fact, the numbers were so high, I started adding, recalculating, and reviewing the figures to be sure I hadn't made some big error.

I worked so hard I didn't realize the end of the day had come. I looked up and saw the time, realizing I had worked right through lunch. Willy never stopped either. Finally, she came in to tell me Eve had gone back to the house an hour previously to start to prepare our dinner.

"She wanted to make a chocolate angel food cake, too. I told her that was one of your favorites."

"I don't see myself having a great appetite tonight, Willy."

"Did you have any lunch?" she asked suspiciously.

"No. I forgot. I bet you didn't either."

"It's not the same thing. I'm not trying to get pregnant tonight. If you're don't take care of yourself, this won't work," she warned. "I'm telling you now that when you get pregnant, I'll be on your ass to make sure you take good care of yourself, so be prepared. No nagging your mother ever did will compare."

"Okay," I said laughing. "I promise. I'll be hungry tonight."

"Better be. Eve would be disappointed, too."

"That's not what I'm worried about," I said petulantly and immediately regretted it, especially when I saw the expression on Willy's face. "I mean, it's really nice of her to do all this for us, but I'm focused on us for the time being, on what we're about to do."

She nodded with that look in her eyes that told me she saw through any false front I could muster.

"Go home, Kate. Get some rest. You don't realize the mental and emotional stress."

"Yes, I do," I said. "But you're right." I closed the books and shut off the computer. "How's it going out there?"

"It's going well. No worries. I'll be home in fifteen minutes," she said and returned to the crew and the equipment. I packed up my things and headed out.

When I pulled into our driveway, I was surprised to see Dr. Matthews had already arrived. I parked in the garage, closed the door and entered the house to the sounds of music and laughter. Eve and Dr.

Matthews were sitting in the living room, having a cocktail. There was a platter of hors d'oeuvres on the coffee table. Dr. Matthews had her hair up and wore a light blue dress that reminded me of a hospital uniform.

"Kate," she cried, standing. "I hope you don't mind my arriving a little early. I had an errand nearby and it was over quicker than I had anticipated. It gave me a chance to catch up on our family news," she added, nodding at Eve.

"Of course not," I said, smiling and gazing at the platter. "I see the party's already started."

"I thought I'd use Dr. Matthews as a guinea pig to test our selections for the White Party," Eve said.

"They're wonderful. I especially like that variation on a crab cake."

"Thank you," Eve said. She had created it so it wasn't entirely out of place for her to take credit. She turned to me. "And don't forget what's waiting for you in the kitchen," she said.

I thought she was referring to the dinner, but Dr. Matthews' laugh suggested something more.

"What's waiting for me in the kitchen?"

"She's referring to the vial of sperm I brought. When we're ready, I'll be thawing it out slowly."

"Where is it?"

"In the refrigerator," Eve said, smiling. "Can I offer her a drink?" she asked Dr. Matthews.

Can she offer me a drink? Whose house was this?

"I'd rather she not," Dr. Matthews said. "I know

you're a little nervous about it all," she said, turning to me. "So I have something that will keep you calm and it wouldn't be wise to combine it with alcohol."

"I don't think I need anything to keep me calm," I said sharply, then turned and went into the kitchen. I immediately saw what looked like a turkey syringe in a closed plastic bag on the counter, beside a small bowl. I froze a moment staring at it and not realizing Dr. Matthews and Eve had come up behind me. When she spoke, Dr. Matthews sounded as if her lips were right beside my ear. I nearly jumped.

"I find that to be the most effective way to transfer the sperm," Dr. Matthews said. "Don't worry. I'll explain it all to you carefully."

I looked from her to Eve who continued to smile. When would Willy be home? I didn't want to talk about any of this without Willy being present.

"We'll wait for Willy," I said pointedly.

"Of course."

"Look at this!" Eve said and opened the refrigerator. I expected her to show me the vial, but she took out a chocolate angel food cake instead. "Yummy."

"Looks wonderful," Dr. Matthews said.

Eve put the cake back and took out a platter of ready-to-fry portions of chicken Kiev.

"I have a secret ingredient that will make this extra special," she said.

"What a feast," Dr. Matthews told her. "I would have come here just for the dinner."

They both stood there smiling at me and although

I couldn't explain it, that made me nervous, even irritable.

"I'm going to change into something more comfortable," I said.

I felt I needed to get away from them for a few minutes, to be alone.

"That's a wonderful idea," Dr. Matthews said. "The more relaxed you are, the better our chances," she said.

Our chances? I thought, and then recalled how she had made the point that every insemination's success or failure reflects on them. I nodded and went to the bedroom. They returned to the living room.

I took my time changing, glancing every five minutes at the clock, wondering about Willy. Where was she? She should have been home by now. It was well over a half hour.

To keep my mind off it all, I brushed out my hair, put on some fresh makeup, and then walked out of the bedroom. The music was louder. I stopped and listened, surprised I could hear Willy's voice and laughter now, too. I hurried to the living room. They were all sitting around, drinking and feasting on a new tray of hors d'oeuvres.

"When did you get home?"

"Just a little while ago? Dr. Matthews told me you were changing. Did you see the cake, the Kiev?"

"I saw everything," I said pointedly.

Eve's smile was really beginning to annoy me. She sat there beaming up at me like some idiot.

"Anything wrong?"

"I'd like to speak with you alone," I said, and turned. I walked out and through the kitchen toward our bedroom without looking back to see if she was coming or not. She entered right behind me and closed the door softly.

"What's wrong, Kate?"

"Everything," I said. "I wanted this to be a very private event, something special between you and me."

"So it will be. All I suggested," she said, smiling lustfully, "is I'll see about making it as erotic as possible."

"I told you I didn't want any party."

"It's not a party. We have to have dinner. You didn't object when Dr. Matthews volunteered to help with the process, and you invited her to dinner, not me."

"Process," I muttered.

"Well, what do you want to call it, Kate, making love with a vial of sperm?"

I glanced at her and sat on the bed.

"I don't want Eve in here," I said. "She's weird. I don't care what you say."

"All right. She won't be in here. I don't see why she would have been in here anyway."

I looked up at her. She shrugged.

"You didn't think I wanted her in here, too, did you?" she asked.

"I don't know what to think. No. I guess not, but she has a way of inserting herself into everything."

Willy shook her head and looked away. I saw she was losing patience with me.

"Look, I am nervous. Just bear with me. I'm sorry."

"Sure. Let's enjoy our meal and then follow the procedure and see what occurs." She smiled, suggesting she was up to something she thought would please me. "All right?"

I took a deep breath.

"All right."

"Great," she said, and opened the door. "Let's eat!" she shouted.

I hadn't noticed before, but Eve had set the dining room table with our fine china. There was a wine goblet at three places. On the plate obviously intended for me, there was a pill.

Dr. Matthews and Willy stood by their chairs. Eve was obviously going to serve. She moved quickly to pull out my chair.

"The guest of honor," she declared.

"What is that?" I asked looking at the pill.

"What I told you about before. Something that will keep you calm, help you get through it all easily," Dr. Matthews said. "I've seen some real blunders when it comes to this," she added, looking to Willy, who nodded as if she had seen them as well.

"What sort of blunders?"

"Just silly things that caused failure. The more relaxed you are, the better our chances are," she said. It was beginning to sound like a chant.

I sat and looked at the pill.

"I don't like taking pills. What is it, exactly?"

"Jesus, Kate."

"It's just a mild sedative, Kate. I wouldn't give you anything more," Dr. Matthews said. "It's something Dr. Aaron recommends and uses, too."

Willy turned her hands over and shrugged.

I took the pill and swallowed it with some water.

Eve began to serve our salad and brought out some fresh, warm bread.

I couldn't say exactly why, but their chatter, their laughter, their obvious enjoyment of the food and the wine all irked me. Maybe it was because the conversation was about everything but me, everything but what we were really here to do. They went from the White Party to politics to a philosophical discussion of the future of mankind and whether or not we were better as a species than our ancestors had been. Willy agreed with Dr. Matthews that people, although far more civilized, weren't any less evil. After a while, their voices droned and I felt as if I were the one who had been drinking all that wine and not any of them. Occasionally, I caught Dr. Matthews looking at me and smiling.

I ate, or at least I thought I did. What I tasted did taste wonderful. I begrudgingly offered up compliments to Eve about her cooking and baking, the whole preparation. I offered to help clean up, but they were all up and around me, plucking dishes and silverware, bowls and pitchers off the table like three vultures. Before I knew it, the table had been stripped clean. I sat there, dazed, until I heard Dr. Matthews at my right ear, her lips grazing it, whisper, "It's time, Kate."

She took my right arm at the elbow. I felt another hand on my left and saw Willy smiling. The two of them guided me to my feet. I laughed.

"Did I drink too much?" I asked.

That brought smiles to their faces.

"No, Kate. You didn't drink anything," Willy said.

"Just relax, dear," Dr. Matthews said.

Eve went ahead and opened the bedroom door. She stood aside and watched as we entered. I glanced at her.

"Good luck," she whispered. The whites of her eyes seemed to bubble around her more rust-colored pupils like boiling milk. She stepped back and closed the door.

"Don't worry. She's not in the room," Willy said.

They guided me to the bed. The blanket had been pulled back and the pillows rearranged. Beside the bed was a small table with the syringe I had seen earlier. The vial was in a small bowl of water. I sat and watched as Dr. Matthews rolled the vial gently in the palms of her hands. I was vaguely aware of Willy's undressing me.

When I was naked, she lowered me back so my head rested on my pillow. I heard Dr. Matthews mumble something to Willy, and then Willy placed pillows under my rear to elevate my hips. To me it then seemed like the lights had been dimmed, and once again I could swear I saw a candle burning in not one, but both our windows that faced the rear of the house.

"Remember this song?" Willy whispered in my right ear. She had knelt by the bed as if she was about to offer a prayer and then leaned toward me. "I asked Eve to put it on for you, for us."

Willy was never one to make big deals over our anniversaries for different events in our relationship. When one occurred, she pretended to be surprised and then reluctantly admit it was reason to celebrate. All the while I knew that whatever it was, it meant as much to her as it did to me. So this was the beginning of Willy's surprise, I thought. Hearing our song put a smile on my face. She leaned over farther to kiss me. I felt warmed right to the heart. We were going to do this in an atmosphere of love and not some laboratory experiment after all.

Dr. Matthews moved around to the foot of the bed, the now loaded syringe in her left hand. She held it up and nodded at Willy, who further surprised me by taking off her clothes, sliding onto our bed, and putting her arm around my shoulders to cradle my head. I felt Dr. Matthews's fingers exploring.

"Locating your cervix," she whispered. She was looking down at me between my raised knees. "Ah," she said. She inserted the syringe. Then she looked to Willy who reached to the right and opened a drawer in the night table. She handed Dr. Matthews a vibrator.

"An orgasm after insemination will help. The uterus will lift causing the cervix to dip down into the pool of sperm, while the contracting orgasm will help move the sperm up into the uterus."

Willy was nibbling around my nipples. Dr. Matthews brought her right hand around to caress my breast. She pressed the vibrator against the inside of my right thigh and gradually brought it closer. My heart was pounding. Willy was kissing me on the lips, pressing her pelvis against the outside of my right thigh. Her moans excited me. She was closing on her own orgasm. Dr. Matthews was doing everything but penetrate. I felt my hips gyrating. It was truly as if something had taken over my body. The excitement rose. I was moaning and crying as much as Willy and then I felt my own orgiastic explosion and screamed. Tears were streaming down my cheeks.

"Good," Dr. Matthews said. "Good, Kate. That's good."

Willy pressed her face against my shoulder. Her breathing was hot and heavy, but soon began to calm alongside my own.

And then the room began to spin. I tried to stop it by reaching up, but before I lifted my arm, I felt myself falling back, falling deeply into a darkness that enveloped me and turned my cry inward to echo and die against all the doors to the outside that slammed shut.

10.

WHEN I WOKE, I was surprised to find myself alone. Sunlight told me I had slept through the night. I felt like I had slept at least a week. I looked at the clock and saw it was just after nine. Willy was not beside me and I couldn't hear anyone moving about in the house.

Nine-thirty! I thought. Wasn't I supposed to have another insemination at eight? Why hadn't I been awakened?

I sat up and gazed around the bedroom. There was no evidence of what had occurred here the night before. It was almost as if it had all been another one of my dreams. I half-expected that when I rose and went out, I would discover that no time had passed, that I had never met Dr. Matthews, I had never been examined by Dr. Aaron, and we had never hired and housed someone named Eve in our casita.

"Willy?" I called, and listened. Except for the sound of the lawn sprinklers starting and running, I heard nothing. Still naked, I went to the door, opened it and listened. I looked into the kitchen and spotted the note on the refrigerator. Willy had written to tell me she had gone to the plant.

I looked at the spotless kitchen, everything neatly in its place. I peered into the dining room and saw how pristine it was. There was simply no evidence of the dinner party until I opened the refrigerator and saw what remained of the chocolate angel food cake and a large platter of leftover chicken Kiev. At least I knew I hadn't dreamed it all, I thought, and went to shower and dress. I didn't think I'd eat much of a breakfast, but when I stepped out of the bedroom afterward, I found I was ravishingly hungry. I drank my orange juice, but then took the time to make myself a cheese omelet with bacon and buttermilk biscuits with jelly. I was more surprised when after I ate it, I still felt hungry, actually hungry for a piece of the angel food cake. The piece I cut didn't suffice either. Before I left the kitchen, I consumed the entire cake, but didn't realize it until I looked down at the cake dish and saw it was empty. I actually recoiled from the sight.

Was I in some kind of self-hypnotic state? How did I eat so much and not realize it? I cleaned up quickly, moving as would someone who was trying to cover up a crime. Then I hurried to my car and drove to the plant.

For a moment after I had arrived, I thought I had entered the wrong warehouse. The new machinery, the tables, the extra conveyor belt, and the additional temporary employees were all there. What had once been a small mom and pop–style operation seemingly turned overnight into a significant little factory. Chatter and noise replaced the once soft laughter and light conversation that had characterized our relaxed, easygoing manner. Willy and Eve were moving about, instructing and inspecting, shouting orders. No one noticed I had entered. I had to shout over the din. Willy turned and waved. I gestured at the office and she nodded, but she didn't come right away. When I approached my desk, I saw that my computer had been turned on and new information had been entered concerning orders and expenses.

"How are you doing?" Willy asked immediately on entering.

"Why didn't you wake me before you left this morning?"

"I thought after what you had gone through, I'd let you sleep longer. I kept looking in on you expecting the noise Eve and I made would wake you, but by the time I left, you were sleeping like a baby yourself. How do you feel?"

"I'm all right," I said, and actually thought about how I felt for the first time since I had woken. I did feel all right. I felt better than all right. I felt more energetic than I had felt lately. "Who was on my computer?"

"Eve put some information in there for you. Did you have breakfast?"

"Yes. I had a big breakfast, a very big breakfast."

Willy nodded and smiled as if she had expected no less.

"Great. It went well," she said. "It was actually very exciting and," she added smiling licentiously, "far from some kind of clinical procedure."

"But I thought there was going to be another insemination twelve hours after the first. Wasn't there talk about Dr. Matthews staying overnight?"

Willy stared at me a moment, her expression freezing on a soft smile.

"What do you mean?" she asked.

"What do I mean? Insemination? Remember Dr. Sperm?"

She laughed.

"Why are you laughing at me, Willy?"

"You had the second insemination, Kate. Then you fell back asleep and I left you, just as I told you."

"What? I had it?" I recoiled and smirked at her. "I think I'd remember something like that, Willy. What the hell are you saying?"

"You had the second insemination. It all went well. Dr. Matthews was pleased. She, Eve, and I had some breakfast and then as I just said, we looked in on you, saw you were sound asleep, and we didn't disturb you. As Lois said when she left, 'It's all in the womb of time now.'"

"I don't remember it, Willy," I said, my lips trembling. "How can I not remember something like that?"

"Take it easy. Maybe the sedative you took confused you. You should have just taken the day off. I keep telling you that this is a bigger emotional and physical experience than you think, but you insist on being a big shot."

"I know. I'm sorry. I don't mean to create any problems for us. Especially now," I added, nodding at the activity I could see through the office window. "But I just can't believe I was that confused. My God."

"It's okay, Kate. Take it easy." She stepped over to me and ran her hand over my hair before leaning over to kiss me. "Mommy baby," she whispered smiling. "Later, we'll both help relax each other."

I couldn't speak. I just shook my head.

She straightened up and said, "Everything's going really well out there. We're going to be a big hit. You know what happens when so many people are impressed at one time. This place is going to expand. We'll need two warehouses, twice the staff. Eve has some interesting ideas for it all. We'll go to dinner and talk about it all one day this week."

"Why such a big expansion? Weren't we big enough, happy enough?"

"Are you kidding? Yes, but why in hell would we let such opportunity pass us by? You want to give our baby the best of everything, don't you?"

"We were doing fine," I said.

"Kate, that isn't very American of you. Where's your entrepreneurial ambition? Besides, you never know. You might like having a child so much that you ask for another, and kids are expensive these days." She started out. "Oh," she said at the door, "Dr.

Matthews has made an appointment for you with Dr. Aaron for next week."

"Next week? We won't know anything by then, will we?"

"Hey, they have better ways now. She says Dr. Aaron can detect human chorionic gonadotropin in your blood as early as a week after ovulation."

"Human what?"

"It's a hormone made by pregnancy."

"Since when do you know so much about this?"

"I sat up into the wee hours with Lois talking about it and learning. Fingers crossed," she said, then smiled and left.

I sat back, my heart pounding. She sat up into the wee hours talking? How come she was so alert?

Could that be right? In a week I'd know? I suddenly felt like someone who had gone too far out on a tightrope to turn back and I was terrified about looking down. As my father was fond of saying, "The die is cast."

I tried concentrating on my work, but my mind drifted continuously. I relived the first insemination and felt myself warm all over with the memory of my orgasm. I still couldn't imagine it being done a second time and not remembering. I drifted off thinking about it. When I glanced at the clock, I was shocked at how little I had accomplished.

"Hi, Kate. How are you?" Eve asked, poking her head through the opened door.

"I'm fine," I replied, not taking my eyes off the computer monitor.

"I hope you don't mind my entering some information for you on the computer. Willy thought it would be okay. We both thought we'd try to make your day easier."

"I'm said I'm fine. I don't need pandering," I said, a little more harshly than I had intended or perhaps as harshly as I intended. I wasn't sure. I knew I felt annoyed and I knew that anyone objective observing would find fault only with me. That bothered me even more.

"Oh, I don't mean to do that. We just want you to be comfortable and happy."

"Right," I said, and thought, what's with this "we" all of a sudden? This was a matter only for Willy and myself. She was just another employee.

"I just want you to know I'm available if there is anything you need done, no matter how small it might seem. You guys have already done a lot more for me than I ever would have anticipated," she said, which only made me feel worse about my reaction. "I'm grateful."

"Okay, thanks, Eve. I'm sorry if I sound short with you. I'm just a little . . . I'm not quite myself."

"Hey, no need to apologize for anything, ever. You're entitled to be as moody as you want. I remember when my sister-in-law was pregnant. My brother was ready to move out. He actually got the shakes himself, but it passes. It gets better as you go along."

"Oh, you know for a fact that I'm definitely pregnant? You, too, have become an expert about pregnancy?" I asked, half curious and again, half annoyed.

She shrugged.

"Hey, I saw how successful the insemination process was for my sister-in-law. If you're not pregnant now, you soon will be, I'm sure, and I just know what I've observed. It's not brain surgery. Don't hesitate to call on me if you want anything. I mean it," she added, and backed out, closing the door.

Not brain surgery? It seemed to me someone would have to be more than a chef to look at a woman and know she was pregnant. That was bigger than brain surgery.

No one came to the office again until lunchtime. Willy, who was busy with one of the machines that needed attention, sent Tommy Ryan to tell me they were ordering in sandwiches.

"Why would you like?"

"A catering business and we can't make our own sandwiches?"

"Willy's got everyone doing something else at the moment and thought it would be the fastest way. I have the Wishing Well's menu," he said, offering it to me.

Just reading the descriptions of the food suddenly turned my stomach. Maybe it was because of all I had eaten at breakfast, but I became nauseated and quickly handed the menu back to him.

"I don't want anything," I said.

"You sure?"

"Yes. Tell Willy to come in here," I said. He nodded and left.

Looking annoyed, wiping her greasy hands with a rag, Willy returned to the office.

"What?" she asked. Before I could answer, she added, "That damn pump on the mixing machine dropped stone dead and it's not even a year old. I've got to send someone to San Bernardino. It'll be hours. What?" she asked again, remembering it was I who had asked to see her.

"I'm going home. I don't feel so well."

"Why? What's wrong?"

"I just feel a little woozy and tired. I probably should have taken the day off and rested as you suggested."

"Want Eve to drive you?"

"No, I'll be fine. I'll just rest, have some herbal tea. Don't worry."

"Okay," she said, obviously eager to get back to her machinery.

"Maybe you're trying to do too much too quickly, Willy," I offered.

"I'm trying to do too much too quickly?" She smirked. "Just go rest, Kate. I can see you're irritable."

Before I could reply, she left me. I wrapped up my things and started for home. Eve came rushing over when she saw me heading for the front door.

"Aren't you feeling well?"

"I'm just tired."

"Okay to drive?"

"I'm fine," I snapped. "Just tired. And leave the computer alone. I don't want to get confused."

I walked out and closed the door between us quickly. She stood by the glass door watching me get into my car and she didn't move until I backed out of my parking spot and started away.

I don't need her haunting me, too, I thought. Her concern about me was over the top. I made a mental note to tell Willy to get her to back off.

Just as I reached the corner and started to slow down for the traffic light, the light changed to green and I began to accelerate, but a tall man with dark-brown hair stepped off the sidewalk as if he were colorblind or something. I had to shift my foot back to the brake quickly. I immediately thought someone behind me would rear-end me, but luckily, there was no one.

The man stood there looking at me through the windshield as if he wanted to be certain I was who he thought I was. He had his hair cut military-style and wore a black shirt and a pair of black jeans. His face was lean, angular, his features distinct, cut from granite. I laid my palm on my horn and he stepped back to the sidewalk. I glared angrily at him and continued. I didn't have the strength to start shouting at him for being pretty damn stupid and almost causing an accident. When I glanced up at him in my rearview mirror, I saw he was standing there and looking after me as if I were the one who had violated the rules and not he.

"Idiot," I muttered, and drove on.

Soon after I arrived home, my nausea was gone and I found I was very hungry again. I considered the sizeable leftover portion of the chicken Kiev. After I put more seasoning on it, I sat at the kitchen table and ate ravenously and consumed it all. I laughed, thinking how crazy I was behaving for someone who was ordinarily so conscious about the food she ate, she would know the total calories to the tenth. However, when I rose from the table to take the dish and silverware to the sink, I was overcome with an urge to eat something sweet. I ransacked the cabinet to find what we had in cookies. There wasn't much of anything. Driven, however, I took out the utensils and ingredients and quickly worked up a batch of chocolate peanut butter cookies.

To my utter amazement, I had the urge to drink Coke with the cookies and was so impatient with waiting for the cookies to cool down, I actually burned the top of my mouth. When I gazed at myself in the mirror, I broke into hysterical laughter. I looked like a little girl who had snuck into the cookie jar. There was chocolate smeared over my mouth, my cheeks, and chin.

The eating frenzy left me exhausted. Ordinarily, I hated taking naps in the daytime. I always woke feeling worse, hating the grogginess. However, the bed looked too inviting. I curled up under the cover and closed my eyes and didn't open them again until I heard voices. Turning over, I saw Dr. Matthews and Eve standing at the foot of the bed. Dr. Matthews had that large syringe in her hand and Eve had the vibrator. They were smiling and separated to come around both sides of the bed toward me. I started to scream.

And then I really woke up, my neck and breasts thick with sweat. It gave me a chill. I sat up, my heart pounding. The room was dark and the house was deadly silent. I practically lunged at the clock and was surprised to see it was after eight. Where was Willy? Why didn't I hear her out there?

A quick walk through the kitchen and living room revealed no one was at home. There were no notes left for me either so I went right to the phone and called the plant. Eve answered.

"We called you earlier," she said. "When you didn't answer, Willy tried your cell phone and then decided you had gone to sleep."

"Decided? Where is she?"

"She's out there supervising. Everything is running like a Swiss clock, but you know Willy."

"Yes, I know Willy. Get her to the phone!" I demanded.

"Hold on," Eve said.

It took quite a while, but finally Willy picked up.

"How could you just assume I was asleep?" I asked as soon as she said, "Kate?"

"Well, you weren't answering either phone and . . ."

"Maybe I was dead or had passed out or . . ."

"If you were already dead, what could I do?" she threw back at me in her characteristically sarcastic manner.

"Thanks."

"C'mon. You're not going to get like that on me so soon. You might not be pregnant yet."

"We never neglected each other like this before, Willy."

"And we're not now. But it goes both ways, Kate. I have a lot on my plate down here. I would hope you would be considerate and understanding. I'm not asking you to work harder."

"I told you this White party was going to be too much for us."

"It isn't if we're both reasonable and considerate. Both," she emphasized.

I took a deep breath.

"When are you coming home?"

"Not for a while longer. You up to meeting Eve and me at Roger's?"

"I don't know," I said, but the vision of one of Roger's fat, juicy burgers flashed across my mind. The restaurant specialized in them, having a variety of burger, cheese, and seasoning combinations, along with the fattest french fries in America. Normally, I wouldn't set foot in the place, and if I did because

Willy wanted one of those burgers, I would order the house salad. "How much longer?"

"Give us another hour," she said. "What have you been doing all this time?"

"I just slept," I said, leaving out the eating and baking I had done.

"So? You probably want to get out for a while, right?"

"Okay, okay. I'll see you there in an hour," I said. The truth was, I wasn't sure I could wait an hour before sinking my teeth into one of those burgers.

I took a quick, hot shower and started to dress, when the phone rang. She's changing her mind, I thought with disappointment. Or she's going to tell me they'll be later than anticipated.

It was Dr. Matthews.

"How are you doing?"

"I'm fine," I said, and then immediately felt guilty for not telling her the truth. "I've just been tired."

"Not unusual. It's traumatic."

"I've also had this inordinate hunger. I can't believe how much I ate already today and I'm hungry again."

She was silent.

"Is something wrong about that?"

"No."

"But isn't such odd eating a usual characteristic of a pregnancy a little further along?"

"Yes, I suppose so."

"You mean you think it means I am pregnant?"

She laughed.

"No, that's not any real evidence. There could be a number of different reasons for your sudden appetite."

"I mean, I couldn't eat fast enough. I made my own cookies because there weren't any, too."

She laughed again.

"You're a healthy young woman, Kate. Don't make anything more of it. I have, however, had clients whose symptoms were accelerated. I swear, I even had a woman give birth in five and a half months to a healthy, normal-size boy."

"Wouldn't that be written up in some paper or magazine?"

"The client wasn't someone who wanted any publicity. She didn't even want people to know she had been inseminated. She went off somewhere when she started to show and when she returned, she told her friends she had adopted a baby."

"Why?"

"Everyone has her own reasons for what they do," Dr. Matthews remarked. "It's none of my business. I did my job, delivered what I promised and that was that."

"You don't have any contact with the mothers afterward?"

"Only a short time afterward." She laughed. "Most don't welcome any further contact. I hope, however, that you and I and Willy can remain friends for a long time."

"Yes, me too," I said.

"Well, enjoy. I'll call you periodically. You have your appointment set with Dr. Aaron, but call me if you have any questions or problems, please."

I wanted to ask her how she knew I had the appointment with Dr. Aaron, but I imagined she had to keep tabs on my progress for selfish reasons. They wanted to announce another successful insemination.

"Thank you."

"Best to Willy. And Eve," she added as an afterthought before hanging up.

I thought about what she had said about that premature birth. Could I, like that other woman, have an unusually accelerated pregnancy? Is that why I was showing symptoms immediately? Or was I being too optimistic to assume the insemination was a success? I paused to study myself in the full-length mirror. As I perused my face and body, however, I thought how ridiculous I am, actually thinking I would see some change in myself after only a day.

On the other hand, what I had just done with Dr. Matthews would be considered science fiction fifty, a hundred years ago. Maybe science would provide techniques that would enable women to get pregnant and have children in half or two-thirds of the normal time. My mind was suddenly buzzing with all sorts of images. I even imagined my baby, lying there on our bed, alert and happy, moving its little arms and legs with impatience, demanding that he continue his accelerated development and be walking and talking in months instead of years.

We'll have a natural wonder on our hands, I thought, a prodigy, a genius, of course. My brain was racing with plans and preparations. I would tell Willy tonight that as soon as we knew the sex of our baby, we should get the nursery ready, get the clothing, hell, even plan his college education. Laughing aloud, I completed dressing, fixing my hair and makeup, and hurried to the car. Contrary to how I had felt earlier, I was full of new energy. I am behaving like a pregnant woman, I thought.

The moment the garage door went up, I backed out and was so excited, I nearly forgot to close the garage door before I sped off, spinning my tires like some speed-crazed teenager. I even turned up my car radio. Were these mood swings another symptom? I wondered.

When I pulled into Roger's parking lot, I didn't see Willy or Eve's car. I started to call to see where they were, but stopped and told myself I've got to give her some space, especially now. I could see Roger's wasn't very crowded. It was late, especially for a restaurant like this.

Roger's was designed on the model of an old-fashioned fifties diner. The booths were in blood red imitation leather with Formica table tops. There was a long counter with imitation black leather stools, and a small rear area for birthday parties and the like parents threw for their children here. The kitchen was open and behind the counter. All the waitresses (there were no waiters) were dressed like high school cheerleaders, wearing light-knit black and gold sweaters and short skirts with white shoes that had tiny bells on the laces.

The aroma of grilled burgers turned me into a hungry vampire. I slipped quickly into a booth and seized the menu when the waitress stepped over. I told myself this wasn't formal dining. I could order my food now. Who knew when Willy and Eve would actually appear anyway? I not only expected them to understand; I thought of it as my right. After all, I'm the one who had undergone the insemination and had to be given any and all consideration.

Before the waitress could ask me what I wanted to drink, I told her to give me the deluxe burger.

"Rare," I added, "and a Coke."

The french fries came with the burgers. She took the menu and went to the counter. I gazed around. There were two couples toward the rear and a tall man with his back to me. I gazed out the window, hoping to see either Willy's car or Eve's any moment. I hadn't even noticed that the night sky had grown thickly overcast. Not a star was visible. The darkness squeezed in around the patches of light cast by streetlights and the restaurant's parking lot lights and signs. The illuminated world was under assault, besieged. Without electricity, fire or batteries, we'd be swallowed into the belly of night.

Just as the waitress brought my Coke, the man who had been sitting behind me walked past on his way out. I glanced up at him and then felt my body tighten, my heart stop and start. He looked like the same man who had stepped in front of my car earlier in the day. He wore the same black shirt and pants, and his hair also was cut military-style. He didn't look at me until he reached the door and then turned back. He stared for a moment, nodding slightly but not to me as much as to confirm something he was thinking. Then he left. I watched him walk through the parking lot and disappear in the wall of shadows on the other side. He didn't even look like he was heading for a parked car.

Moments later, Willy and Eve pulled in. They were in Eve's car. Willy was laughing when she stepped out. I could see they were both in a jolly mood. They saw me in the window and waved. The waitress brought my burger as they entered and headed toward the table.

"Well, who can't wait?" Willy asked.

"I had no idea when you were showing."

She slipped in beside me, taking a french fry off my plate. The waitress waited for Eve to get into the booth and handed them both menus. Willy eyed mine.

"Since when do you eat the deluxe? I couldn't get her to order the petite whenever we were here," she explained to Eve, who smiled and nodded as if she had been with us for years. "I will have a petite, medium," Willy told the waitress. "Without the pickle," she added.

Eve ordered the Jack cheese burger and both ordered bottled water.

"Great. Make me out to be the pig," I said. I bit into my burger.

"Don't tell me you're having cravings already," Willy said. I told her about my conversation with Dr. Matthews and the pregnant woman who had delivered the perfect baby months too early. "Could that be?" she asked Eve.

Why was she suddenly the expert? I wondered.

"I do remember hearing something about that particular birth."

"Well, if you're not pregnant, you've certainly had an identity reversal," Willy told me. I had nearly finished my burger.

I gazed out the window again and then told them about the man in the black shirt.

Willy shrugged.

"So? It's not a big city. People see the same people in different places all the time."

"It was the way he looked at me both times."

Willy stared a moment and then looked at Eve. They both smiled.

"Oh give me that old paranoia," Willy began to sing to the tune of "Old Time Religion." "That old time paranoia to make me feel important."

"Very funny."

"If he's around when I am and he gives you any weird looks, I'll kick him in the balls so hard, he'll have a new pair of ears," she said.

They laughed and then started talking about the plant and the business and this idea of a bigger expansion. Once again, I felt left out. I was torn between my impending motherhood, should I be pregnant, and my interest in the business and life Willy and I had created together. I could see Eve slipping into my seat behind my computer and spending most of the day with Willy while I sat at home.

But wasn't this what I had wanted? I had to get past my petty jealousies.

Besides, I thought, when the baby is born, Willy will be a parent too and that will bind us in ways neither of us could imagine. That was always our plan, our dream for ourselves and our child.

And that's what will happen, I told myself.

But I was unable to prevent the small voice within me from throwing up a challenge and asking, "Are you sure?"

I looked at Willy, her face so vibrant with new excitement, the excitement that should have been reserved for our impending parenthood and I had to admit to the voice, to the challenge, that I didn't know. I couldn't be certain.

And that made me afraid.

It made me almost wish the insemination had failed. If it did, I thought, I'd put off trying again until this new business venture was completed.

Or maybe . . . forever.

11

WHEN I WENT TO SLEEP, I slept like a contented baby. Willy lay beside me talking in what felt like a stream of rhythmic phrases threading together comments about the work, people she met, and our future as though she were weaving a tapestry of our past, present, and future. For me it had the effect of a lullaby. I had a wonderful, restful night and woke when she did. Back into myself, I showered and dressed, feeling renewed. Eve came over and the three of us had breakfast. Even my interest in the plant and our project was heightened. I saw how pleased Willy was, so when we arrived at the warehouse, I went right to work and our day just clicked along. Representatives for the White Party came to talk to us. They were pleased with all our plans and preparations. Amazingly, none of them even mentioned poor Glen Isler anymore. However, Tommy told me he heard the investigation of Isler's accident and death was still ongoing.

My appetite, although still bigger than usual, was nothing like it had been that first day. I didn't crave sweets as much either. I know my temperament improved. I didn't view Eve as any threat and in fact began to see how she was really assisting Willy and lessening her workload. She had quickly become a true right-hand man, an assistant manager. I saw, too, how the other employees were treating her with more respect, recognizing her expertise.

Because we still had our regular customers to service, our days had few dead spots. Keeping busy diminished any of my concerns about the insemination's success or failure, and as the day of my first post appointment with Dr. Aaron drew closer, I anticipated and suffered little anxiety. Eve didn't ask to go along with us, but I saw she wanted so much to be part of our lives now so I asked her if she would like to go. Her face instantly brightened. Later, Willy thanked me.

"That was kind of you, Kate. The more I'm with her, the more I see how she's alone in the world. What she had of family has really drifted away from her. I learned she doesn't have all that much contact with her sister who works for Dr. Aaron. She thinks of us now as her sisters."

I nodded. I was feeling magnanimous. The more I enjoyed my health and energy, the less threatened I felt. If I were pregnant, it was true that women were at their best when with child, I thought, even this early into it. More pleasing to me was Willy's admiration for me, which seemed now to be growing. She wasn't teasing me anywhere as much as she used to. The increased warmth between us was palpable.

When we arrived at Dr. Aaron's office and were buzzed in, I immediately saw and felt the strain between Eve and her sister. They didn't hug or kiss each other, and her sister's questioning of how she was getting along was full of negativity. I sensed a terrible sibling rivalry, a frenzied feeding in the trough of envy. She kept looking to us hopefully to see if we would show any displeasure, especially looking to me. We left her out in the lobby when we went into the examination room.

"I like the glow in your face," Dr. Aaron said as soon as she entered, and looked at me. "Women are like candles. Pregnancy lights them up."

"Hear that, Willy?"

"In this case I'd rather be in the dark," she responded, and we laughed.

Dr. Aaron took some blood, did a quick examination of my breasts and stomach and then asked us to wait.

"I am equipped here with state-of-the-art diagnostics," she explained. "Why don't you two have a cup of coffee or tea? Bea will take care of you."

We returned to the lobby to wait. I was surprised to see Eve wasn't there. There was another patient waiting to see Dr. Aaron. She didn't look much more than a teenager. From the way she kept her attention on the magazine she was reading and avoided eye contact with me or Willy, I assumed she wasn't happy about being here. Another unwanted pregnancy, I surmised. It made me a little uncomfortable. Did Dr. Aaron perform abortions in this same office where she assisted and encouraged healthy births?

Willy and I exchanged a look revealing she was probably on the same wavelength.

"Where's Eve?" I asked her sister.

"Oh, she wanted to get some air and went for a walk," she told us. "Is she really doing as well as she claims?"

"Yes, she is," Willy said. "We're lucky to have her."

"I'm happy for her. And for you, of course," she added, but not with any real sincerity.

I stepped out of the office and Willy followed.

"I know why she'd rather have us as sisters," I said.

"Ditto."

We saw Eve walking slowly a good block and a half down the street. She had her hands in her pockets and her head down. I called to her and she turned and waved. Then she started back. Just as she started to cross the street, a car came around the turn behind her, the engine roaring.

"EVE!" Willy shouted.

If there were two inches between her and the bumper of that car, there was a lot. The wind it created and the shock of its sudden appearance spun her around. We both screamed. The car sped past us, the driver not looking back or slowing down. I had only a brief glance, but it was enough to send chills up my spine. Willy was running to Eve, who had her hand over her heart and looked incapable of moving. I hurried behind her.

"Are you all right?" Willy asked.

"I think so," she said. She was taking deep breaths.

"The bastard didn't even slow down after he almost hit you."

"It looked like he wanted to hit her," I said.

Eve looked at me and shook her head.

"He just didn't pay attention when he came around the turn and I didn't anticipate a car. He shouldn't have been going that fast, but it was just as much my fault for being so oblivious."

"If we didn't have to wait for Dr. Aaron, I'd go after the son of a bitch and send his balls to a taxidermist to make something I could hang on my rearview mirror instead of big dice," Willy said.

Eve laughed.

"He wanted to hit her," I emphasized.

They turned to me.

"C'mon, Kate," Willy said.

"The driver . . . I'm almost sure he was the same man."

"What same man?"

"The same man I almost hit. The same man I saw in Roger's who gave me that look again."

"Why would he want to hit her, Kate? That doesn't make any sense."

"I don't know. I sense something evil."

Willy started the hum the theme from *The Twilight Zone.*

"I'm all right, Kate," Eve said. "It was just a stupid driver. Don't make anything more of it. I'm sorry you had this happen now. I should have stayed at the plant."

"It's not your fault, Eve," I said. "How could that be your fault?"

Willy seconded it, but she, like me, could see something troubled her.

"Is anything wrong?" she asked her. "I mean, other than this stupidity."

"My sister is such a horse's ass. We never got along that well. She's always been jealous of my ability to make close friends. It's her own fault. She puts people off. Silly sibling rivalry, but I wish she'd grow up," she added. "I'm sorry. I shouldn't be laying all this on you guys, especially now."

"Forget it," Willy said.

"It's all right," I said. "I'm not in a fatal illness."

"That's debatable," Willy quipped. "Children can cause premature aging and encourage parental suicide."

"You're such an idiot," I said.

Eve laughed, and the moment lightened up for us.

Suddenly, we heard Bea calling to us from the office entrance.

"Don't mention this close call to her, please," Eve said. "She'll only see it as my fault anyway."

"I wish I would have gotten his license plate number," I said.

We entered the lobby. The teenage girl who had been sitting there reading her magazine had apparently been taken into the examination area. As it turned out, Eve's sister had seen everything through the window in her small reception area.

"You almost bought it," she told her. Eve tried to ignore her. "You never watch what you're doing. You never anticipate . . ."

"Will you stop it, Bea," Eve snapped.

"You should know better," Bea apparently had to add.

What kind of a thing was that to say to an adult? I wondered. I was starting to dislike her as much as Eve did.

"You just love criticizing me, Bea," Eve told her and accompanied us into the office. "Jerk-off," Eve muttered. Willy laughed.

"Don't let her bother you," she told her, and then put her arm around her and shook her. She smiled at me and at Willy.

"I'm sorry, Kate," Dr. Aaron said as soon as she entered the examination room. "I'm really surprised. I was so confident we'd get it this first try, but don't be discouraged. It's more the case than not."

Both Willy and Eve were staring at me. Willy put her arm around my shoulder and gave me a squeeze.

"It's all right. It'll happen," she said.

I felt my eyes starting to fill with tears so I quickly turned away, took a deep breath and held my lids closed.

"You want a moment?" I heard Dr. Aaron ask Willy.

"I think we're fine. Hey, Kate, we'll try again as soon as it's opportune."

"I'm sorry I don't have good news for you this

time, but when I do, I don't envision any complications with your pregnancy, Kate. You're healthier than most of my patients."

"She's Vitamin Kate," Willy quipped. "Between her herbal teas and natural foods . . ."

"I have one suggestion," Dr. Aaron said reaching into her lab coat pocket. "Take one of these every day. The pills are a combination of herbal and hormonal ingredients that could very well enhance your chances next time."

"Why didn't you give them to me before?" I asked immediately.

"You were such a perfect candidate, I didn't see the need, but there are so many factors that involve themselves in this event, Kate, including anxiety, stress, so many we can't anticipate. The pills cut down on that sort of interference."

"Can't hurt her, can they?" Willy asked.

"Oh no. They're made from only natural substances. You can take your regular vitamins, eat how you wish, drink alcoholic beverages. Nothing contradicts them and they contradict nothing. They're just a little hedge," she added.

Willy looked at me and then widened her eyes. I reached out and took the pills.

"Thank you," I said, then bit down on my lower lip, forced a smile at Dr. Aaron, and started out. "I want to get back," I said.

"Thank you, Doc," Willy told her. She and Eve followed me out, Dr. Aaron trailing behind.

"I'll be on the phone with Dr. Matthews later in the day," she told us. I paused. "I'm sure she'll be calling you. In the meantime, continue your normal daily routine. Two months from now it will all be different, I'm sure. They'll be a he or a she coming into your lives."

"When would we know that?" Willy asked.

"Know what?"

"If the little being is a boy or a girl?"

"Oh, well some don't want to know."

"We'll want to know, won't we, Kate?"

"Let's not get ahead of ourselves," I said. Her face darkened with my negativity. "Yes," I said quickly. "We would want to know."

"Ultrasound is the best way, usually between 18 and 26 weeks," Dr. Aaron told us. "There are other ways, but sometimes they're not accurate."

"Four and a half months?" Willy asked. "Seems you'd know that earlier."

"We can't hurry nature," Dr. Aaron told her. "It's how the fetus forms."

"Really?" I said. "Dr. Matthews told me about a client of hers who gave birth in a little more than five months to a healthy child. Did you have her as a patient?"

"No, that one got past me," she said, smiling. She continued to walk us out. "Be sure to call me with any questions, Kate. Anytime. And try those pills, one a day, okay?"

"Okay," I said, but not with much enthusiasm.

"And how are you doing, Eve?" she asked her.

"Great, thanks. It's a pretty exciting business."

"I'm happy for you. That's nice. It's nice to hear good news," she said.

As we walked down the hallway, I glanced through a slightly opened door and saw the teenage girl prostrate on a table. She had a damp cloth over her eyes. Dr. Aaron saw where my gaze went and reached out without looking to pull the door completely closed.

"Okay, then," she said when we reached the lobby, "I'm sure I'll be seeing you sooner than you think."

We walked out. Eve paused at the receptionist's window.

"How's Lil?" she asked her sister.

"She's doing well. Nice of you to remember your niece," she added caustically. Eve glanced at us and swung her eyes.

"Okay, Bea. I'll be seeing you," she said, and walked out ahead of us.

I looked at Bea quizzically and then, feeling Willy's hand on my arm, continued after Eve.

"Hey," Willy said, getting into the car, "remember. You can choose your friends, but not your relatives."

"Too bad," Eve said, looking out the window. Then she turned and smiled at me. "Anyway, if you go back far enough we're all related."

"Right," Willy said. "Eve."

They laughed. I sat back and closed my eyes. I'm not pregnant, I thought. I am not going to have my own baby as soon as I had hoped. Someday, however, he or she will be a part of me and I'll be part of him or her forever. I have to keep telling myself that or I'll just burst out in tears.

The phone started ringing as soon as we entered the house. It was as if someone was watching our home and called to tell Lois Matthews we were there.

"I know you're terribly, terribly disappointed, Kate. I feel I added to that by being so overconfident," she told me. "I've discussed it with my associates, and we've decided that next month's insemination should be on us. It won't cost you and Willy anything."

"The cost wasn't upsetting me," I said, "but we appreciate your offer."

"Good. Now just take care of yourself, use the pills Dr. Aaron gave you, and let's keep a stiff upper lip. I'll check on you from time to time and of course, we'll schedule you in at the opportune time."

"Thank you," I said.

"Give my best to Willy and Eve."

"I will," I told her and then told Willy what she had said.

"They should pay," she said sharply. "She shouldn't have made it seem a slam dunk."

"I guess that's the right analogy," I told her, and she laughed.

"That's my Kate," she said, hugging me. I knew she was anxious to get back to the plant and told her to just go. I'd be fine.

Although I ate somewhat more than I usually did during the week that followed, I no longer saw any radical changes in my eating habits and I did not develop any unusual cravings. Previously full of expectation and hope, I had downloaded a booklet describing what I should expect during my pregnancy. I read it all carefully and some of what had been happening to me suggested I had become pregnant. This added to my disappointment.

What surprised me, however, was the weight I gained. I was never one to gain weight that quickly, and with my normal eating habits and my otherwise neurotic concern for my figure, I rarely indulged in foods that would impact on my weight dramatically. Willy was always astounded by the fact that I could eat well and, despite not doing a tenth of her exercise, not gain an ounce. Of course, the explanation rested with my metabolism. For better or for worse, mine simply burned up calories.

Not now, however, and at the start, it didn't alarm me, especially because my face didn't bloat or show signs of any weight gain, but when I stepped on the scale, I recoiled at the report that I had gained five pounds and this in less than ten days since I had been given the blood results and told I wasn't pregnant!

I called Dr. Aaron to see what she thought. I wondered if it had anything to do with the pills she had given me to enhance my chances next time.

"Well, they might have a slight effect on your metabolism. Five pounds isn't terrible. You say you haven't dramatically changed your eating habits?"

"No, not really. Certainly not enough to gain five pounds in a week."

"How are you feeling overall?"

"Good. Despite being a little depressed, I have more energy. I'm actually surprised I'm sleeping well."

"Most of that is, I'm happy to say, a result of the pills I gave you. So, I wouldn't stop taking them, but don't hesitate to call me if you have any questions or concerns. Anytime," she emphasized and then to underscore that, she gave me her cell phone number and her home phone number.

She did make me feel better about it and I stopped worrying. I hesitated to mention anything to Willy anyway. She and Eve and the crew were deep into the preparations for the White Party now and I didn't see any reason to stir up concerns, especially when I considered that I did feel good. I knew Willy would just ridicule my concern about my weight.

Every day I looked for something different in my face, but saw no bloating despite the weight gain. Even my legs remained the same shape and size, but my belly looked a little distended. How odd, I thought, and weighed myself three days later to discover I had put on another three pounds.

Something else began to happen. I found myself sweating unusually at different times. The next day I woke in a sweat, showered, dressed, and went to work. Two hours after I was at the plant, I broke into another heavy sweat. For a few moments, it was so severe, I went into a little panic. Willy was shouting at one of the employees for approaching a table without wearing his hair cap. I never heard her so strident and even from the office window could see her face was crimson. I retreated and took deep breaths, drank some cold water, and tried to calm and relax myself. The perspiration diminished, but then I thought I felt something in my stomach.

My eyes opened and widened. I held my breath and waited, and then I felt it again, a distinct feeling of something moving within me. I sat there dazed, shocked and astounded. Willy came barging into the office to make a phone call, mumbling to herself about the employee and didn't even look my way until she lifted the receiver and began her call.

She stopped poking out the numbers and lowered the phone from her ear.

"What's wrong with you? You look like you've seen a ghost or something even worse."

"I could swear I felt something move inside me."

She smirked and raised her eyes toward the ceiling.

"You're not pregnant, Kate. We both know you have a remarkable imagination. I'm sure it was just gas," she added, smiling, and shook her head and returned to her call.

I waited while she took a supplier to task for failing to make a delivery. With our added buying, her power grew proportionately and she was not afraid of welding it like a club. Whoever was on the other end was pleading, promising, and apologizing profusely.

"You have an hour," she told her and slammed the receiver down on its cradle so hard, she made me jump in my seat.

"Damn," I said. "This new enterprise is supposed to be something good for us. You look like you're on the verge of a heart attack."

"People take advantage of you if you let them," she replied.

"They never did before."

"Of course they did. We couldn't do as much about it as we can now. Don't worry about it. I'm not getting sick over it; I'm just flexing our new muscle."

She started out of the office.

"Something else is happening to me and I'm not imagining that," I said.

"What is it, Kate?" she asked with controlled impatience.

"I'm breaking out into these sweats. It's common in the second trimester of a pregnancy."

"Maybe it has something to do with the pills Dr. Aaron gave you. Did you call her and discuss it?"

"No, it just started."

"So?" She raised her arms. "Call her. Jesus."

After she left the office, I had to admit to myself that she might have been right about my active imagination. I didn't feel any more movement in my stomach. However, I did feel discomfort around my waist. When I stood up, I found my skirt was so tight, I had to lower the zipper. Something's bloating me, I thought. I became more and more anxious about it and decided that for a while, I should just lie down on the settee in our office. I closed my eyes and didn't realize I had fallen asleep and slept through a good part of the afternoon. If either Willy or Eve had seen me, neither apparently wanted to wake me.

The sound of Willy screaming at the top of her lungs was what finally woke me. I sat up, confused, even a bit dazed and shocked at the time that had gone by. The shouting grew even louder. I stood up and went to the door. Willy was in the process of firing someone, one of the new employees, a lean, dark-haired man a few inches shorter than Willy. I recalled he had a very soft, mild manner about him. Willy was very aggressive, standing inches from the cowering man. We had hired three days ago. His name was Anthony Salani.

I opened the door to hear more clearly.

"What are you, a saboteur?" Willy screamed. She raised her fist toward his face. He shook his head, turned and walked out of the plant. Willy stood there fuming.

"What's going on?" I shouted, trying to be heard over the machinery. Willy turned and walked toward the shrink wrapper. I felt a little dizzy and backed into the office to get myself some water. When I brought it to my lips, however, a strong wave of nausea rippled up from my abdomen and I leaned over the sink where I started to dry heave and then, after a terrific cramping that terrified me for a moment, suddenly felt incredibly better. It was such an instantaneous recuperation, I simply stood there holding my breath and waiting for a second shoe to drop. None did.

I straightened up, took a few deep breaths, and looked at the cabinet where we kept our snacks. How could I be so hungry after that? I wondered, but went to it and plucked out one of Willy's hi-protein bars. Normally, I thought they were nauseatingly sweet, but I gobbled it up like some stray dog, nearly biting my own fingers and then, astounding myself, reached in for another.

Eve came in just as I finished the second.

"Hey, how you doing?" she asked.

"I fell asleep, woke up, felt nauseous and now I feel . . . ravenous. It's crazy."

"I get like that sometimes. Many times," she said, smiling. "That's why I look like a balloon someone's squeezing." She went to Willy's desk.

"What happened out there?"

"Oh. That new guy Father Rossi recommended screwed up the computerized mixing tank and we lost the whole batch of the crab cake mix. Before that he broke a bulb on the box packer and the shards of glass were all over the place. Whatever experience he claimed he had was probably bogus. Willy wants to tell Father Rossi a thing or two, but I calmed her down. Priest can't be responsible for what one of his parishioner's relatives does. He meant well."

"She's too high-strung," I said. "I'm worried."

"She'll be all right once we get past today. It should be smooth sailing after this," Eve assured me. "You need anything?"

"Looks like another late night, though," I said, gazing through the window at Willy.

"Afraid so."

"I think I'd better leave and get home to relax," I said. What I really meant was I didn't want to wait for dinner.

"No problem. I don't want to interfere, but if there's anything you want me to do on the billing, ordering."

I gazed at the pile of invoices I had yet to enter.

"Okay," I said. "If you can, enter those. I'll follow up tomorrow. Just be sure you back up continually. I'm paranoid about computers."

"I hear ya," she said. "No worries."

I looked at the shelf of snacks, glanced at Eve, and then took another protein bar.

"Tide me over until I get home," I said.

"Oh. I forgot. I prepared a meat loaf Stroganoff you might like. Just heat it at . . ."

"I know how to heat it," I said quickly.

"Right. It's a recipe I learned from this Hungarian chef I worked with two years ago. I hope you like it."

"Thanks," I said.

I gathered up my things and headed out. Willy turned from the machinery and held up her hand to signal I should wait. She spoke to Tom Ryan quickly before heading in my direction.

"I saw you were fast asleep before. You okay?"

"I wasn't for a while there and then suddenly . . ." I smiled. "I feel great."

"Did you call Dr. Aaron?"

"Not yet. I will when I get home."

"You're going home?"

"Yes. I'd better take it easy nevertheless and besides, the way you're going here, I'd be starved to death by the time you decided to eat."

She laughed, hugged me, kissed my cheek, and whispered, "My beautiful prospective new mother." She kissed me again and returned to her work. I told myself I should be grateful she was so busy she couldn't be despondent about my failure to get pregnant and my need to continue this insemination process. I had half expected her to throw up her hands and say forget it, it ain't meant to be, but she had yet to even suggest such a thing.

My drive home was uneventful, but I did drive faster than I normally did. As soon as I got home, I looked for the meat loaf, smelled it, and smiled. The aroma was delicious. I got started on reheating it and changed quickly into a robe. My skirt actually made pink ripples in my skin. How could I have grown too wide for this skirt so quickly? I wondered. My stomach hadn't receded either. The bloating was not a simple, temporary event. I was actually showing like someone who was pregnant, I thought, and now my legs looked bigger, too.

A thought occurred to me so fast I wondered why I

hadn't considered it before. I went right to the phone and called Dr. Aaron. As soon as she picked up the receiver, I rattled it all off to her and ended with, "So, do you think it's possible you misread the results?"

"I don't think that's possible, Kate. We don't read them once only."

"But . . ."

"Please come see me. I can feel your anxiety and I'd like to help relieve your tension. Will you come tomorrow?"

"Yes," I said, and she gave me an appointment.

I couldn't help feeling a deeper disappointment. I had harbored the hope that she would tell me it was possible, the results could have been misread. She would retest and then a wonderful thing would occur, my pregnancy would be confirmed. Another fantasy, Kate Dobson? I asked myself, and turned to my dinner.

Normally, I hated eating alone. For one thing, when I ate alone, I usually ate too quickly. It was more like eating than dining, doing something necessary for life and health and not something enjoyable. Willy loved to make that distinction with the hope that our work, our catered food was treated with respect and not brought in and eaten "like some fast-food take-out." In fact, although she was disdainful of religion, she was fond of saying that good food was a gift from God. The one and perhaps only thing she liked about the world's various religions was the emphasis their holidays put on festive dining, convivial dining wherein families, friends, anyone was brought closer together because of the food.

"Take all the hocus-pocus out," she told me, "and all the holidays make sense."

"If you take out what you call the hocus-pocus, you take out the reason for the holidays."

"Food should be reason enough," she quipped. She loved goading some of our more religious friends into these arguments.

I thought about all that as I sat alone in our dining room and began eating the meat loaf Eve had prepared. It was so good, I really thought it was like a religious experience. I had to give the devil her due. I would have to compliment her. She had definitely outdone anything I had created or prepared.

I drank some wine and had some of the honey-wheat loaf we made in our own plant. I was enjoying my meal so much, I didn't even consider that I was eating alone. Strangely, I felt as if I weren't alone anyway. I even talked to myself aloud just the way I would if someone was sitting across from me. Was I becoming a schizophrenic? I laughed at myself, drank some more wine and definitely overate or what I would normally consider overeating. It was weird. I didn't feel full. I stopped because the sight of most of the meat loaf already gone surprised me. Once again, I had eaten so ravenously, I had lost track of what I was consuming.

Maybe I have been overeating, I thought. Maybe what I told Dr. Aaron wasn't entirely true. There was a logical reason for my weight gain. It was all going to my midsection. After all, if I put together the calories of the bars I ate at the plant, the food and wine, I was way beyond my usual intake. There was nothing mysterious here, I told myself. You've become a little hog.

I rose and cleaned up and then poured myself something I never cared to have before, a créme de menthe over a scoop of vanilla ice cream, and went out to the pool to lounge and relax while the night sky gave birth to more and more stars. For a little while, because I was so contented, I felt guilty about enjoying myself so much while Willy worked slave hours at the plant. Before this, neither of us would ever think of leaving the other behind to work and work while she relaxed unconcerned.

It was easy to rationalize away the guilt, however. I had been undergoing a very traumatic experience. I had been on an emotional roller coaster and it had and continued take a toil. Willy would just have to put up with my self-centeredness for a while. After all, when the insemination took, we would become more than a couple. Both of us would have to make sacrifices. No matter what she said at the end, she apparently had come to the point where she wanted this as much as I did, I thought and closed my eyes.

I almost fell into a deep sleep, but the phone rang. We had extension line outside so I rose and, feeling a little groggy, went to the receiver hanging on the outside wall. It's probably Willy checking up to see if

I was okay, I thought, and smiled to myself as I said hello.

"Get an abortion," I heard.

"What?"

"Before it's too late. Get an abortion."

Even though I heard the caller hang up, I shouted, "Who the hell is this?"

I stood there with the receiver in my hand, my heart pounding.

And then I felt it again.

A stirring in my abdomen as if there really was a fetus developing within me and it had heard the threat and woke with terror inside my womb.

12.

WILLY AND EVE WERE THERE so quickly I thought they must have broken a speed record on their way home. I had retreated to our bedroom and closed the door. I was actually shivering and had a blanket wrapped around me. They both stood in the doorway gaping in at me. I was sure I was a sight, my hair wild, my face flushed.

"What happened?" Willy asked. I had babbled it so quickly and incoherently when I called her that she didn't fully grasp what I was saying. She just said she would be right home.

As calmly as I could, I described the phone call and the warning.

"You didn't recognize the voice?" she asked.

"No. Who do we know who would do such a thing anyway? One of your many jealous admirers, maybe?" I asked her, my voice dripping with sarcasm.

She smirked and glanced at Eve.

"Don't be a cunt, Kate," she said.

"Well, who would do it?" I screamed back.

"My sister-in-law had something similar happen to her," Eve told me in a little more than a whisper.

"What? Why do you mean something similar?"

"They really should warn you about it before they sign you up," she added. She looked at Willy. "All these insemination companies are aware of them."

"Of whom?" I demanded. I could feel the strain in my neck. "What the hell are you talking about?"

"Take it easy," Willy said, moving closer to me. "I'm sure you're making much more of this than needs to be and you're going to get yourself into a terrible state."

"I already am in a terrible state," I said. "It wasn't just what he said. It was the way he said it. That voice . . . like a voice from a nightmare."

"Kate . . ."

"No, Willy, you didn't hear it. I did."

"Okay, okay, I believe you."

"So aware of whom?" I asked Eve, trying to sound a little less frantic.

"There's some right-wing religious group who believes this whole insemination process, using sperm like this, is unholy. They're a branch of the same people who fight abortion, stem cell research, et cetera, fanatics who have gotten a taste of power and have become bolder and bolder. They threaten everyone, doctors included."

I thought for a moment, wondering how she knew all this, and then I widened my eyes with suspicion.

"Could they have had anything to do with what happened to your sister because she went through a similar insemination process? Could they have anything to do with her dying in childbirth?"

"Kate."

"Let her speak," I snapped back. Willy actually took a step in retreat.

"I told you about that, Kate," Eve said.

"You didn't tell me why she died, just that she died in childbirth. I should have asked for some details, but I didn't want to hear anything that would change my mind," I admitted. "So? What happened to her, exactly?"

"She died of an aneurysm bursting as a result of her efforts with the delivery. It happens rarely, but it happens," Eve said softly, looking to Willy as she spoke. I had the sense that they had spoken of this before and Willy knew all the grisly details. They had decided they would avoid telling me probably for the very reason I avoided asking about it, but Eve obviously felt that telling me now was the lesser evil. "As far as I know, no one can induce such a thing."

"How often did they . . . bother her?" I asked.

"I don't know. My brother didn't know all of it, perhaps. My sister-in-law wasn't the type to panic or put any worry on anyone else," she added.

I couldn't help but feel it was a little dig at me. She saw it in my face.

"Not that it was a wise thing for her to do," she added quickly. "She should have spoken up more often and not taken so much on herself. The stress didn't do her any good, I'm sure. Besides, we're here to help. We're your fortress, Kate," she added. "It's not going to happen to you. We'll make sure of that."

Willy nodded.

Since when did Eve take such a commanding position? I wondered, but I did like what she was saying.

"I'm not even pregnant!" I cried. "Why would they call and say such a thing?"

"How would they know if you were or weren't?" Eve said softly.

"She's right, Kate. They just assume."

"We find out who did that or see someone bothering you, that person will be dog food," Eve said.

"I wouldn't do that to a dog," Willy said.

"Food for worms, then."

I felt myself calming. The shivering stopped so I lowered the blanket and sat up to run my fingers through my hair and brush back the strands dangling over my face.

"How did they, could they have found out about me?" I asked.

Willy shook her head and looked at Eve, who had suddenly become our resident expert on fanatics.

"They might have spies, someone on the inside in these places or maybe someone you've spoken to here blabbed it openly in a public place and one of them happened to overhear it. Then their attack dogs were triggered."

"You make them sound like the CIA. They're that organized?"

"Apparently," Eve said. "I really don't know all that

much about them, Kate, just the little I was able to glean from my sister-in-law."

"What about now? Are they still bothering your brother?"

"He hasn't said anything about it to me." After a moment she added, "Remember, I told you he remarried and then soon after that, he moved."

"Moved?"

"Even with a new wife, he had a hard time remaining in the same house, the memories. So, he picked up and took his family to Wyoming. He's living in Jackson. I haven't spoken to him for a while."

"So you don't know if they followed him there or if they are still bothering him?"

She stared, silently.

"If this happens again, we should call the police," Willy muttered. "Harassment."

"Never mind that. Eve's right. Why didn't Lois Matthews tell us about them?" I wondered aloud.

"Maybe her company hasn't had any problems with them," Willy said. Eve nodded.

"I doubt that. Genitor seems to be growing more and more according to what she told us. They stand out and if these people are targeting such companies and women who use their services, she must know about them. It's upsetting to know she knew but didn't at least give us some warning, Willy."

She sighed and nodded.

"Don't jump to conclusions. I'll get on the phone with her."

"Let me make you some herbal tea," Eve said. "Just try to relax you."

I leaned back on the pillow and then I sat up quickly.

"Wait. What about that man?"

"What man?"

"The man in black, the one who stepped in front of me when I was driving, the one I saw at Roger's, the one who almost ran Eve over at Dr. Aaron's? Could he be one of them?"

Willy shook her head.

"Bastards. See what's happening? They'll turn her into a paranoid," she told Eve.

"As far as I know," Eve said, "they just try to intimidate. They haven't hurt anyone physically."

"As far as you know. You did say you don't know all that much about them and your sister-in-law hid most of it."

"What do you want to do, Kate, go into hiding until you get pregnant and give birth, for Christsake? We'll make sure to stick closer to you."

I looked at her.

"Call Lois Matthews," I said. "See what she tells you now."

"All right. Make her some tea," she told Eve, and walked out.

"Sorry," Eve said. "Sorry these people have risen so boldly in this country."

"How do you know it's only in this country?" I muttered.

"I don't. I'll make you some tea," she said, then left.

The movement in my stomach hadn't reoccurred, but I did want to discuss it with Dr. Aaron. I just didn't want to do it in Willy's presence. She thought I was neurotic already as it was. A minute or so later, she stuck her head in the doorway and told me to pick up the phone.

"Lois wants to speak with you."

I picked up the receiver next to me and said hello.

"I'm so sorry, Kate. I should have warned you about the possibility. We haven't had anything like this happen for a while so I thought these people had gone on to plague some other company. We've assured ourselves that there is no one working for us that is in any way connected with them, but when you deal with so many different people . . . some relative of one of our clients could be involved, for all we know."

"At least if I had known they existed, I wouldn't have been so upset by the call."

"Yes, of course. It's all my fault. We've discussed this before at Genitor and my colleagues are willing to provide you with some security."

"Security?"

"Absolutely. I'm going to have someone see you tomorrow to set up surveillance and give you some peace of mind. I know how trying to become pregnant can make you anxious in and of itself, much less have something like this occur."

"So no other client of yours has had this happen recently?"

"No, not for some time actually. If she has, she hasn't let us know like you did."

"I just thought that . . ."

"Not that I'm complaining. I'm grateful. The quicker we show these people they can't intimidate us, the better it is for my company as well as for our clients. We have a big interest in your success, remember?"

"Okay."

"There'll be someone there first thing in the morning. Let me know if there is anything else I can do. Don't hesitate for a second."

"Thank you," I said.

"No, thank you, Kate. It's disgusting. It makes me sick to my stomach. I'll be up to see you soon. I have another potential client in Palm Springs."

"Oh?"

"That's all I can say about her."

"I understand."

"Except it has something to do with you indirectly. As I was hoping it would. Word of mouth is the best advertising."

"Word of mouth? I can't recall telling anyone any details about my insemination, much less mentioning your company, Lois."

"No mystery. She heard you were trying to get pregnant through insemination and went on a search to find us. See you soon," she added. "And once again, I'm sorry about all this."

"Thank you," I said.

"Well?" Willy asked seconds after I hung up.

I told her about the security company being assigned to me through Genitor.

"That's only right," she said. "I like Lois and was just as disturbed as you were that she hadn't mentioned the lunatics," Willy said.

Eve came in behind her with my cup of tea.

"I put a little honey it for you," she said.

"Thanks."

"Genitor is assigning some security to us," Willy told her.

"Great. My sister-in-law never mentioned anything like that. I don't think she was with a company half as efficient or as responsible."

I sipped my tea.

"Lois told me they have another client from Palm Springs. She thought it had something to do with us, word of mouth. Did either of you mention Genitor to anyone?"

"Not me," Willy said.

"No, but they're becoming more and more well known in the field."

"Yes," I said. "Lois thinks she found them on the Internet because we did reveal I was trying to inseminate."

No one spoke for a moment.

"You guys should eat dinner," I said.

"Meaning you have already?"

"That meat loaf was delicious, Eve."

"Oh, I'm so glad."

"I'm afraid I didn't leave much."

"We brought home some steaks," Willy said.

"I'll get right on it," Eve said, and left.

Willy came to the bed and sat at my feet.

"I don't know why people just can't leave other people be. Freedom and independence is in a life-and-death struggle in the one place the world thought it would flourish. How did this all turn?"

"You're not going to start talking politics now, are you?"

She laughed.

"You have to admit it's pretty ironic . . . all of us living here in the bastion of conservatism."

"There are the Log Cabin Republicans."

"Please. That's like black soldiers fighting for the Confederacy."

I laughed. It was such a relief to do so.

She rose, took the cup of tea from my hands, and kissed me softly on the lips. I moaned.

"Maybe an hors d'oeuvre before dinner," she whispered, and slipped under the blanket beside me, kissing my neck, sliding her hand under my blouse. I moved to make more room for her. "My," she said, helping me undress, "I hadn't noticed, but your breasts look two sizes bigger."

Braless, I hadn't felt my inflated bosom and didn't realize it for some reason until this very moment.

She pulled back and smiled.

The phone rang before I could comment. She picked up the receiver, said hello, and then handed it to me.

"Dr. Aaron."

"Hello."

"Kate, Lois Matthews just called concerned about you. I'm sorry about what happened. How are you feeling now?"

"A little shaky," I said.

"It's no wonder."

"I was going to wait until tomorrow to tell you," I said, "But besides the weight gain," I said, eying Willy. "I've been having some strange symptoms."

"Like what?"

I hesitated.

"It's almost as if I'm in my third trimester, according to the pregnancy chart I downloaded on my computer. That's why I asked you to check again on my results."

"What specifically are you referring to, Kate?"

"I . . . my breasts are larger," I blurted.

"Really?" Her voice dripped with skepticism.

"Yes. You know I downloaded one of those charts on the stages of pregnancy and . . ."

"I hate those charts," she said. "That's why I don't give them out. They make it all seem so mechanical, as if everyone is exactly the same. We're all different. That's what makes us interesting. But getting back to my reason for calling, I want to be sure you don't get yourself upset because of these wackos. They've called here with threats and profane remarks, as well."

"Oh, have they? Do you have security, too?"

"We do."

"I didn't notice any," I said.

"Imagine if our patients saw armed guards about my office. I'd be a starving physician," she said, laughing. "So, I'll see you then at two tomorrow afternoon?"

"Two tomorrow?" I looked at Willy.

"Eve will drive you," she whispered.

"Okay."

"Great. For now, take one of those pink pills I gave you."

"Pink pills?"

"Oh, right," Willy said. "Tell her I have them."

"What pink pills?" I asked Willy.

"She gave them to me for you when you were in the bathroom at her office getting her a urine sample. I forgot. They're in the kitchen."

"What are they?" I asked Dr. Aaron.

"They just mild sedatives to help you relax. Just don't drink any alcohol with them," she advised. "I'll see you tomorrow and we'll make sure everything is all right."

"Okay," I said. "Thank you for calling so quickly."

"No problem. We're all interested in you eventually having a successful pregnancy," she said.

I hung up. If one more person said that to me . . .

"I'll get you the pill," Willy said, rising.

"How could you have forgotten to tell me about them?" I asked her.

She raised her eyebrows.

"I think I've had a little on my mind, too, Kate. What's the big deal? You didn't have any need for them before," she added. "Right?"

"I don't like taking so many pills."

"What's so many? One pill? You can't count the pill that enhances your chances of getting pregnant as you would an ordinary pill. You heard her. It's made up of natural ingredients, herbs."

"Lois gave me that sedative before the insemination," I reminded her.

"So? That was then; this is now. It hardly constitutes taking a lot of pills, Kate, and the doctor knows best, right?"

"I suppose."

She went out and returned with a glass of water and the pill.

"Don't fret. I'll be close by," she said. "Take a rest."

She fixed my blanket, kissed my cheek, stroked my hair, and left me.

I didn't want to fall asleep yet, but the pill was amazing. It was almost an anesthetic. My eyelids closed, and in seconds I was gone.

I didn't wake until morning and was shocked I had slept clear through the night. At least I woke early enough so that Willy wasn't yet gone. She was sleeping so soundly herself that I made every attempt not to wake her. After all, I thought, she's surely overdoing it and now I've added additional stress and worry to her plate.

I slipped out of bed and went to shower and fix myself to face the day. When I stepped out of the bathroom, I was surprised to see that Willy had still not woken. Practically tiptoeing, I went out to the kitchen and started to make some coffee. I thought I would prepare some scrambled eggs as well. Glancing through the patio door that faced the pool, however, I paused.

Eve was talking with an African-American man built like a football player. He had a shaved head and was wearing a suit and tie. They both stopped talking as if they sensed they were being watched and turned to look at me through the patio door. Neither smiled. I had no reason to be afraid, but I felt a cold chill, and then a hot shiver rippled down my spine.

I opened the patio door.

"What's going on?" I asked.

Eve smiled, glanced at the man and then nodded at me. They both approached.

"This is Sterling Plunkett," she said with obvious excitement. "I recognized him immediately."

"Well, who is he?" I asked, not hiding my annoyance. Why was she having a visitor this early in the morning? And why didn't she tell us someone was coming?

"I work for Genitor," he said, smiling. "I was just

waiting around for y'all to get up, when Eve here spotted me. She's pretty good security herself."

"I saw him patrolling the property."

"Just learnin' the lay of the land," he said. "With your gates and wall, we got a pretty good situation. You have good lighting, too. I'll check out your alarm system and see about intercepting any alert."

"Sterling is in the Football Hall of Fame," Eve said. I could see she thought she was in the glow of some major celebrity.

"I'm running interference for you, back to blocking," he quipped, and they both chuckled softly.

"Lois Matthews sure moved quickly," Eve said.

"I thought she would," I said. I was still upset about her not warning me that such people existed and were a threat to my well-being.

I considered Eve, dressed, looking fresh and awake.

"You were up early. You don't seem to sleep very much," I said.

She smiled.

"I never have. I'm like Napoleon. I read he needed only three, four hours of sleep. I think he was about my height, too. Maybe that's got something to do with it. I'm sure I have his personality."

"You going to conquer the world, too?"

"Just a little piece of it," she replied.

"C'mon. I'm making some scrambled eggs." I looked at Sterling Plunkett. "I'll throw on some bacon."

"Sounds like this is going to be a perk and not another job," Sterling said.

They followed me into the house.

Willy had risen and come out wearing a bathrobe.

"Lois Matthews didn't waste a moment," I said and then introduced Sterling to her.

"You look familiar," she told him, and Eve recited his biography, rattling off his amazing statistics as if she were a walking sports encyclopedia.

"How long have you been in the security business?" Willy asked him.

"About two years. They made me a junior partner. So far, it's been an easy buck," he told her.

"Let's hope it stays that way," I muttered over the eggs.

While we all ate, Willy and Eve gave him our work schedules and locations. He took notes but said he would mainly be sticking to me and watching the property. When he heard about my doctor's appointment, he volunteered to take me.

"I'm going to put some sensors of our own around your property as well," he said.

"Have they hurt anyone?" I asked, now more concerned than ever because of all the preparation and attention he was giving me.

"Not that I know, ma'am, but we don't take chances with a client's safety and well-being."

He reached into his inside pocket and produced a device no bigger than a playing card.

"I'd like you to hold on to this. It couldn't be any

simpler. If there is any reason you want me right beside you, if anything disturbs you, you just press the red button in the center here and it sends a signal to me."

"I thought you said you would be sticking to me."

"Well, sure I will, ma'am, but there are places you'll go that are private," he said, his ebony eyes glittering impishly.

"I'd hope so," Willy said.

I took the device.

"Besides," he added, "if I do my job correctly, neither you nor anyone else should know I'm around. I'm going to disappear and you might think I'm not here anymore. Thanks for breakfast," he said, pushing away from the table. "I want to finish looking over the property and the neighborhood. Y'all going to the plant this morning, then?"

"Yes," I said before Willy could suggest I take off the day.

"Why don't you just rest until you have to go to see Dr. Aaron?" she asked.

"I have to keep myself busy, Willy. I don't want to sit here and shiver all morning."

"Okay, okay. Yes, we're all going," she told Sterling.

"Fine. Y'all shouldn't do anything different. Patterns are what the bad guys look for, but that's good because they give themselves away when they get into the same groove."

"How many times have you guarded someone against these people?" I asked him.

"Oh, it don't matter who the intruders are. Intruders are intruders, threats are threats. Let's just say, I've been busy," he added smiling. "You know what they say . . . without criminals, cops be out of work. I'll be there about 12:30 to take you to the doctor," he said, then rose and left.

"How did he know what time I had to be at Dr. Aaron's?" I realized and wondered aloud.

"Oh, I told him," Eve said. "I thought he'd better know as much as possible as soon as possible."

"Good thinking," Willy told her. They exchanged a smile so conspiratorial it made me jealous. "I'd better get a move on," she added, then rose and went into the bedroom to dress for work while Eve cleared the table and helped clean up the kitchen.

"Sterling's a pretty intimidating man. I wouldn't want to have him breathing down my neck," she told me. "I hope it makes you feel better, Kate."

"Yes," I said, but the truth was, it didn't. The very fact that I found myself needing such a man in my shadows heightened my tension and stress.

Willy insisted we go to the plant in two cars.

"I want you to be able to go home if you feel the need to rest, Kate. We've got this thing under control. You have to take care of yourself," she said. "Make yourself as comfortable as possible."

When we left, I looked for Sterling, but I didn't see him or his any car that might be his. It was a very quiet, warm morning. There was an unseasonable heat wave sweeping into the desert on the back of what we called Santa Ana winds. It didn't bring humidity, but the sun seemed to draw itself closer to the earth. We were headed for triple digits.

At the plant I dove into my work. Eve had loaded in almost all the invoices, but I had to prepare the information for payroll and that was now more work because of the added employees. Willy wasn't wrong about my needing to find ways to make myself more comfortable, however. Suddenly, I was developing lower back pain and had difficulty sitting in the same position for long period.

I hadn't thought again about my enlarged bosom until I was at the plant either. None of my bras were comfortable. My stomach remained bloated and my legs felt as if they were filling with more water every hour. I had to get up and pace about and soon found myself doing it every twenty minutes. It put me in a small panic.

Through the window, Willy saw me when she was passing by.

She came into the office.

"Something wrong?"

I shook my head, bit down on my lower lip and then just started crying. I couldn't help it. In the middle of all that was happening, I hated myself for being such a mess. She rushed over to embrace me and move me to the settee. She sat with me.

"I can't sit; I can't work. My body feels as if it's

expanding every minute, my boobs, my waist, and now my legs," I said lifting my skirt to show her my thighs.

"They don't look any bigger than they have, Kate," she said softly. "Except for your breasts and waist, I don't see any dramatic changes in you."

"Oh, it's all in my mind? Even the ache in my lower back?"

"I'm not saying that," she replied, speaking as if she had to be careful, as if I were some sort of mental case. She checked her watch.

"It's not right. I'm going to stop taking those pills."

"Why don't you wait until your doctor's visit? Are you hungry?"

"No." I looked at her guiltily. "I ate three of those damn bars," I confessed, and she laughed.

"So? That's why we made sure the cabinet was restocked."

"What do you mean, we?"

"Eve likes them, too," she said. "All right, take it easy. Sterling should be here any minute. You'll see Dr. Aaron and get some answers, I'm sure."

I could see from the way she was glancing into the plant that she was concerned about the work and I was distracting her.

"Go back. I'm okay," I said.

She kissed my cheek and left. I tried to do some more work, but the aching was so intense, I found myself taking deep breaths. The moment I saw Sterling enter the plant, I grabbed my purse and headed out even though we would be going earlier than I had planned.

"I just came early to looking things over here," he explained.

"That's all right. I want to see the doctor as soon as possible."

"But don't you have a specific appointment?'

"I want to go now," I said firmly. "If you can't leave yet, I'll drive myself."

"No, it's all right. Let's go," he said. "Things quiet here?" he asked me as we headed out.

"Hardly," I said, nodding at the machinery and the employees scurrying about.

He laughed and opened the door for me. His car was right there, a black Town Car, the engine running. He opened the rear door for me.

"I'll sit up front," I said.

"Oh, sure." He opened that door and I got in quickly.

I knew it was selfish of me, but I wished Willy were taking me, instead of a stranger. I would even rather it were Eve, but to take either of them away from the plant today would be mean. The party was less than a day away now. The preparations were bigger than anything we had done or even contemplated doing and we had handled some sizeable weddings in the past, too.

"I think it's pretty nice, you two planning a family," Sterling said as we drove off. "Seems to me more people than ever are running away from family re-sponsibilities, not running toward them."

"Where are you from?"

"I was born in Dallas. After my mother deserted us, my father moved us to New York, where his sister and brother-in-law lived. As it turned out, me and my sister got brought up by them. I won a football scholarship and got picked up by the Giants. Being tough and fast saved me from the street life."

"What about your sister?"

"She was always a good student, a real reader. She became a nurse and works private jobs in Los Angeles."

"Does she have a family?"

"Nope. Never got married. She ain't gay," he added quickly. "She's just scared of it, I think."

"How old is she?"

"Thirty."

"Well, maybe she'll meet someone. That's far from too old."

He looked at me as if I were a dreamer.

"Can't you drive a little faster?" I asked him when I felt that stirring in my stomach again. "You're not even going the speed limit."

"Oh, sure," he said. He accelerated, but he didn't look happy about it. The way he was driving, how-ever, we would have been late for my appointment instead of early.

He almost made a wrong turn, too, when we exited the freeway.

Finally, we arrived at Dr. Aaron's office. Like a chauffeur, he got out quickly to open my door for me.

"I'll be out here, waiting. And watching," he added.

"Thanks," I said, pressing the door buzzer. When I heard the buzz, I entered the lobby. Eve's sister was not behind the counter. There was no one waiting in the lobby either, so I went up to the window and called for someone. Who had let me in? I wondered when no one responded. I waited, realized I had broken into a sweat, and then called again.

Suddenly, the door opened and I looked with surprise and shock as Janet Madison stepped out. The sight of me brought a look of pain into her face.

"What the hell are you doing here?" I instantly demanded.

"Oh, damn," she said. "I was hoping to keep it a secret for a while."

"Keep what a secret?"

"I'm going to be a surrogate." She leaned toward me to whisper. "I've been offered twenty-five thousand dollars and with the new rules at the school, even unmarried women can take a maternity leave."

"How did you find this doctor?"

"Dr. Matthews," she replied.

"Then you're the one from Palm Springs who contacted Genitor?"

"No, they contacted me."

"Contacted you?" That wasn't what I was told, I

thought. "How did they find out you had any interest in such a thing?"

"I dabbled a bit with it on the Internet and one day found an e-mail from Dr. Matthews, describing this couple's desire to have a child and how much they were willing to pay."

"Oh. They have a way of tracking people who show interest." That explains it, I thought.

"I told myself if you were doing it, I could, especially since I don't have to care for the baby or raise a child. Can you keep it to yourself awhile, Kate. Please. No one else knows about it, not even Willy," she said, "although I'm sure she'll know now."

"Are you pregnant already?"

"Just found out for sure," she said. "I won't show until the summer, maybe. She's great," she said, nodding toward the inner office. "Good luck with your pregnancy. See ya," she added, and left.

I watched her go and then I turned to see Dr. Aaron standing there.

"You got here quickly," she said. "I had planned for her to be gone. She was hoping to keep it a secret."

"That's a secret you can't keep very long," I said. "It's stupid to think so. I never would have imagined her doing this, even for money."

"Everyone has a price."

"Not me," I said.

"That's wonderful, Kate. The devil will never knock at your door. Now, let's get you in here and see what's going on," she said, smiling.

Bea was suddenly there inside the window smiling at me, too.

It was as if they could both materialize out of thin air.

Just like the figure I had seen sitting beside Lois Matthews that first night.

13.

AFTER DR. AARON EXAMINED ME, she sat back and made some notes while I dressed. I sensed she was being somewhat hesitant and I thought she looked like someone trying to workout how to explain something terrible in a euphemistic fashion. It made me even more anxious.

"Is there something very wrong?" I finally asked.

She looked up from her papers.

"Well," she began, "it's not something terribly wrong. I've seen this condition before and . . ."

"What condition?"

"There isn't any terminology as such for your particular situation, Kate."

"You're frightening me," I said with an underlying note of anger. "Whatever it is, just tell me, for godsakes."

"I am. I am," she said. "It's sort of a combination between something real and unreal."

"What?"

"There's a condition, a disorder that's been written about since antiquity. In fact Hippocrates set down the first written account of it around 300 B.C., and recorded twelve different cases of women with the disorder."

"What disorder, Dr. Aaron?"

"Well, the term for it is pseudocyesis," she said.

"Pseudo? Something false? What?"

"False pregnancy," she replied.

I smirked and shook my head.

"How can anyone be falsely pregnant?"

"With pseudocyesis, women have symptoms similar to true pregnancy. They have morning sickness, tender breasts, gain weight, suffer abdominal distension, and many report they experience the sensation of fetal movement, known as quickening, even though there is no fetus present. There are even breast changes, uterine enlargement, and softening of the cervix. They can go into false labor.

"The most famous case on record is the case of Mary Tudor, the Queen of England, who believed on more than one occasion that she was pregnant when she wasn't."

"So you're telling me I have pseudocyesis?"

"Yes," she said coolly and calmly. "I'm afraid that would be my diagnosis, Kate."

"Maybe the results were wrong after all, despite what you think."

She stared a moment.

"Okay," she said. "Let's retest you."

She went about it and then left me in the examination room. I sprawled out on the examination table where she had provided me with a pillow. Less than an hour later, she returned, closed the door softly, and smiled.

I sat up, feeling a little dazed.

"Well?"

"I'm sorry, Kate. It's the same result. You're definitely not pregnant. You have the characteristics, the symptoms of someone suffering with pseudocyesis."

"Why would I have that? Why?" I practically screamed at her.

"The obvious cause for pseudocyesis is a woman's intense desire to become pregnant. In some cases, the intense fear of becoming pregnant or the displeasure inherent in looking pregnant causes the internal conflicts and changes in the endocrine system which mirrors the symptoms of pseudocyesis."

"Why would someone make herself look pregnant if she hated the thought of it?"

"To get it over with. I'm not saying that's you. Other depressive disorders have triggered the same symptoms. You'd have to go to some therapist to get out the root cause and frankly, soon it won't matter."

"So what you're saying is I'm causing all the false pregnancy symptoms myself? Emotionally, mentally, whatever, I'm causing my breasts to enlarge faster, my abdomen to distend faster, all of it, even the quickening I feel?"

"Yes, I believe that is it, Kate." She shrugged. "Hopefully, after the next insemination, it will all be physically valid and accountable anyway, so I wouldn't put you through any therapy. We'll deal with it just the way we would if you were that far along," she said, and flashed a smile.

"What happens to these women who are not really pregnant?"

"Some are cured through hypnosis, purgatives, opioids like endorphin, fentanyl, and methadone or . . ."

"Or what?"

"Some have what we call hysterical childbirth."

"You mean they go through it all as if they're actually giving birth?"

"Yes, and then it's over."

"But there's no baby."

"But there's closure," Dr. Aaron said. She stood up. "Try to relax. Do other things. Don't think about being pregnant so much. Distract yourself. You're still taking the pill I gave you?"

"Maybe that's causing all this," I said.

"No," she said, smiling. "Hardly. Believe me, it's psychological, but if you stop taking the pill, you'll reduce your chances of really becoming pregnant."

"I feel trapped," I muttered.

"Nonsense. This will pass. You'll be fine. You don't need to do anything else right now and I certainly don't want you to treat yourself as if you were someone with an illness, Kate. Take it easier, of course. No heavy work. Nothing that will strain you, but do you normal routine. I'm always here for you," she added. "Okay?"

I nodded and stood up.

"This and now those religious fanatics annoying you can be quite a weight to carry. I know," she said, putting her arm around my shoulders to lead me out. "But we're all looking after you, watching for you. You're not alone. Don't ever feel alone," she said.

I looked at her a bit surprised.

"I never feel that, Dr. Aaron. I couldn't ask for a better partner than Willy. We don't let each other down."

"I'm sure. You are lucky. Call me whenever you want," she said, and then closed the door between us the moment I stepped out to the lobby.

I looked at Bea, who was smiling at me from behind the glass. She opened the door and leaned forward.

"Tell my sister our father called and said he was very happy she's doing better."

"Why didn't he call her himself?" I shot back. I didn't know anything about their father. Eve had never mentioned him and I was in an irritable state of mind.

"It's easier to reach me," she replied. "Eve understands."

She closed the window. I can see why Eve avoids her, I thought.

Sterling jumped out of the car the moment I emerged from the office and rushed to open the door for me as if I were already nine months into the pregnancy that I just learned had yet to even start despite my symptoms. I felt like some kind of nutcase regardless of how Dr. Aaron had tried to describe me. How was I going to explain this to Willy?

Sterling closed the door and looked around carefully as he strolled back to his side and got in.

"Everything all right?" He asked.

It sounded funny to me and I laughed. He turned with surprise.

"Yes," I said. "Everything is just wonderful." I closed my eyes and lay back.

"Back to the plant or home?"

"My car's at the plant," I said. Now I was wishing I had taken Willy's initial advice and not gone at all to the plant. I hadn't accomplished all that much there anyway.

This time I didn't have to tell Sterling to drive faster. He drove as if we were being pursued and a few times, I did catch him studying the traffic behind us before deciding to accelerate and weave around cars.

When we pulled into the plant parking lot, I got out before Sterling could come around to open my door, and I hurried into the plant. Everything was humming along. Four members of the White Party committee were there beside Willy and Eve watching the production. Willy saw me, excused herself and followed me into the office where I told her what Dr. Aaron had diagnosed as my problem.

"That's incredible," she said. "Characteristics of false pregnancy?"

"She didn't come right out and say it, but I think she believes I have this pseudocyesis because I'm trying to speed up my pregnancy and get it over with as quickly as possible. In other words, I'm a contradiction. I wanted the baby, but I don't want to be pregnant after all. I can't stand the idea of losing my figure and going through these symptoms."

Willy nodded, thinking.

"Makes sense to me," she said.

"Thanks."

"Hey, it's not a fatal illness, Kate. So what did she tell you to do?"

"If I wasn't going to continue with the insemination process, she'd have me see a shrink, but under the circumstances, there's nothing to do. Behave as if it's all natural, I suppose. Ignore the entire thing."

"And the pill she gave you?"

"She claims it has nothing to do with any of this, but if I stop it, I'll reduce my chances for the next insemination."

"So, keep taking it," she said, nodding. "And do what she says, behave as if it's all natural. Ignore it."

"Like I'll be able to ignore looking and feeling pregnant when I'm not?" I came back at her in a voice so shrill that it was strange even for me to think of it as mine."

She winced as if I had reached out and slapped her.

"I'm sorry," I said, seeing the troubled look on her face. After all, I was pulling this right in the midst of this tremendous effort to produce for the biggest party in the whole Coachella valley.

"Don't worry," she said. "We'll deal with it. I know how you are about your figure and I love you for it, but this is why many women choose to have surrogates, I guess."

"That brings me to the pièce de résistance," I said. She raised her eyebrows.

"There's more?"

"Janet Madison has gone to Genitor and become pregnant. She's using Dr. Aaron."

"What? Get out of here. She's a single schoolteacher. Why would she want a child?"

"She doesn't. It's what you just said. She's getting paid to be a surrogate. Twenty-five thousand."

"No shit." She smiled. "Wait until she starts to suffer symptoms and show. She's such a sissy puss."

"Lois never mentioned that part of their enterprise, procreating surrogate mothers."

"Hey, she's not asking us to invest in Genitor. Who cares?" She gazed through the window into the plant. "Eve's going to get a kick out of this. She isn't exactly fond of Janet."

"I told her I'd keep her secret for now."

"Like she would keep yours. Screw her," Willy said. "Besides, I don't expect to give it another iota of thought. We're too busy with important things."

"Oh. Bea asked me to tell Eve their father called and was happy to hear she's doing well. I got the sense Eve and her father aren't getting along that well and Bea isn't exactly upset about it. Sibling rivalry with capital letters."

"Don't go there," Willy said. "We're too busy to become involved in other people's family problems."

"Whatever. Give her the message. I'm heading home," I said. "I'm sorry I can't be of more help."

"Don't worry about it. Just take it easy. I'll call you later. It's going to be a long night."

She hugged me and then walked me out to the car. Sterling was nowhere in sight.

"I don't see my bodyguard," I muttered.

"That's the idea," Willy said. "If they see him, they'll keep their distance."

"Isn't that what we want, them keeping their distance, lots of distance?"

"No. We want to catch them and bathe them in acid. You sure you're okay to drive yourself home?"

"Yes," I said. We kissed and I got into my car and started away.

It wasn't until I stopped at a traffic light that I saw the envelope on the passenger's side. My name was on the outside. I just stared at it. The light turned green and I continued driving, avoiding looking at it until I pulled into the driveway and then into the garage. When I shut the engine and saw the garage door close behind me, I opened the envelope.

There was only a picture inside but it was gruesome, a mass of red bones and blood, twisted flesh and what looked like a face in the center with yellow eyes and jagged teeth. It looked like a form of fish with the scales developing into limbs. Below the picture were the words, "This is living in you."

I tossed it to the floor and screamed, struggling to get out of the car quickly and nearly falling in the process.

The sound of the garage door rising threw me into another panic. I screamed until I saw Sterling Plunkett standing there. He had a pistol in his right hand.

"What is it?" he asked, gazing around the garage.

I nodded at the car.

"In the car on the floor in front," I managed, and backed up toward the door into the house.

He moved quickly to the car, opened the passenger side door and immediately found the envelope. He looked at the picture and then put it all in his inside coat pocket.

"I'll take care of it," he said.

"Take care of it? How did that get into my car? I left it locked."

"Getting into a locked car ain't hard to do, Kate. Look how easily I arranged to get into your garage. The code for your garage remote is accessible. So is the car key."

"What do you mean, you'll take care of it? What are you going to do with that disgusting picture?"

"I'll have it processed. Might give us a clue as to exactly who they are and where they are."

"They got into my car; they can open the garage; they can get into my house!"

"Not with me around," he said. "I promise."

I looked at the door.

"My sensors don't indicate anyone entered your home."

I didn't look convinced. He hurried to the door and opened it. Then he entered the house with his pistol still in hand. I walked in behind him and watched him check every room, every closet, and then the pool area. He looked into Eve's casita as well.

"All's well," he said. "I'll be planted out front like one of your palm trees," he assured me.

I didn't realize how much the shock of finding the picture had upset and nauseated me. I tried lying down and resting, but the image kept replaying inside my eyelids. I wanted to call Willy to tell her, but I knew she was right in the thick of it now and she would feel she had to rush back to see me. Instead, I opted to take another one of those pink pills. If I didn't, I was sure I wouldn't sleep.

Just as before, it worked like an anesthesia and I was out moments after I swallowed it.

When I woke, it was pitch-dark in the house. Glancing at the clock, I realized I had slept almost six hours. It was nearly midnight. I flipped on the lamp and sat up. Despite my sleeping like a dead one, my body was stiff all over, especially in my lower back. I groaned and stood, rubbing it vigorously as I walked out to the kitchen. I saw the answering machine was blinking with two calls.

The first was from Willy.

"Hey. Tried you twice and finally reached Sterling, who told us all was well. He checked on you and found you had gone to sleep. Probably a good idea. We're going to be here until about one or two supervising the packing of the refrigerated trucks. Call me if you want anything. Love ya."

I thought the second message was her checking in again because for a moment there was nothing and then I heard that now familiar voice, raspy, scary.

"Get an abortion quickly. It is draining your very soul."

It clicked off. I stepped back as if the voice could come out of the answering machine and materialize into some horrific creature right before my eyes. It took me a few moments to calm down and then I hurried to the front door. Sterling should hear this, I thought.

At first I was surprised and then grateful to see his car in our driveway. He had told me he would stay out of sight, but perhaps after they had managed to get into my car while we were at Dr. Aaron's office, he thought he should make his presence more obvious.

The heat that had come in during the day lingered because the sky was overcast. It was still well into the nineties, even this late. Our house and grounds were well lit. The palm trees were highlighted and the driveway itself had a line of fixtures on both sides. However, Sterling's Town Car had heavily tinted windows so they behaved more like mirrors than windows. As I approached, I saw my image in the glass. I had fallen asleep in the clothes I had worn to Dr.

Aaron's and was still wearing them. My unbrushed hair seemed to bubble around my head in rebellious clumps. Perhaps because of the glow of the lights in the darkness, my face looked ashen.

I knocked on the passenger's side window and waited.

There was no response, so I went around and looked through the windshield. I didn't see him in the car. He's patrolling the grounds, I thought.

I called to him and waited.

It was quieter than ever. Because of the late hour, there were no cars on the streets around our home or leading to it. I saw some planes crossing east to west, their blinking lights clearly visible against the overcast inky night, but I didn't hear them. Even the coyotes were asleep and not howling as they usually did making their way down the wash, hunting for food. It was almost as if this were all a dream or I was walking in my sleep. In a moment I would wake up in my bed.

Sterling didn't respond nor appear after my additional calls. Either he didn't want to show himself for some reason or he didn't hear me, I thought and headed back to the house. I need him to hear this though I told myself and found the transmitter he had given me. I pressed it and waited and listened and then pressed it again. Still I heard nothing. The silence was very unnerving.

Willy will surely be home soon, I told myself, and went to the kitchen. I was surprisingly not hungry for a change, but I was thirsty. I drank a full glass of ice cold water and then went to the rear patio door and looked out at the pool. I didn't recall putting on the pool light, but it was lit. It put a greenish-yellow glow around the decking.

For a moment I thought I was imagining someone there, but then I realized it was Sterling. It actually brought a smile to my face. He had sprawled out on one of the lounge chairs and looked asleep. No wonder he didn't hear me calling or hear the transmitter. Some bodyguard, I thought, and then told myself even he had to get some rest. I was sure he had some alarms set up anyway.

I opened the patio door.

"Sterling," I called. He didn't respond.

I closed the door behind me and walked to him. He was really in a deep sleep, I thought, and called to him again. He didn't move nor open his eyes. Alarm bells rang inside my heart. I stared down at him and then I reached out and nudged his shoulder. His body barely moved and he didn't open his eyes. I pushed him harder. He didn't move. His eyes remained shut. I shook him and shook him. His head rocked from side to side, but he didn't awaken.

When his head fell to the left, I saw a small dartlike object in his neck.

With a gasp that seemed to emerge from the very bottom of my soul, I backed away. For a moment or two, I froze. Then I looked about fearfully. I saw no one, not a movement, but every shadow seemed threatening, seemed poised to leap in my direction and cast a dark blanket over me. The terror I felt was drawn up from my feet as if I had stepped into a pool of ice water. I turned and rushed to the house. Just as I closed the door behind me, the phone rang. I stood there staring at it.

It rang and rang until the answering machine came on with Willy's wiseass greeting.

"We're not answering either because we're not here or we don't feel like it, so do what you're supposed to do at the buzz."

It buzzed and I heard the voice say, "Now you know why it's almost too late."

The phone went dead with a long, deep, and annoying tone before the machine went off and the message light began to blink.

I couldn't move. I heard myself gasping, which brought on a strange feeling. It was as if I were out of my body observing myself. I wondered, is that me? Am I struggling to breathe?

My stomach constricted and the cramp brought me to my knees.

I fell over on my side and closed my eyes. I descended into a pool of black quicksand as warm as blood. Crimson-faced fetuses danced around me on feet that looked like the roots of flowers. They grimaced and shed putrid green and yellow tears. My ears were stuffed with the howling of wounded beasts drowning out my own desperate cries for help. I was spinning, shrinking, folding into myself until I began to resemble one of the gruesome fetuses and lost my voice.

It was the cold washcloth on my forehead that brought me back to consciousness and rescued me from my own horrific dream. I looked up at Willy, who had tears streaming down her face. She lifted my head first to kiss my cheek and then she got me into a sitting position.

"Kate, oh damn, Kate, are you all right?"

I heard Eve coming in through the patio.

"He's gone," she said. "It looks like some kind of poison dart."

"Poison dart? Kate," Willy said, "what happened? Who was here?"

I tried to speak, but didn't utter a sound. My eyes felt as if they were bulging with the effort.

"Let's get her to bed," Eve said, and knelt to take my left arm. The two of them stood me up. I leaned on Willy and we made our way into the bedroom.

Gingerly, they laid me down and made me comfortable, fixing the pillow under my head. Eve sat beside me on the bed and took my hand in hers.

"You'd better call the police," she told Eve.

"Is that wise?" she replied.

"What do you mean?"

"With the party and all tomorrow . . . a scandal like this?"

"It's not a scandal. A man was murdered on our property."

"You're going to have to explain who he is and why he's here."

"So?"

"I'm just telling you . . . anticipate reporters, television . . ." She nodded at me. "Think about her."

"Well, what are we supposed to do, Eve? Leave him out there for a while?"

"Call Genitor, Lois Matthews. Let them handle it," she suggested.

It was so odd. I heard their conversation, watched the changing expression on Willy's face, but it was as if I were watching a television show, as if I really wasn't in the scene itself. There was a distance, a chasm I couldn't get across yet. Just like before, I felt caught in a dream.

"Yeah, maybe," Willy thought aloud. "Get her opinion about it anyway."

"I'll call," Eve said. "The number's right by the phone in the kitchen, right?"

"Yeah."

Eve hurried out and Willy turned back to me.

"How you doing, Kate?" She rubbed my hand. "Did anyone hurt you? Why did you faint?"

I took a deep breath as if I were about to dive underwater.

"I found him," I said in nothing more than a whisper.

"Damn."

"It all started with the picture in the car," I added.

"What picture?"

"I found a picture in my car when I left the plant. It was horrible, a horrific-looking fetus. Whoever put it there wrote that it was inside me."

"Where is this picture?"

"Sterling put it in his jacket pocket. He was going to have it processed," I explained. "I took one of those pink pills and fell asleep."

"Yeah, he told me that when I called earlier this evening."

"They called, too."

"Who? You mean they? The wackos?"

"Yes. There are two messages on the machine out there," I said. "I went out to tell Sterling and I found him on the lounge chair. He wouldn't wake up. When I saw the dart in his neck, I realized he was dead and came into the house to call you. The phone rang and it was them again. They must have been watching me and knew I had come back inside, and then I guess I passed out."

Eve appeared in the doorway.

"Someone's on the way. She understood the problem and said it was smart to call her and let the company handle it. She's making sure there's another security guard assigned."

Willy nodded, looked at me and then stood.

"I want to check him for something," she said.

"What?"

"A picture Kate found in her car earlier."

She hurried out.

"I'll get you a glass of cold water," Eve told me and followed Willy.

I closed my eyes and tried to calm down. Eve returned first with the water and then Willy came in shaking her head.

"What?"

"No picture in any of his pockets. I checked his car, too. Nothing."

"Maybe whoever did that to him took it, or he had given it to someone to check out. He said he was going to do that," I suggested. She nodded. "Did you listen to the answering machine, Willy?"

"No."

"Go listen, Willy. You should hear that voice, too. Go ahead."

"Okay, relax," she said.

She went out. Eve remained smiling down at me.

"It'll be all right."

"Someone killed him, Eve. How can things be all right? You said as far as you knew, they didn't do anyone physical harm."

She shrugged.

"They're getting more aggressive. Maybe they're frustrated or they just feel their oats."

"It frightens me."

"I know."

"Are you absolutely sure of your sister-in-law's cause of death?"

"Yes. She was a picture of health, but as I understand it, that can happen even to people who have no other symptoms. Besides, she was in a hospital. No one was shooting darts at her."

"There are many ways to kill people in a hospital," I said.

"Don't get yourself worked up. Your imagination will run havoc."

Willy returned.

"Well?" I asked immediately. "What do you think of that voice?"

"I didn't hear it, Kate. There weren't any bad messages on the machine. You must have erased them."

"I didn't," I said pushing myself up with my elbows.

"I'm sure there's nothing on the machine."

I looked at Eve, and she looked at Willy.

"You two think I made it all up, the picture, the phone calls?"

"No, but you could have just inadvertently hit the delete button, Kate. No big deal," Willy said.

"I didn't, damn it! I never got to that machine. I fainted, remember?"

"Okay, okay. I'll check it again," she said.

"Stop humoring me!" I screamed after her.

"Easy," Eve said. "C'mon, Kate. Calm down. You'll get yourself sick."

"I am sick," I said. I lowered my head to the pillow.

"Maybe you want to get out of those clothes," she suggested.

"What? Oh. Yeah."

I sat up again and she began to help undo my dress.

"I can do it myself," I said sharply.

"Okay."

Willy returned, shaking her head.

"Look, I realized even my message is gone, Kate. You hit the button. That's it. You probably don't remember doing it."

I stared at her.

"I'm going to take a shower," I said, "and then get some sleep. I'm sorry. I know you have a lot on your mind and you've got to get up early."

"Kate?"

"No, let me alone," I said, waving at her.

Eve stepped back as I rose and headed for the bathroom.

"But are you sure you're stable enough?" Willy asked me.

I paused and looked at her.

"I've been threatened by some fanatics, diagnosed with pseudocyesis, discovered my security guard was killed by some sort of poison dart at our pool, and passed out on the floor. Considering I'm still moving about all right, I'd say I'm pretty stable," I replied.

Willy smiled.

"You're such a dyke," she said.

We heard the doorbell.

"If that's them, that's pretty quick," Willy told Eve.

"More than likely they had some sort of backup nearby," she said.

"Take your shower, Kate. We'll handle it," Willy told me.

I nodded and went into the bathroom. When I came out, Willy was getting undressed to prepare herself for some sleep.

"It was them?"

"Yeah. They took him away and his car as well."

"What about that dart? What do they think?"

"They said they would let us know, but they left someone out there tonight. We'll have a new man on the job tomorrow. He'll introduce himself to you. I'll be at the plant," she said. "And then the convention center, unless you aren't feeling well and we have to get you back to Dr. Aaron."

"I'll be all right."

She nodded and went into the bathroom.

When she got into bed beside me, she reached for my hand and then turned over to kiss me softly.

"It's going to be all right," she said.

"I'm nervous about not calling the police, Willy."

"I'm not. I think Eve's right about what would happen, Kate, and they should be taking care of this mess. We have a lot on our plate. Besides, they're better equipped at it than we are. It's the best way. I'm confident of it."

"I'm glad one of us is."

She laughed.

"I don't know how you can laugh. Go to sleep, you idiot. You have to be exhausted and I'm not getting blamed for making you sick," I said.

"Okay, boss."

She turned over, but I lay there staring into the darkness, afraid to close my eyes, afraid of falling into that black quicksand again.

And then I had the quickening, that symptom of pseudocyesis Dr. Aaron had described.

If my imagination was that powerful, I should try to put it to good use, I thought, and imagine myself on some South sea island drinking a piña colada.

However, before I could try, I thought the stirring inside me was followed by the wail of an infant so shrill it vibrated through my spine and shook the very foundation of my being.

As silly as it sounded, I hummed a lullaby my mother had sung to me. Fortunately, Willy was already asleep and didn't hear me or she would surely think I had gone over some deep end. I kept humming to drown out the cries echoing inside my ears.

Soon it worked and I fell asleep as well, the two of us, me and whatever it was within me that had shuddered with fear.

14.

FOR THE FIRST TIME since I began this insemination process, I suffered what anyone else would assume was severe morning sickness. Of course, I knew there were many other possible reasons for the nausea, and since my doctor's visit I looked to one of those. After what had occurred the night before, I didn't sleep well at all and my nerves were sizzling so much, I had enough static electricity in me to light a movie marquee. That alone would upset my stomach. Willy heard me in the bathroom and wouldn't leave until she was assured I was all right. I felt even more terrible because this was happening on what I knew to be the busiest day for her and our business. I struggled to put on a good face and ease her concern.

"I hate leaving you here. I know you're nervous as hell, but they are sending another security person to protect you. Nevertheless, you'll call me to let me know how you're doing," she demanded. "You promise, Kate, or I'll just keep coming back here."

"I promise. I'm not stupid about it, Willy. If I have any other problems, or something more serious occurs, you'll be the first to know, big payday for us or not. I know my priorities."

"Yeah, you know," she said skeptically. "Okay, even so I'll call in periodically. Either Eve or I will stop by around lunch time."

"I don't need either of you to do that," I said sharply. She raised her eyebrows. "Look, I'll be fine. I'm feeling better already and I might very well go to the plant and the convention center."

"Whatever," she said. I hated to see her losing patience with me.

Eve came in to bring me a box that had been delivered during the night and left out front.

"What could this be?" I asked. Willy tore it open with her pocket knife and plucked out one maternity outfit after another. There was a note inside.

"It's from Lois Matthews, from Genitor. Apparently, she spoke with Dr. Aaron and had this delivered to make you feel comfortable. There are five outfits in here."

I stared at them in disbelief.

"Why would she do this?"

"She's only trying to be of some help. It's very considerate," Willy said.

"I'm not going to wear these things until I absolutely have to."

"Fine. At least you know you have them," she said.

Eve prepared one of her herbal teas for me before they left and then I went back to bed. I didn't get up again until I heard the doorbell. I slipped on my robe as I started out of the bedroom. My head was heavy, more symptomatic of a hangover than anything, but the nausea had passed soon after I had drunk the tea, and I was actually starting to feel a little hungry.

I checked through the peephole and saw a woman in a dark black suit. She had short reddish-brown hair, trimmed in a style resembling a page boy. I saw she had no makeup, not even lipstick, no earrings either. Her eyebrows were more like a man's eyebrows and she had a sprinkles of tiny freckles splattered over the crests of her cheeks.

"Yes?" I asked through the door without unlocking.

"I'm from Genitor," she said. "New security."

She held up an open ID wallet to show me her picture and her name, Trinity Masters. The same security company as Sterling's was identified.

They sent a woman? I thought, and opened the door.

"Good morning, Kate," she said, sounding as if we had known each other for years. "Sorry to disturb you, but I wanted to introduce myself right away and get you into a comfort zone. I'm Sterling's replacement."

"What exactly happened to him?" I asked without passing through introductory small talk.

"He was hit with a dart that had been dipped into a very potent poison."

"What do you mean, potent? What kind of poison?"

"You want the technical answer?"

"I want any answer," I said visibly annoyed. "Poison darts aren't exactly common around here."

She smiled.

"This dart was dipped in batrachotoxin, which comes from the skin of what are known as *Phyllobates terribillis*, more commonly called poison dart frogs. They're usually found in South America and used by certain primitive tribes. These frogs are very dangerous. Okay?"

"Are you saying a frog killed him?"

"No, of course not, or at least not directly," she said, smiling.

"I don't see this as in any way humorous. The man is dead, killed while protecting me."

"I'm sorry. I don't mean to sound flippant," she said, truly dropping the smile as one would drop a hot potato. "Assassinations have become quite sophisticated these days, so I'm not so surprised by the device used. We all liked Sterling very much. He had a sense of humor about his work and was quite competent. We're all highly trained."

"Isn't this unusual work for a woman?" I asked, still not stepping back to let her in.

She laughed.

"Now, Kate, you, of all people, don't want to be accused of gender discrimination, do you? There are women FBI and CIA agents, of course, as well as regular police, highway patrol, and private detectives. I assure you I have been as well-trained as any man in our company, and I have nearly twenty years of experience in the security field. Actually, more time than Sterling had."

"I'm sorry," I said. "All this has made me . . . nervous. Please. Come in."

I stepped back and she entered and closed the door.

"I've been fully briefed up to the events of yesterday," she said. "Can you bring me up to date after that, I mean, after you returned home from the plant?"

"Yes," I said. I felt a slight trembling through me just thinking about reliving the events, however. She saw my hesitation.

"Just the broad strokes. You don't have to go into great detail."

I nodded.

"I was just going to make myself some coffee. Would you like some?"

"Sure," she said. She looked about. "Very nice house and beautiful area."

"Thank you."

I led her into the kitchen and told her to sit at the table in our nook. As I prepared the coffee, I described the events of yesterday, breaking them up into the incident with the photograph, the phone calls, Sterling's death and my own troubled reactions. She listened, taking some notes and then before I served her any coffee, she asked if she could look through the house and check out the grounds around the pool and the casita.

"I'm making myself a toasted cheese and tomato

sandwich, baby bib lettuce and Spanish onion. We make our own dressing. Would you like one?"

"No, thank you. Just coffee. I'll be right back," she said, and went off to do her reconnaissance.

I had just sat at the table to eat my sandwich, when she returned. She carried a plastic bag with what looked like plain paper in it.

"What's that?"

"Sometimes, people who use this particular poison load their dart into the blow gun with a funnel to keep themselves protected. This looks like one. I found it behind one of the bushes out there. I'll have it checked for fingerprints. We have something of a list of the people and full files on each involved in this sort of intimidation."

"Intimidation? It's more than intimidation. They killed him."

"I meant what they are trying to do to you."

"Yes, why didn't they kill me, too?"

"They're hoping you'll take their orders and get an abortion," she said. "In their way of thinking, they see you as being a victim."

"A victim?"

"Seduced into doing this unnatural, evil thing," she said, "which can result only in an evil child."

She smiled and hummed the theme music to some horror movie.

"And if I don't get an abortion?"

She stopped smiling.

"They're determined. I'll give them that," she

replied, and had some coffee. I didn't take much comfort in her answer, nor did she look like she was trying to sugarcoat anything.

"You seem to know a lot about them. You've had experience with this group before then?"

"Yes," she admitted. "But not working for Genitor specifically."

"Are they always this violent?"

"Not until just recently. Up until now they were mainly a pain in the ass and we could usually scare them off, but their success in pressuring politicians and getting their way on other issues as well has swelled their ranks and brought in some more, shall we say, proactive members?"

"So what do I do?"

"Nothing. We'll do it all," she said.

"Like Sterling did it all?" I countered. If she was going to be blunt, so could I.

She shrugged. I imagined she had to have a thick skin to do the work she did. Staying calm, being centered was critical and could mean life or death. For a moment I envied her. She reminded me a little of Willy with that inner strength, that muscular self-confidence.

"As I said, we liked Sterling. He was good, but I don't think he took this particular assignment seriously enough. You don't relax on the job, not for a second. I wouldn't exactly have sprawled on a pool lounge at night."

"He had the pool light on as well."

"Or they put it on."

"They put it on? Why would they do that?"

"So you'd find him quickly," she suggested. "Remember, they're trying to intimidate you."

"That light is worked from a control inside my house. Are you saying they were in the house?"

She shrugged.

"If that's the only way it gets put on, obviously yes."

"How familiar are they with my house?"

She shook her head, glanced about and then said, "My guess is one or more of them have been through it recently. Maybe even when you were in it."

"When I was in it? You make them sound more like ghosts."

"Maybe you were in a deep sleep. They are what they are and as I said, not to be underestimated. They killed a pretty good man, saw an opportunity and took it."

"Sterling did tell me they could easily get into the house without triggering any alarm."

"Most people have a false sense of security because of what these alarm companies claim," she said.

If she was supposed to be providing me with some comfort and self-assurance, she was failing miserably, I thought.

"My partner couldn't find the picture on him when she went out and searched him."

"Picture?"

"The picture I just described, the one in the car."

"Oh yes." She shook he head and sipped some coffee. "I heard nothing about it. As far as I know, he didn't turn anything over to us. Maybe he was planning to do that today."

"If he didn't turn it in and it wasn't on him and it's not in his car, where did it go?"

"The killers took it, I imagine."

"Why would they take it back?"

"Who knows?" she said. "Maybe to cover up their tracks, make you question your own sanity. They love doing that. They get their targets questioning what they saw and didn't see."

"There definitely was a picture," I stressed. "No matter what you've been told."

"No one told me either way," she said. "Why would anyone doubt you?"

"I don't know. I don't know anything anymore."

"Try to take it easy. Rely on me."

I couldn't help looking skeptical. It only brought a smile to her face.

"We'll get you through it, Kate. Once you give birth, they'll disappear."

"How do you know that?"

"They'll have failed to prevent it; they'll move on to someone else. That's been my experience with them."

I thought for a moment.

"Well, they're not that smart. They don't know that I'm not pregnant yet."

"Oh, you're not?"

I didn't want to get into the whole story of pseudocyesis. "No, but my next insemination is already scheduled."

"Right. Well, that's enough to get them to work on you," she said. "And continue to work on you. We have to assume they know your schedule, your doctor's visits, etc."

"I have a friend here who has just become involved with Genitor."

"Oh?"

"Janet Madison. She's a schoolteacher and lives alone. She should be warned about them."

"I'll look into it," she said.

"I don't think it's right for Genitor to protect its interests by risking the health and welfare of its clients," I added firmly. "She should have been told before she agreed to their insemination program. I should have been told. Not that it would have dissuaded me. It's just good to know what could happen."

Trinity nodded.

"I'll make sure that's understood," she said, but not with any real enthusiasm. "What I'll need from you every day is your schedule, where you want to go, how long. I work differently from how Sterling worked. I'll be sticking so close to you, you'll try to brush my teeth."

I had to smile.

"You're not afraid of another dart?"

"You can't protect yourself or anyone from everything possible, Kate, but if you let them intimidate you and make you afraid to move, they've won without blowing a single dart your way. It was smart to call us to take care of Sterling, by the way. Keeping it out of the papers and away from anyone else's attention denies them the publicity and the chance to intimidate other people.

"In fact, if the media stopped reporting terrorist attacks, they'd lose their reason to attack."

"But what about protecting people by warning them, making them more aware and alert?"

"It's a trade-off that in time would work. That's my opinion," she said. She rose. "I'm going to phone this in and have someone pick it up," she said holding up the plastic bag. "I'll be right outside and I'll be making periodic sweeps around the house all day. Are you going anywhere today?"

"I thought I would check on my business," I said.

"Good. Follow your normal routine," she said, and left.

Feeling a little better, I showered and dressed. I was excited about the preparations for the White Party and wanted to be a part of it. After all this was my achievement as much as Willy's, maybe even more. I should at least show my face, I thought.

I put on a relatively new skirt and blouse with matching sandals, fixed my hair, and put on some makeup to get rid of the dragged-down, dark look I had been wearing. Cheered by my bright, revitalized appearance, I hurried out to first visit the plant and then go to the convention center to see how the preparations were preceding. Trinity was waiting outside the garage as the door lifted and I backed out.

"Why didn't you come out to tell me you were leaving already?"

"I just assumed you would follow me."

"You can't assume anything anymore, Kate. I'll ride along with you, if you don't mind," she said.

I waited for her to get in.

"Going directly to the plant, then?"

"Yes."

"I put a tracer on your phone line, by the way. If you get any more calls like that at home, try to keep whoever it is talking a while. Chances are, he or she is using a cell phone, but we can track that location pretty quickly."

"Okay."

"This business, the things they do, are enough to discourage anyone," she said. "I'm happy you're not intimidated."

"Oh, I'm intimidated," I said, "but I'm still going through with it. We want a child."

"That's what I meant," she said.

"How did you get into this line of work?"

"I was with the FBI. I hit the glass ceiling and left when I got an offer from the Godfather."

"What?"

She laughed.

"You know, an offer you can't refuse. It was too good an opportunity and far less demanding work. I enjoy meeting people, too, and in my line, you meet them from all walks of life."

When we arrived at the plant, we saw Eve running the loading operation. She told me Willy was over at the convention center overseeing the setup of the various kiosks and organizing the supply line and the kitchen. The plant buzzed like a hive of frantic bees. I noticed that even though Trinity moved about to look at various machinery, products, she kept a close steely eye on me.

"Who is that?" Eve finally broke away to ask.

"The new security from Genitor."

"She's kind of sexy in an androgynous sort of way," she whispered. She smiled licentiously. "Or have you already noticed?"

"I hardly think I'm in the mood to be thinking those thoughts, Eve."

She shrugged and went back to work.

Trinity worked her way around the plant.

"Do you know everyone working here?"

"Not anymore," I said. "Eve and Willy hired the new employees relatively recently."

"When I get a chance, I'd like to look over what they have on everyone. The easiest way for the creeps to infiltrate your life would be through the business."

I nodded and gazed around suddenly more keen to the way any of them were looking at me. Maybe she was better than Sterling. He never mentioned this possibility.

"Let's go to the convention center," I told Trinity, and we left and got back into my car.

"Quite an operation you guys got going. I'm impressed. I didn't expect so much," she said as I pulled away.

"It wasn't until recently. Almost overnight, matter of fact."

"Impressive," she said again, nodding. I saw her making some notes in a PDA.

I found Willy in the thick of it at the convention center. One of the committee members was not happy with the way Willy had designed the arrangement of the kiosks. Willy was trying to explain how her way made for easier restocking.

"It's like planning a battle," she explained. I could see the frustration in her face, the slight redness in her cheeks, trickling down into her taught jaw. The committee member wasn't convinced and went off to talk to other members.

"What a dork," Willy said. "You run into these self-important assholes every time you deal with any committees. They compensate for their otherwise empty lives," she muttered, and then finally realized I was at her side. "You okay?"

"Fine."

She looked over at Trinity.

"Who's that?"

"My new security agent."

"No shit," she said. "She looks like she has a pair of balls."

"I haven't gotten to know her that well yet," I said. Willy laughed.

"You look good," she said. She kissed me.

"I feel better."

"Great. Do me a favor, will you. I'm going into the kitchen. You check out the setups for the mixed drinks. I don't trust Tommy with the job. I trust him with the actual intercourse, but not with the necessary foreplay."

"Okay," I said, laughing.

Trinity watched me cross the room. I noticed how she kept back, but moved almost precisely with my every twist and turn as if there were invisible wires connected to us. I began to feel as if I were being guarded by the secret service.

Tommy did look overwhelmed. I started to check the stock and saw immediately that he had under-stocked club soda. Soon, I was in the thick of it, confirming glasses, mixes, condiments. There were so many new employees, I did not know names and I thought again about what Trinity had said. I knew many were only temporary, but one blond-haired man of about thirty-five looked familiar. I noticed he had an air of self-confidence about him and other employees were listening to him.

"Hi," I said, approaching him. "I'm Kate Dobson."

"Yeah, I know," he said shaking my hand. "I'm Peter Teller. I used to manage for Isler. We've done this party for the last five years."

"Oh. I'm sorry about him."

"Yeah, it was quite a shock, especially with the new information."

"What new information?"

"Everyone believed he suffered heart failure and drifted into the opposite lane."

"Didn't he?"

"Autopsy report said he had no heart problem and the police now believe it was the truck that had drifted too far to the right. Here's the best part. The truck driver has disappeared, or should I say evaporated?"

"Evaporated? What do you mean?"

"That truck wasn't supposed to be on the road and the driver not only had what the police think now was a phony license, he never worked for the company."

"Oh, my God."

"Yeah. Poor Glen. Wrong place, wrong time. The driver was probably stealing the truck," he said.

"I'm so sorry."

"Well," he said, looking around. "I can't blame you guys for jumping in. This is a major payday. What do they say, someone's bad luck is usually someone else's good. Thanks for hiring me at least," he said, and jumped quickly when an employee nearly dropped a case of tequila.

I watched them for a while and then, when I turned, I found Trinity so close behind me, I almost turned into her.

"You all right?" she asked.

"Yes, why?"

"Just checking. That's my job," she said. She looked at all the activity and the employees. "Any one of these people could be planted," she repeated.

"You know you're scaring me a lot more than comforting me," I said.

"Sorry. It's not my intention. We just want it all to go well for you and when you're pregnant, the baby," she added. "Everyone has an interest in your having a successful birthing."

If I were told that one more time, I'll scream, I thought, then sucked in my breath and went to see how Willy was doing. I was still quite disturbed about the news concerning Glen Isler, and I wondered how much of it Willy knew.

She shook her head when I told her and said she hadn't heard anything like that.

"Doesn't it just make you sick, Willy?"

"Unfortunate, but we can't dote on it."

"Dote on it? We have all this because of that truck driver apparently," I said, thinking about my conversation with Peter Teller.

"Look, what were we supposed to do, turn down the opportunity?" she snapped. "You know how long it would have taken us to get to this point? And we got it because we deserve it, because we have the capability to jump in with such short notice."

Her face was getting red again.

"I didn't say we should have turned it down, Willy, I was just pointing out . . ."

"Okay, okay. This just isn't a good time to talk

about the good and bad in the world," she said. "If you're strong enough, check on things at the plant."

"I've already been there," I said, but she was already walking away, looking for something else to steal away her attention.

It wasn't like her to be so short with me, I thought, and I can't blame it entirely on the pressure of this enormous party. It frightened me. Were events quickly changing us or were the changes always in us, dormant, waiting to be nudged and brought out of hibernation? She and I had a conversation on this topic once, and Willy proposed that no one changes; he or she simply becomes whoever he or she really is. She called it the Dr. Jekyll and Mr. Hyde phenomenon. "Mr. Hyde is always there, brooding under the surface, waiting to pop out like some kind of latent cancer."

Maybe he already had, I thought, and turned to leave. I was suddenly feeling very tired again, and there wasn't all that much I could do here anyway. Trinity was at my side so quickly I had the feeling she was standing there all the time. She wasn't exaggerating when she told me I'd feel like I had to brush her teeth. I knew I should be grateful, but it was becoming more annoying to have a second shadow.

"Where to?"

"Home," I said sharply. "I suddenly need to rest."

"Understood," she said, as if I had just translated from a foreign language. "You've been through quite a bit over the past twenty-four or so hours."

I didn't want to talk about it. I walked faster. Just before we reached my car in the parking lot, I felt the ground turn and reached out for her.

"What's wrong?"

"A dizzy spell," I said.

"Take it easy. I've got you," she said, and led me to the car. She took the car keys out of my hand. "I'll drive. Lucky, I decided to come along in your car," she added. She opened the passenger side door and I slipped in and quickly lay back, closing my eyes.

That damn quickening occurred again before she got in, and I held my breath. How many times had I seen someone put their hand on a pregnant woman's stomach to feel the baby moving? I had done it a few times myself. It sure felt similar. Was I going completely crazy?

"You all right? Want to go to the doctor?" Trinity asked. I guess I looked a little white in the face.

"No, just take me home," I said. "Wait," I added.

"What?"

"Do me a favor. Put your hand on my stomach."

"What?" she smiled.

"Just tell me if you feel anything."

She shook her head.

"What would I feel?"

"Could you just do it?"

She shrugged and put her palm over my exposed stomach when I lifted the blouse. I felt the quickening again and looked at her face.

"Well?"

"It's a very nice stomach, but I don't feel anything unusual."

I lifted her hand away.

"Okay. Take me home," I said. I could feel tears under my lower eyelids threatening to spill over. I closed my eyes and swallowed back the tightness in my throat.

When she started the car, I opened my eyes, and as we backed away, I saw Peter Teller step out of the convention center to light a cigarette. He watched us drive off. I closed my eyes again and dozed off, waking when I heard the garage door going up.

I got out of the car quickly.

"I'm going to lie down for a while," I told her. She nodded and watched me go into the house. I heard the garage door close and her coming into the house behind me as I made my way to our bedroom.

I was so frustrated with myself, with my fatigue, nausea, and dizziness. When would this stop? I was beginning to feel like an invalid, more like someone suffering a fatal illness. I should have asked more questions about the pseudocyesis, I thought. I slipped off my shoes and lay back, staring at the ceiling. My lower back was aching again. I was so uncomfortable I had to keep changing my position. I felt like screaming. Finally, I sat up and decided to go throw cold water on my face.

Standing there at the sink and looking into the mirror, I felt a tightness around my bosom and unbuttoned my blouse to expose my breasts. I studied them in the mirror. They looked two sizes bigger and I saw the distinct stretch marks. How could anyone's mind make such a thing happen? It literally took my breath away. I seized the edge of the counter and held it tightly for a few moments.

Suddenly, I heard the sound of someone running in the house, chairs being pushed aside in the kitchen and the sliding door slammed open. Before I could turn to walk out to see what was happening, I heard the crack of a gunshot. I froze and listened. Then I charged forward out of the bedroom and into the kitchen. The sliding door was open. I peered out and saw Trinity walking back from the wall on the east side slowly. She put her pistol back into its holster and headed for me.

"What was that?"

"One of them was at your bedroom window."

"What? Oh, my god." I pressed my hand to my heart. "Did you shoot him?"

"He moved too quickly. He was like a gazelle. I couldn't believe how easily he hopped over that wall. By the time I got to it, he was gone down the wash. Bold bastard," she said. "You left that window open?" she asked.

"I don't think so."

"It's open. Let me check your bedroom," she said, and I followed her back.

The screen on the window had been edged up. She studied it a moment and then turned and looked at the bed.

"Son of a bitch," she said.

"What?"

She walked slowly to the bed and, using a piece of paper, carefully lifted a dart to show me.

"I'd better call this in," she said.

"They want to kill me!" I exclaimed. "But I thought . . . they would only try to intimidate me."

She wrapped the dart in the paper and then looked at me.

"Obviously, they're convinced you're pregnant," she said. "And they don't think you'll abort."

15.

I was terribly conflicted.

Willy had to know what had happened, but if I called her now, I'd be calling her right in the thick of it. I knew she would be angry when she found out all this had happened and I hadn't called, but I couldn't pull her away from the convention center. I sat in the living room, dazed and still shaking. Trinity returned.

"Okay, we're going to have an additional member of the security team assigned to you so you'll feel more secure. He'll be here in less than an hour. He was pulled off another job nearby."

"That's fine, but we should be calling the police," I said.

"I wouldn't do that."

"Why not? Someone tried to kill me!"

"We'll have to explain what happened to Sterling, why you called us to take care of it . . . it'll lead to all sorts of complications. We're on this. Don't worry."

"You're on this? What did the killer miss me by, a few inches?"

She stared at me as if I were being uncooperative and behaving like a spoiled brat.

"It won't happen again," she said.

I looked away, my heart pounding.

"I'm glad you're so confident. Maybe I should put an advertisement in the newspaper announcing I'm not really pregnant yet or put up a billboard announcing it on my front lawn. That way they'll leave me alone."

I felt the strain in my voice. I was tottering on the balance beam of sanity and close to falling into hysteria.

"Just try to calm down," she said. "We're directing more resources to you. You'll be fine, but for now, please stay inside and avoid standing in windows or patio doors."

"Calm down? Stay inside and avoid windows and doors?" I started to laugh. "You want me to be a prisoner in my own home? What kind of a solution is that?"

"I'm going to do another sweep of the grounds. You should go rest," she said, not replying to my question and left. *She has about as much sympathy as a Nazi SS officer with a hangover,* I thought.

My lower back started aching again. I decided I should go lie down and considered taking one of those pills. I rose and started for the bedroom when the phone rang. It froze me for a moment. After the third ring, I picked it up. It would go to the answering machine on four rings and if it were Willy, she would be upset.

"Hello."

"Don't believe them," the raspy voice said. "You

are pregnant and we're not going to let it happen."

Just as he hung up, Trinity came rushing in through the open patio door.

I stood there holding the receiver away from my body as if I believed the speaker could somehow poison or attack me through it.

"What?" she asked, seeing how I was standing there. "Was it them?"

I nodded.

"Good."

"Good? Good?" My voice rose. "He threatened me. He was on all of ten seconds."

"It doesn't matter how long he was on. Our devices will have picked him up."

"You were right. They think I'm pregnant. They say I shouldn't believe what I've been told."

"Don't listen to them. You oughta know if you're pregnant or not," she said. "They're playing with you. I told you they want to make you crazy. I'm going to my car to check on what we just learned. I'll be right out front and the second guard should be here momentarily. Go relax," she told me, and headed for the front door.

I realized I was still holding the receiver and cradled it as if I believed the caller remained connected. I stood there fighting back a more desperate urge to call Willy. I needed her, needed her strength, but it was only a matter of a few hours now until the big extravaganza began. I knew how busy she was at this very moment, coordinating it all, working with so many new people. I feel guilty enough about not being at her side. How could I draw her away, even after this?

I stepped back and turned quickly to go to the bedroom. I closed the shades and, still trembling, looked for the pills. If I didn't take one, I thought, I would surely not rest and I would only get worse and worse until my hysteria drove me to either run to Willy or call her. I was perspiring so much, I felt as if my skin had just been greased. Before I took a pill, I washed my face in cold water.

Pausing, I gazed at myself in the mirror. Was it part of what I could only call my madness now? My face looked somewhat bloated, my features larger. The weight gain I had felt only in my breasts and stomach, and a little in my thighs appeared to have seeped upwards, thickening my neck and filling my cheeks. There was even a tracing of a double chin.

Shuddering, I backed away.

How could this be happening?

How could my twisted brain be capable of affecting my body this way? Maybe, just maybe, I was imagining it.

I glanced at the scale and then took a deep breath and stepped on it. It was as if I were in a church bell tower. The ringing echoed from one ear to the other and bounced around in my head.

According to my scale, I had gained nearly twenty-five pounds!

Was all this, could all this, even the reading on the

scale be a figment of my imagination? Was I caught in some dream? Was pseudocyesis that powerful a mental aberration? I couldn't have gained this much weight this quickly. I wasn't eating as ravenously. If it were true, surely it was water retention, serious water retention. I need to see the doctor.

As if to reinforce that decision, I felt that damn movement inside me, that quickening again. It was even more vivid causing me to gasp. A wave of nausea came over me and then another and another. I dry heaved for a few moments and then, feeling very dizzy now, headed toward the bed.

I never made it. The room spun and the floor went out from beneath my feet. I felt myself falling and falling, but never hitting the ground. I was descending forever into the deeper and deeper darkness, accompanied by a horrendous howl, the cry of some prehistoric beast giving birth in a delivery so painful, it spit out her insides with the fetus and left her soaking in pain and blood, eagerly welcoming the embrace of Death.

When I woke I was in bed.

I had no idea what time it was, but I saw it was dark outside. After a few deep breaths, I turned and saw Willy sitting in the lounge chair, her feet up on the ottoman. Her head was tilted to the right and with the little illumination from the outside lights spilling in around the closed shutters, I could see she was asleep. Bracing on my elbows, I sat up and saw it was four o'clock in the morning. How could I have slept so long? How did I get into the bed? I was naked. Who undressed me? Had Willy come home and found me on the floor?

I needed a cold drink. My skin felt clammy and my throat was so dry that I was afraid if I swallowed too hard, I'd scratch it. When I pulled the blanket completely away and shifted my legs to get off the bed, Willy opened her eyes and scrubbed her cheeks with the palms of her hands quickly.

"Kate? How are you?"

"Why are you sleeping in the chair? When did you get here? How did I get into this bed?"

I fired my questions at her, but she just sat there staring at me in the dark.

Then she leaned over and turned on the standing lamp. The brightness stung my eyes.

"I came home about an hour ago. The party went on and on," she said, "but Trinity found me and told me you had passed out and she had gotten you into bed. She said you woke and were confused so she was told to give you one of the pills."

"Trinity found me and gave me a pill? I don't remember any of that."

"She said you were confused. I understand."

"Well, I don't," I said sharply. "Who told her to undress me and put me in the bed?"

"Don't be so upset about it. It wasn't a bad thing to do for you at the time, Kate."

"You know they tried to kill me?"

"Pardon me?"

"The dart Trinity found in my bed . . . the poison dart!" I cried when she continued to stare. "Didn't she tell you all about it?"

"No, she didn't mention any dart. All she told me was you received another one of those threatening phone calls."

"What?"

"She said they traced it to a pay phone in the Palm Springs Airport."

"She didn't mention any dart?"

"They went to the airport but they didn't spot any of the people they knew from the fanatic organization," she continued.

"Aren't you listening to me? Someone blew the same kind of dart with this poison frog stuff that killed Sterling Plunkett at me through the opening in the window there," I said pointing. "She found the dart inches from where I was and then she went after the assassin. They're trying to kill me, Willy. They think I'm pregnant for sure and they vow they won't let me have the baby!"

"Take it easy," she said, rising. "You want to go to the bathroom?"

"No, I don't want to go to the bathroom. Where's Trinity now?"

"She's out front. She and another security agent are outside watching the house."

"Get her in here."

"Kate, it's after four in the morning."

"I don't care. I don't see how she could leave out

the dart story. If there was no attempt on my life, why did they send a second security guard, Willy?"

She didn't reply.

"Well, why would they do that?"

"She said you were quite hysterical after the phone call and she thought it would help."

"What? I need to talk to her now!"

"Okay, okay, we'll talk to her, but let's wait until morning when we're all bright and alert and we'll sit down with her and go over it. I'm exhausted," she said.

I settled back. Of course she was, I thought.

"Do you want anything before I go to sleep?" she asked.

"I need a glass of cold water. My throat feels like sandpaper."

"Okay. I understand. I'll get it."

"What about Eve? Where is she?"

"She remained behind to finish up. She's still not back. It was an enormous job, but it went well for us," she added. "We had many compliments on the food."

"Terrific," I said, but without any enthusiasm. "I'm sorry," I quickly added. "I'm not exactly in a mood to celebrate yet."

"I understand."

"Stop saying you understand."

"Okay. I'll be right back with your water," she said in the tone of voice of someone trying to placate a mental patient and left.

I looked down at myself. My stomach was even more distended. Pseudocyesis or no pseudocyesis, how could it grow so large so quickly? Was I going to get to the point where I would simply explode?

She returned with my water.

"Look at me," I said when she handed me the glass. I put my hand on my stomach.

She stepped back.

"Yeah, so?"

"Don't you see how big I've become?"

"You're bigger, yes, but Dr. Aaron explained it all to us. It's not unexpected, right? It's part of that psychosomatic condition, pseudo something or another."

"Pseudocyesis."

"Exactly."

I drank some water.

"I can't believe it."

"Stranger things happen," she said.

"Not to me. Did Trinity tell you what he said to me on the phone?"

"Who?"

"Aren't you listening to anything? Them, whoever . . . he said I shouldn't believe that I'm not pregnant. I've been thinking. Maybe . . . maybe I am. Maybe I don't have pseudocyesis. Just maybe the report was erroneous."

Willy smiled.

"You think that you could possibly be this far along in a real pregnancy in this short of time, Kate?

Get a hold of yourself. You, yourself, told me you were having symptoms characteristic of a woman in her second trimester."

"It's more like the third trimester," I said.

"So that's even more implausible. Third trimester?"

"Yes, third trimester! I've gained nearly twenty-five pounds, Willy. My lower back aches every time I sit for more than fifteen minutes. My breasts are even more enlarged. Look at this," I said, pointing to my stomach and then to my breasts. "Look at these stretch marks."

She nodded.

"I think we should go to a therapist, Kate."

"Oh, WE should go?"

"What happens to you, happens to me, remember?"

"Your breasts and your stomach aren't bulging. Mine are!"

"Okay, we should take you to a therapist. Dr. Aaron gave me the name of someone nearby."

"I thought she said under the circumstances it would soon not matter whether I went to one or not."

"Obviously, for you now it matters."

"Oh, just for me."

"I know you're upset and testy, Kate, but I'm trying to do what would be best for you."

"Upset and testy, the weaker one again. I wonder how you would be after someone tried to hit you with a poison dart and then called you and called you to scare and threaten you. Even you, Willy the Super Dyke, might crack."

"Stop it, Kate."

"Even you might crack after you found a man dead in your pool lounge chair with a dart sticking in his neck."

I felt the tears streaming down my cheeks.

"Are you going to get hold of yourself or what?" Willy said approaching.

I stared up at her. She looked as if she might strike me and it frightened me. I imagined that was her intent.

"I want it to end," I said and looked down.

She was silent and then she put her hand softly on my hair and drew my head to her. I felt her lips on my forehead. She took the glass from my hands and guided me back into the bed.

"I know. That's why we should get you some treatment. I really am exhausted," she said. "Let's talk about it all in the morning, late morning."

She began to take off her clothes. I watched her undress, turn off the standing lamp, and then slip under the blanket beside me. Her lips grazed my cheek and her left hand slipped up and over my ribs to caress my breast.

"I'm not physically distasteful to you?"

"You're voluptuous," she whispered.

"Yeah, right."

"Relax," she said, bringing her mouth to my breasts and nipples and then kissing her way down and over my distended stomach. The moment her lips moved below my belly button, I felt a terrific rumble within, a distinct quickening. I seized her head at her temples and kept her face buried in my stomach until she pulled away.

"Did you feel it?" I asked. "Well? Didn't you?"

"Feel what?"

"Damn it, Willy, that movement inside me, what Dr. Aaron called the quickening. Couldn't you feel it?"

"I didn't feel anything, Kate. I'm sorry."

First Trinity felt nothing when I did and now Willy. I wanted to scream. I did open my mouth and I did scream, but inside myself.

She shifted away from me.

"I guess we both should just get some sleep. It will all seem different in the morning. Late morning," she added. She kissed my cheek and turned over. I lay there with my eyes open looking into the darkness.

"I'm sorry," I said after a few minutes. My head was so heavy. It felt clogged with thoughts, fears, images. "I should have asked you more about the party."

I waited, but she didn't respond. I could hear her heavy breathing. She is spent, I thought. She was going to make love to me just to help me feel better. I'm such an ungrateful bitch. She was right. There wasn't anything we could do right now anyway, but why didn't Trinity tell her about the dart? That was far more important than another threatening phone call. They tried to kill me.

Maybe Willy did know but was pretending she didn't just to keep me calm, to prevent my hysteria from getting worse. Maybe I would see the therapist. Maybe he or she would help me bring this condition to an end and we could start anew. If I did that, if I lost all the symptoms, perhaps those fanatics would learn about it and leave us alone. It was worth a try. It comforted me to think so.

The ache started in my lower back again. I turned on my side and closed my eyes. Get some sleep, I told myself. Don't let events take over. Get control. I felt myself drifting off and smiled with gratitude, grateful to a body that was finally being cooperative. For a few hours at least, I wasn't going to be at war with myself. I wouldn't feel as if I were separated from my own flesh and blood. I wouldn't feel like I had lost it, like a Kate Dobson trapped inside someone else.

I slept.

When I awoke in the morning, I discovered Willy had already risen. It was nearly noon. I called for her, but heard nothing. I did feel stronger and rose quickly, put on my robe and went out to look for her. There was a note on the kitchen table. She said she wanted to let me sleep and she had gone to the plant to handle the cleanup and setup after the big event. She told me to call her as soon as I had gotten up. I was about to do so when I out of the corner of my eye, I saw someone moving in the direction of the casita.

I went to the patio door and watched Trinity, gun drawn, moving very slowly, a bit in a crouch. I watched, mesmerized.

A very tall, caramel-colored man, who looked more like a professional basketball player than a security guard, came up on her right. She nodded at him and they drew closer to the casita. I saw her pause at the door and then nod at him and go in. He followed. I waited. After a good five minutes or so, they both emerged, their guns holstered.

I opened the patio door.

"What's going on?"

The tall man went toward the rear of the property. Trinity came my way.

"We thought we saw someone run across the yard and go into the casita," she said.

"And?"

"No one there. Kerry Barnes is checking out the grounds again. How are you?"

"Why didn't you tell Willy about the dart?" I asked.

She shrugged.

"I didn't think she was that interested in it."

"What?"

"The poison you mean?"

"No. The dart in my bed? The attempt on my life? Hello," I sang.

She shook her head.

"I don't know what you're talking about," she said and started away.

"What? What do you mean? Trinity!" I screamed.

She turned and looked at me.

"You had a bad night, Kate. Leave it at that," she said and continued toward the front of the house.

I stood there, my jaw hanging.

"This is bullshit!" I screamed and backed into the house, slamming the patio door closed.

Few a few moments, I just stood there trying to make sense of it all, my heart thumping as if something was trying to break out of my chest. My whole body was shaking. I drank some cold water and calmed myself. Then I looked at Willy's note and hurried to the phone. It rang so long, I thought I had dialed the wrong number.

"Hey," she said when Tony put her on. "How are you?"

"I think I'm going crazy, otherwise, I'm just a perfect example of pseudocyesis."

She laughed.

"You sound stronger."

"I thought I was, but this woman, androgyny, whatever she is, is trying to make me think I'm going nuts."

"What do you mean? What woman?"

"Trinity, my security guard. The one who didn't tell you about the poison dart in my bed, remember?"

"So?"

"I asked her why she didn't tell you and she made me feel as though I imagined the whole thing."

Willy was quiet.

"I didn't imagine it, Willy. I saw the dart. I saw her take it away."

"Okay, okay. I'll speak to her as soon as I can get free. We're overwhelmed here."

"I swear it happened. Maybe she didn't tell you because they're afraid of your knowing how dangerous this has become for me. Maybe they think we'll cancel the next insemination. Maybe . . ."

"Kate, you don't need anyone to drive you crazy. You're driving yourself crazy. I told you we'll get to the bottom of it. For now I've got my hands full getting this place in order, machinery, products . . . on top of which, we still have our regular customers."

"You should have woken me when you woke so I could get there to help."

"It's under control for the moment, but I'll need you back here as soon as you can get yourself together and drive over, okay? There's a ton of paperwork to be entered into the computer and the phones aren't stopping. The party was so successful for us that we're getting tons of new inquiries and Tommy isn't exactly an ideal receptionist. He still thinks yeah is a synonym for hello."

"Eve isn't doing any of it?"

She was silent too long.

"Where is she?" I asked.

"We'll talk about it when you get here."

"What do you mean, we'll talk about it? She's not there? She's not here. They just checked out the casita. Where is she? What's going on, Willy? Did she quit on us? Why would she quit on us immediately after such a success?"

"Look, take a shower, have your breakfast, get dressed, and come over to the plant."

"Willy, I'm not hanging up until you tell what's going on with Eve," I said firmly.

"Don't freak out on me," she replied.

"I'm not freaking out."

"I'm warning you. I can't come running over there right now, Kate. You'll be on your own or I'll just make a call to the paramedics."

"I said I won't freak out, Willy. I'm better, stronger, despite what my security guard is doing to me." I stiffened myself for any new blow. "Well? Tell me!"

"She had a family tragedy," she said.

"What? You mean, something happened to her father, her sister, the one who works for Dr. Aaron?"

"No. Her brother, his new wife, and their child. It happened early this morning."

"What happened?"

"A house fire. They're all dead," she replied. "She had to go to Jackson to identify the bodies. I felt very bad for her. She was exhausted and then hit with this terrible, terrible thing."

I didn't speak.

The receiver felt soft in my hand. It was as if it were turning into putty and it would simply fold over into a mass of nothing. With it would go Willy's voice and all she had just told me.

"You're freaking, aren't you? I knew I shouldn't have told you."

"Do they know what caused the fire?"

"She didn't know any more than what I just told you. I'm sure it's an ongoing investigation. They lived in one of those fancy log cabins. Dried logs . . . out in the woods beyond any fire hydrants. It was probably something electrical. They were apparently caught fast asleep and trapped, probably dying of smoke inhalation."

"No alarms?"

"I don't know, Kate. She woke me very early and told me what I told you. She promised to call tonight."

"Do they suspect arson? Well, do they?" I followed before she could answer.

"I just told you. Eve didn't know any more than that."

"They killed them," I said in a heavy whisper. "They wanted to be sure they killed the baby."

"What?"

"The child was created through the same insemination process and Eve told us her sister-in-law was harassed just as I'm being."

"Stop it. Kate, do you hear me?"

I felt a deep and heavy shuddering inside me which caused a swift surge of icy cold up my spine. However, that was immediately followed by a warmth at the tips of my nipples. With my free hand, I opened my robe and looked at my breasts.

The receiver fell out of my hand, the wire swinging it into the wall. I could hear Willy calling for me.

"Kate! Kate, damn it."

I picked up the receiver.

"Willy."

"What is it? Are you freaking out on me? Kate?"

"Willy, my breasts. . . ."

"What? Damn it, Kate. What?"

"They're leaking," I said. "Just as they would for a woman in her third trimester."

16.

I RETURNED TO BED.

Twenty minutes later, Willy appeared in the bedroom doorway.

"C'mon," she said.

"What?"

"Get up, Kate. I'm taking you to see the doctor now. C'mon," she ordered, her hands on her hips, snapping a command like a marine drill sergeant.

There was no sympathy or compassion in her face, just raw rage. I rose quickly.

"You didn't have to come running home, Willy."

"Yeah, right. You're gaining weight every minute. People are blowing poison darts at you and your breasts are leaking. I'll just hang in there and make sure the shrink wrapper is greased."

"Willy . . ."

"You'll remember I wasn't for this," she muttered as we started out of the house. "You'll remember I said it would bring on serious problems."

"I'm not blaming you for anything, Willy. Don't worry about it," I said.

She was silent.

I got into the company van she had parked in our driveway.

"Where's Trinity?" I wondered aloud as I looked over the front and the street.

"Forget about Trinity. Let's just concentrate on you," Willy said, started the engine and drove out so fast, we bounced at the end of the driveway. I hadn't even put on my seat belt.

"Jesus," I screamed, hurrying to do so.

"I told you not to freak out on me, but no, you had to hear about Eve's family. You just had to know it all right away."

"I didn't freak out, but I can't explain this," I said gesturing at my breasts.

She was silent, her face cast in an iron mask of blatant rage.

"Just when things are really happening for us," she muttered, "you have to come completely apart and become mental on me."

I started to cry.

"Don't," she said. "Or I swear I'll drive into a tree."

"Where are we going? To Dr. Aaron?"

"No," she said, and handed me a business card.

It read, Dr. Sandra Yan. Individual and couples therapy.

"You should take me to our doctor, Willy. I'm not a nutcase."

"Let's just see what this therapist has to say. Please," she added. "Just cooperate or soon I'll be going to see the therapist and not you."

"Okay. I'm sorry. I really am!"

She looked at me and her face softened.

"Okay, like you said. Let's not blame anyone for anything, Kate, not even ourselves. We'll get through it," she said with her characteristic confidence. It did feel good to be leaning on her again.

We drove to Palm Desert and turned onto the beautiful El Paseo area, where the streets were lined with upscale clothing stores, art galleries, restaurants, and offices for plastic surgeons as well as dentists. As soon as we turned up a side street, she pulled into a parking lot and found a space.

I looked back at the buildings behind us. There were three restaurants, a gift shop, and an art gallery in this section.

"Where's this therapist?"

"Upstairs," she said, nodding at a stairway that went to the second floor. I saw no sign.

"How did you know where to go?"

"I called," she said. "How do you think? Let's go," she ordered and stepped out of the van.

I followed her up the stairs. The door had a gold plaque with the engraved name, Dr. Sandra Yan. It said nothing else. She pressed a buzzer and brought her lips to a small microphone in the wall.

"Wilma Radcliff and Kate Dobson," she announced, and we heard the door buzzing.

She seized the handle and we entered a small lobby, if I could even call it a lobby. There was only a settee, a round hard cherry wood table and a standing lamp with a very ordinary yellow shade. There was nothing on any of the walls. Across from the settee was another door. It opened and a petite Chinese woman with her ebony hair in a tight bun smiled at us. Wearing an alluring lace cheongsam, she looked like a receptionist in a Chinese restaurant.

"Good afternoon," she said. "Please, come in."

She stepped back and we entered a somewhat larger room with the traditional psychiatrist's couch, a chair, and a desk and chair. I saw some framed degrees on the walls and an abstract painting that looked like something extracted from a Rorschach test on the wall to my left.

"I'm Dr. Yan," she said, extending her hand to me and then to Willy.

"Willy Radcliff. This is Kate."

"Pleased to meet you," she said.

"What do I do, lie down on the couch?"

"Most comfortable way," she said smiling. "But of course you can sit. You can even stand," she added, still smiling. She looked at Willy.

"How long will it be?" Willy asked.

"An hour. Not longer," she said.

"No paperwork?" I asked. "No insurance cards, forms to fill out?" Willy shot fire from her eyes at me, but I couldn't help it.

"Time for that later. From what I've been told, more important we address your problem quickly. Please," she said indicating the couch.

I went to it and sat.

"I'll be back in an hour," Willy told me. "Kate?"

"Okay," I said. "I'm all right. Go."

She left and Dr. Yan picked up a pad from her desk and sat in her chair. I couldn't help thinking of Tony Soprano. Psychoanalysis still felt like Voodoo medicine to me.

"I have spoken at length with your doctor," she began. "You know your diagnosis?"

"Yes, but I can't believe these physical changes are a result of a mental condition."

She widened her smile.

"Oh, you'd be surprised at what the mind can do to the body. Women who suffer false pregnancy have all the symptoms you have. Depression can alter the activity of the pituitary gland, mimicking symptoms."

"Even leaking breasts, secreting milk?"

"Absolutely. Sometimes, even false positives on a pregnancy test, otherwise, I would just do one for you and show you, but if we had a false positive, it would damage our therapy. You've come to believe you really are pregnant, right?"

"I don't know what to believe. How can I have symptoms that occur in the third trimester?"

"Exactly. Not possible. Even in premature births, the mother will not be in third trimester. Let's talk about your desire to have a child," she said. "Tell me when you first thought of this and how your partner reacted."

I began. She took me back to my childhood. We

talked about simple things like playing with dolls, imitating a mother, a woman's natural instinct to have children. As the session progressed, I became more and more comfortable with her. Her insights to my feelings, even my most inner thoughts impressed me.

"In time," she said, "you will come to understand yourself and then confronting your problem will be easier. Dr. Aaron makes a good point. Hopefully, you will become pregnant and psychosomatic symptoms will merge into real symptoms."

"It's like being pregnant for 18 months instead of nine," I said, and she laughed.

"Maybe you give birth to elephant. Gestation period last about twenty-two months, longest of any mammal."

"I'll commit suicide if that happens."

She laughed again and then grew serious.

"Stay on the medication Dr. Aaron provided. It is a good tranquilizer." She looked at her watch. "We talk again one week from today, same time?"

"Okay. But what do you really think about me?"

"You are a classic case. No problem. We'll work it out together, make you more comfortable and ease you into a smooth transition to real pregnancy."

She reached over to her desk and plucked a card from small box.

"Here are my numbers, cell phone included. You call with any questions between now and then."

I looked at it and then I thought about the fanatics. Would it complicate things to bring all that up? We heard the door buzzer.

"That must be your Willy," she said. It was. We walked out to the small lobby.

"How'd it go?" Willy asked immediately.

"She'll be fine," Dr. Yan said. "We see each other in one week, unless necessary before."

"Great. Kate?"

"It's okay," I said.

"Do we pay you anything now?" Willy asked her.

"We keep tab," Dr. Yan said. "Like bartender."

"I could use a stiff drink," Willy told her.

We left the office and headed for the van.

"So?" Willy asked me.

"I like her. She makes sense. She helped me understand my deep desire to have a child and how that could lead to this condition."

"Feeling better, then?"

"A little, yes."

We got into the van.

"I heard from Eve," she told me as she started the engine and backed out of the parking space.

"And?"

"It's what I thought, an electrical problem caused the fire. It started on the lower floor. The bedrooms were upstairs and they got caught unaware. By the time the fire department arrived, the cabin was fully engulfed in flames. Her sister flew up to be with her."

"That's so sad. When will she return?"

"In a couple of days."

"Well, you can't carry this load on your shoulders only. I'll just go to the plant with you," I said. "This invalid role doesn't suit me anyway and there's no time for any of this self-pity now."

"Aren't you suddenly the big shot?"

"I'm far from a big shot, but I should keep my mind off everything and work is the best solution."

"Now you're talking," she said smiling.

"However, to get back to the other situation, I do want us to have a real heart-to-heart with this security guard, Willy. I did not imagine the dart in my bed."

"Will do," she said.

"Besides, how did they let us get away from the house and not follow us? What kind of protection are they providing now?"

"I'll call Lois when we get to the plant," she said.

Once there, I did dive into the paperwork. I couldn't believe what had piled up for us. Willy hadn't exaggerated the new orders, the inquiries and the wrapping up of the White Party business. The tips of my fingers started to ache from tapping out numbers on the keyboard. Either I was too involved or my imaginary symptoms were subsiding after only one session with my therapist, but I didn't have any aches in my lower back the whole time and I had no incidents of the quickening. For a while at least, it seemed we were back to some semblance of normalcy in our lives. As happened often, I even forgot about having any lunch and didn't even crave a nutritional energy bar.

During the entire time I worked, Willy had been out in the plant organizing the production team. We had what I couldn't imagine ever having, ten more full-time personnel. When I glanced through the window, however, I was surprised to see Marlee Peters from The Meadow talking to Willy. I imagined she was congratulating us, more specifically Willy, on the successful White Party. Marlee, like a number of women I knew in our circle, never missed an opportunity to flirt with Willy. This didn't look that way to me, however. They were off to the side talking and Willy had that serious posture she took on when something disturbed her. She leaned against the wall, folded her arms across her breasts and looked like a manikin.

After a good fifteen minutes or so, Marlee left, both of them looking toward the office before parting. Willy turned to an immediate mechanical problem, but I kept my eye on her. Finally, she came to the office. As she approached, I could see from the expression she wore that something unpleasant was happening or had happened. We still didn't need words at all to transmit our thoughts to one another. She entered, closed the door and leaned against it. I waited for a few moments and then asked, "What is it, Willy?"

"Janet Madison is dead," she told me.

I shook my head as if the words were mangled in my ears.

"What?"

"Before you think anything wild, she apparently had some sort of heart valve problem. She died at home. Paula found her sprawled on the kitchen floor. It happened early this morning."

"Heart valve? No one ever mentioned such a thing." I thought a moment. "Why would she go climbing up mountain trails with you if she had that sort of problem? Why did she decide to get pregnant as a surrogate? Why . . ."

"Just maybe she wasn't aware of it," Willy said. "You know not everyone has a decent annual physical."

"Wouldn't there be some warnings, some symptoms?"

"I don't know. Maybe. Maybe she just ignored them. No one wants to believe there's anything wrong with her. It doesn't make a difference now anyway. Hindsight is always twenty-twenty."

"When is the funeral?"

"It won't be here. Her parents have had her body shipped back to Ohio."

"Maybe the pregnancy did something."

"Kate . . ."

"I'm just saying, maybe. I mean physically, Willy. I'm not saying those nuts had anything to do with it."

"Good. Speaking of the fanatics, I spoke with Lois a short while ago."

"And?"

"She's investigating what went on between you and Trinity, but we both think you should postpone the next insemination."

"Really?"

"She wants you to be stronger, emotionally, physically. It makes sense, Kate."

I nodded.

"Except I had the impression from Dr. Aaron and now Dr. Yan that when I became pregnant for real, this pseudocyesis would come to an end."

"It will anyway," Willy said. "It has to."

"Okay. We didn't eat any lunch you know."

"Let's just go for an early dinner."

"It'll be very depressing out there," I said.

"I know, but no matter what, she was a friend and our gang needs us. We need each other, especially at times like this. I told Marlee we'd stop by The Meadow."

"Whatever you think," I said. "How sad."

"Yes. I've got a few more mechanical issues out there. I'll be back in a while. How you doing?"

"Almost caught up. I keep looking at the bottom line in disbelief. Willy, we're way beyond anything either of us imagined possible when we began."

"That's the American way," she said, smiling.

"I never really understood why they came to us after Glen Isler was killed. Why would they turn to a company as small as ours?"

"Someone recommended us to the people who control it."

"Who?"

"I never found out," she said. "Who cared? They came around and we certainly weren't going to turn it away. When would we ever get such an opportunity? It could have taken years."

"All this new business."

"Kate, relax. Can't you accept good luck as easily as you accept bad?"

I looked at the billing statements and shrugged.

"Got no choice," I said. "Have to be rich."

She laughed and left.

Later we did go to The Meadow, and as Willy had predicted, most of our friends had gathered to talk about and mourn poor Janet. I was surprised at they did not know she had undergone the insemination process and was pregnant. I didn't mention it. I just waited for someone to tell me. No one did.

"Isn't that odd?" I asked Willy.

"No. She wasn't ready to tell anyone probably. Remember she had tried to avoid meeting you at Dr. Aaron's. Forget about it. It'll just make everyone even more depressed to learn two people died."

"Two people?"

"The fetus and Janet."

"Wasn't it too early to consider the fetus a person?"

"Not to Janet and I'm sure not to the people who were paying for her to be their surrogate."

Of course, she was right. I hadn't thought of it that way. I wondered if they would feel obligated to attend her funeral since their progeny was being buried along with Janet. It all suddenly seemed so surreal.

"So what happened to my bodyguards?" I asked when we left for home. I saw no signs of Trinity or her backup.

"Lois said she was going to ask her to be less in your face and less obvious. I assume they're around. Maybe they're in a different car. Whatever."

I imagined she was right. They weren't at the house and afterward, when I looked out front and in the back, I didn't see them or any car. Despite that, perhaps because of all that had happened during the day, the tremendous roller coaster ride of emotions, I was too exhausted to care. Willy made sure our house was secure, checking the alarms, the doors, and the windows. Both of us fell asleep so fast, it was as if we had drunk some sedative together.

We woke about the same time in the morning. Despite my new sense of confidence, I still had to urinate more frequently, noted the darker pigmentation of my areolas and nipples and still suffered some leakage. My breasts didn't diminish, nor did my stomach and I had to wear the maternity clothes Lois Matthews had sent over. I did my best to put it out of mind and dive into work at the plant. The quickening occurred a few times before the end of the day, and the following morning it actually woke me before Willy woke. I screamed because it felt like something inside me was now determined to punch its way out. It was as if I were having a natural Caesarian.

"What?" Willy asked, groaning and turning.

I described what I had felt.

"You were dreaming for sure," she told me. "Might as well get up," she said and we did.

Late that afternoon, Eve returned to the plant. She was apologetic about having left us in the lurch.

"You had much to do after the White Party. I'm sorry," she told us in the office. She looked drained and exhausted. Willy told her to go directly to the casita and rest.

"We've got it all under control here, Eve. Obviously, it wasn't your fault. You haven't let up since you came to work for us. We're both grateful."

She looked at me and I seconded her comments. I did ask her if the investigators had firmly concluded the fire was an accident.

"As it turns out, the builder used cheaper materials, wires, than the code required. They're pursuing him now. He might be charged with manslaughter or something."

"He should be," Willy said. Then she told her about Janet.

I knew from what Willy had told me and how Eve had always been around Janet that she hadn't been all that fond of her, but she was sorry to hear it.

"She never looked very healthy to me," she said.

"What do you mean? I never noticed that," I said.

"She looked pale, peaked, like someone who had just recently been visited by a vampire," she said. "I guess I'd better go home and rest. We should take better care of ourselves," she added looking my way.

Willy walked her out. When she returned, she told

me she had seen Trinity and Kerry Barnes patrolling around our plant.

"I still want us to talk to her, Willy. I want her to tell me to my face that I imagined that dart in my bed. Call her in here."

"Why don't we just leave it for now, Kate? I'm so tired of it all, aren't you?"

I was, but I still wanted the satisfaction of having her admit she was sugarcoating the situation to keep Willy from freaking. However, I wasn't going to push it and make her more unhappy. She did look tired, too, and after what Eve had just said about us taking better care of ourselves, I backed off. All I needed now was Willy to get sick and I would surely drive myself off a cliff.

Nevertheless, when we left for the day, I looked for signs of Trinity and Barnes. I didn't see them and thought they were good at disappearing into the background. I told myself to take comfort in that at least.

Despite her depression and fatigue, Eve had managed to work up a gourmet dinner for us. She had prepared a lobster fra diavolo. I thought the spice might be too much for me under the circumstances, but it was so delicious, I threw caution to the wind and ate more than I should have. We drank two bottles of a delicious French wine Eve had brought with her when she had first moved in with us. Our talk was mainly about the great success at the White Party and the new long list of customers we were going to try to accommodate. The food, the wine, the great new prospects lifted the three of us to a state of euphoria. It was good to hear laughter and feel hopeful again.

I overslept the next morning and discovered Willy and Eve had gone to the plant without me. Once again, there was a note in the kitchen, telling me they didn't want to wake me and I should take a day off, especially now that Eve was back. My aches and pains had returned and I felt even heavier, especially in my breasts. Maybe I would take the day off, I thought and went to make myself some breakfast, but in the middle of it, I experienced more intense quickening. It lasted much longer than it ever had and actually took my breath away. I had to return to bed where I waited for it to subside.

"How can this be? How can this be?" I screamed.

I started to reach for Dr. Yan's card and stopped when the phone rang. Assuming it was Willy, I plucked the receiver quickly off its cradle. I wanted to tell her how intense the quickening had been and still was.

"Willy?"

"Listen to me," the raspy voice said. "Dr. Aaron recommended Dr. Yan. Dr. Matthews sent you to Dr. Aaron. You are really pregnant."

"Who the hell are you?"

"Eve's not who you think she is either, or she is what you think she is. You always knew, didn't you? She lied about her brother. We were there. We stopped him and we'll stop you if you don't listen."

The phone went dead. I sat there, gasping for breath, holding my stomach and then I and went to my computer. Quickly surfing through a search engine, I located the newspapers that covered the events in Jackson Hole, Wyoming. Scrolling down, I found the story updated.

It was a clear case of arson.

It was no accident. It had never been described as such. Fighting back the onslaught of nausea and dizziness, I dressed myself in one of the maternity outfits and then, staggering a bit, but determined, I made my way into the garage and to my car. I half expected to find Trinity waiting for me when I backed out, but she was nowhere in sight. With tears streaming down my face, I sped away.

Twenty minutes later, I pulled into a parking space at the Tahquitz medical center and got into the elevator. When I entered Dr. Malisoff's office, I saw the lobby was already full with his patients. Debbie Marks, his receptionist, looked up surprised.

"Kate?" she said as if we hadn't seen each other for years and years.

I realized she was shocked to see me in a maternity outfit.

"I realize I have no appointment, Debbie, but I've got to see him. It's truly life and death."

"When did you ..."

Dr. Malisoff emerged from one of his examination rooms and looked at me with just as much surprise. The sight gave him real pause. His patient said something to him as she left the room, but he barely acknowledged her. He stepped toward me and I rushed down the hallway.

"What's this?" he asked. "You're pregnant?"

"I'm not sure," I said. I couldn't stop myself from crying. "Please. . . . please help me."

17.

DR. MALISOFF'S NURSE, Rhoda Green, led me into another examination room where she checked my blood pressure and body temperature, as well as my pulse, while he started another patient in another room. I had never been in this particular room where there was far more medical equipment. I quickly understood it was the examination area for his maternity patients.

"Just relax, Kate," Rhoda told me. "The doctor will be in to see you as soon as he can. Can I get you something in the meantime? Water, perhaps?"

I shook my head. After my outburst in the hallway, my throat tightened so that I thought I would choke on anything. She patted me on the hand and went out.

Normally, Dr. Malisoff, a tall, slim man with a perfectly trimmed black mustache and a head of coal black hair so thick that it resembled a tightly knit wig, took so much time with each of his patients that he always ran behind. However, his curiosity about me, as well as my mental state, caused him to abbreviate his examination of the other patient, and in less than ten minutes he was beside me. In the meantime

Rhoda had me lie on the examination table, where she had placed a pillow.

"What's going on, Kate?" he asked as he checked my vitals on the chart Rhoda had begun. "You do have low blood pressure," he muttered. "Which I should say is characteristic of pregnancy, so tell me, what do you mean by you're not sure? You're wearing a maternity outfit." He smiled. "That's not some new fad I missed, is it?"

Through my tears and sobs, I related the past few months and the diagnosis Dr. Aaron had given me. He listened with those inscrutable dark eyes and then nodded.

"I'm familiar with the condition," he said, speaking of the pseudocyesis, "but to be honest, I've never seen a patient with it. Without further tests, I couldn't tell you if you are suffering from it or not, but in any case, I'm not qualified to diagnose mental conditions."

"What tests?"

He turned and nodded at a machine and a screen.

"That's a real-time scanner, ultrasound. It's an indispensable tool for early diagnosis of many things, including an ectopic pregnancy. You know what that is?"

"I don't know much at all when it comes to pregnancy. I'm obviously new at this, despite how I look," I said trying to find some room for humor.

He smiled.

"I imagine so. Ectopic pregnancies are commonly called tubal pregnancies, a pregnancy in which the fertilized egg implants outside the uterus. It can also implant in the ovaries, abdomen, or cervix. As the fetus grows, it bursts the organ that contains it, which obviously can endanger the mother's life. There is also something we call molar pregnancy and the ultrasound is good at finding that as well."

"And what is that?"

"An abnormality of the placenta caused by a problem when the egg and sperm join together at fertilization. There are two kinds, complete and partial molar pregnancy. Complete molar pregnancies have only placenta parts. There is no baby. It's an empty egg. Nevertheless, the placenta grows and produces the pregnancy hormone."

"HCG."

"Yes, you know that. Good. The patient believes she is pregnant. She believes a fetus is forming as well. How would she know otherwise? The ultrasound will show there is only the placenta, no baby. As I said women with molar pregnancy feel pregnant, have vaginal spotting, develop nausea and vomiting. Cysts can form from the abnormally high amounts of HCG."

"You think that could be my problem?"

"I don't know yet, Kate." He smiled and shook his head. "Insemination. I have to say I'm pretty surprised. I had no idea raising a child was something you and Willy desired. I can't recall you mentioning the idea, especially the idea of actually having the baby yourself."

"It took us time to talk ourselves into it. For me to talk Willy into it," I corrected. "It was always primarily my idea. I've been told that this condition, pseudocyesis, could be a result of my deep desire to be pregnant," I said, mimicking Dr. Aaron and Dr. Yan. "It can be traced back to my childhood, in fact. As you can tell, I've been to a therapist recently to explore the causes."

"I see." He returned to his doctor's face, scrutinizing eyes, intense. "Give me an idea about all these symptoms you've been experiencing."

I described it all and as I added the weight gain, the leaking of my breasts and the increased quickening, his eyes widened and began to lose their inscrutability.

"I've been told I can even produce a false positive on a pregnancy test."

"Yes, that's true, but considering the time period you're describing, I think we can establish or eliminate your concerns today."

He nodded at Rhoda who had been standing by with an expression of disbelief. Like most people, apparently, she had never heard of pseudocyesis or didn't know the full extent of its symptoms. She immediately began to set up the ultrasound.

Dr. Malisoff was always good at describing what procedures he would be using, what medications he would be prescribing, and he was always good at explaining a diagnosis. He was a master at helping patients understand their own issues and giving them a sense of comfort and security with the treatments he would prescribe.

"This, the transducer," he said, holding it above my stomach after lifting away my blouse and lowering the skirt, "emits very high frequency sound waves. I place it in contact with what we call the maternal abdomen and move it about as if it were a light shined from a torch to look at any particular content of the uterus. The ultrasound beams scan a fetus, if there is a fetus, in what we call thin slices. Not literally slices of course," he added, smiling. "They are reflected back to the transducer, and," he said, nodding at the monitor, "composed into a picture on the ultrasonogram."

"This is a 3-D ultrasound," he continued. "State of the art. You know me and new, innovative equipment."

Rhoda smiled and nodded.

"Anyway, it's a great tool for picking up a fetal heart beat and possible malformations, but parents love it because they can visualize their child better and there's some evidence that it has a catalytic effect for mothers to bond to their babies even before birth. We, in the business," he said, smiling, "refer to them as reassurance scans.

"Sometimes, because the ultrasound demonstrates an embryo but no clear-cut heartbeat; therefore, a missed abortion may be diagnosed."

I shuddered at the sound of that and even cringed. Was there something dead inside me? Had that been causing all these symptoms?

"However, looking at you," he said, smiling, "and listening to your description of the symptoms, which, as you properly described, are characteristic of a woman in her third trimester, and given the time period you have also described, I would have to say, we're not going to find anything resembling a fetus, Kate. You can watch the screen then and see for yourself and end this anxiety."

"Why didn't they prescribe this to me before? It would have been so much easier and I wouldn't need any psychotherapy. It certainly would have spared Willy. I've been impossible to live with."

"I don't know exactly why or why not you never had an ultrasound, but as you told me, your OB/GYN thought it was going to go away with real symptoms shortly and your therapist might have been concerned about the dramatic psychological impact such a discovery would have."

He held the transducer above me, hovering.

"In fact, now that I think of that, I have to say I'm not completely comfortable about doing this without consulting the therapist. Perhaps I should have a quick phone conversation with her. You are quite upset and . . ."

"No," I said, afraid he wouldn't go forward. "I need it to be proven or disproven to me. Besides, as you suggested, maybe I have some sort of growth, some sort of tumor, cyst, whatever! I can tell you that no one checked me for a molar pregnancy. No one even mentioned the possibilities you've been describing and supposedly I've been going to a specialist. I'm sorry I let them talk me into it. I should have been here from day one."

He looked at Rhoda as if he wanted her to be sure to make mental note of what I was telling him to do. *Everyone is worried about lawsuits these days,* I thought.

"Okay," he said. "Let's get it over with."

He began. As the information was fed back to the transducer and interpreted on the monitor, Rhoda edged closer. The three of us watched.

"There's a heartbeat," he said in a low, incredulous whisper.

I put my hand over my mouth to smother a gasp.

The fetus began to take form on the monitor.

He shook his head.

"Kate, you are really pregnant."

I was at once relieved, but that was quickly followed by a feeling of shock and terror as well.

"Is it . . . normal, healthy?"

The picture continued to take form.

"Prenatal ultrasound cannot diagnose all malformations and problems of an unborn baby, but from what I see here, it's looking good, but . . ."

"But what?"

"The femur . . . the longest bone in the body . . ."

"What about it?"

"The length of this femur . . ."

He looked again at Rhoda who was now staring at me as if I were from another planet.

"What?" I nearly screamed.

"It's about 7.8 centimeters. The biparietal diameter is about 9.5 centimeters."

"What's all that mean?"

"It means this is a baby at term, Kate or it's going to be one helluva giant. I can tell you what sex it is," he added. "You want to know?"

"Yes."

"It's a boy, Kate."

He continued shining that torch, his metaphor for the ultrasound.

"As far as I can tell, he looks like he'll be about seven, seven and a half pounds. I feel comfortable saying this is a rather healthy pregnancy, but we'd had to watch it. I just can't imagine it going much longer," he concluded and stepped back, lifting the transducer away.

I stared at the monitor for a moment and then looked at him. He took a step back from me as if he thought I might just explode and the baby would pop out of me like some science fiction creature. He had lost all his inscrutability. He was looking at me as if I were some nutcase after all.

"What is it?" I asked. What more would he tell me?

"You have to be wrong about all these dates, this insemination, Kate. I haven't seen you for nearly a year, according to our records. It's just not possible for a fetus to develop this quickly and for you to be this far along in a pregnancy. If I announced it, you'd make the cover of the *American Medical Journal*."

"Then I haven't been imagining these trimester symptoms. They're not psychosomatic. None of it is psychosomatic. When I felt what my doctor called a quickening, I was feeling the baby kick?" I asked. I needed to have him confirm it in no uncertain terms.

"Yes, I would say so, absolutely."

"And when I was having the quickening, anyone else could feel it if she wanted to feel it?"

"Most likely," he said. He looked at Rhoda. "Ask any man close to being a father. Men love putting their hands on their wives' abdomens and feeling their soon-to-be-born child move about. You can see the pride and excitement in their faces, no matter how big and strong they pretend to be. I recall it with all my children, and I'm sure Rhoda would say the same thing, right, Rhoda?"

Rhoda nodded and forced a smile but then lost it again when she looked at me. She thinks I'm a raving lunatic, I thought. Probably, they both do.

All of it, all that had happened to me, was happening to me, came rushing back. I couldn't speak. I couldn't even move. I just lay there looking at the doctor. I could see he was trying to figure out how to handle me, but I wasn't crazy. I wasn't.

"Let me speak with this doctor you've been seeing. What was her name, Aaron?"

As if to respond for me, the male fetus within kicked hard. I put my hand on my stomach and felt him kick again and again. The cold shudder that had fallen over me like a blanket of ice lifted and I felt a comfortable warmth. My cheeks were probably glowing.

"No," I said, swinging my legs off the examination table and sitting up to fix my clothes. "It's not necessary now. It won't make any difference."

"What do you mean?"

"She'll lie to you."

"What?"

"They'll all lie to you, Dr. Malisoff. Forget about it. None of that is necessary."

"Lie? Why should the doctor lie to me? What are you saying, Kate? Why isn't it necessary to get to the bottom of this?"

"I've got to go," I said. "Willy needs me at the plant. We did the big White Party, you know." I turned to Rhoda and smiled. "We're swamped with new business, business beyond anything we dreamed we'd have."

"Kate, listen to me."

"I'm sorry, Dr. Malisoff. I'm sorry I threw off your patient load here. It wasn't fair. Please apologize to each and every one of them for me."

He stood there, staring at me. So did Rhoda. The two of them actually looked quite comical to me. I smiled and opened the examination room door.

"Just send us the bill," I said. "It doesn't matter. We're rich now, very rich."

"Listen, Kate, just sit here for a while," Dr. Malisoff said stepping toward me. "I'll call Willy and . . ."

"Oh, I can't. There are so many things to do. Don't

worry about me. I'm fine now," I said. "Really. I'm fine. Thank you for helping me understand. You'll never know how much you did for me."

I walked out and closed the door on them. As I strolled down the hallway, I smiled at his receptionist and then at the patients waiting in the lobby.

"Sorry," I told them, and left the office.

I waited for the elevator and then traveled down to the parking garage. Just as I got into my car, my cell phone rang. Of course, I had expected it. I didn't even have to look at the phone to know who it was.

"Did you hear, Willy? Did he tell you all of it? Tell you it's a boy, tell you his size and his weight? He's a sure athlete in the making."

"Kate, where are you?"

"I'm in the garage at the medical center. I just got into my car."

"Wait right there. Don't start the car. You're not in a good state of mind. I don't want you driving."

"Afraid something might happen to me? To our baby?"

"Of course."

I looked around the parking garage.

"I don't see Trinity, but she's here watching over me. I'm sure of that, Willy. No need to worry. They won't let anything happen to me. They're probably very excited about it all. Who knows how often they fail and how rare someone like me really is?"

"Kate, I agree with you. None of this makes any sense. I'm sure we'll get to the bottom of it. We'll go to another specialist. Eve and I are coming for you. Just sit tight, you hear me?"

"Eve and you?" I laughed. "I never told you, Willy, but remember that first night when I saw someone with Dr. Matthews? I always had the feeling it was Eve. She doesn't sleep, you know. She's not human."

"Kate, you're talking nonsense."

"No, I'm not. I went on the Internet and checked out the story about her brother's and his family's deaths in Jackson. The police always suspected arson. They never thought it was accidental and now they've determined it was arson. They were murdered, Willy, and I think we know who did it and why they did it."

"Kate, your imagination is running away with you."

"No, it's not, Willy."

"You're just not thinking clearly. I'm sure there's an explanation for all of it. Right now, you're overwhelmed, mentally exhausted. It's all happened so fast and we've been so busy. If . . ."

"Yes, it has happened so fast. We are overwhelmed. How did we get the White Party, Willy? How did we get all this? They killed Isler, you know. That accident, that phony driver . . . they set it up, but maybe you were always aware of that. Were you, Willy?"

"What are you talking about? Jesus."

"What did you do to get it all, Willy? What did you promise them?"

"Get it? Kate, oh my God."

"Yes, oh my God."

"Listen to me. You're very upset. I understand, but you have to calm down and wait for me."

"I'm calm. I'm finally calm, actually."

"I'm getting into my car, Kate. I'm on my way. I'll come there without Eve, okay? I promise."

"They told me everything in the last phone call. They made it clear. Don't you see how it all falls into place, Willy? Dr. Matthews pushing us to use Dr. Aaron, and this Dr. Yan recommended to us by Dr. Aaron? We should have thought about all that, Willy. The fox guarding the henhouse. We should have thought about it, or I should have. You didn't want to think about it. You wanted only to build the business, and at any price, any cost."

"Keep talking to me, Kate. Accuse me of anything you like. I'll stay on the phone all the way," Willy said.

I started my car.

"Sure, I'll keep talking to you. Dr. Malisoff thinks I'm confused about time. He basically said it was physically impossible for me to be carrying a fetus this developed in this short a period. He thinks I'm a nutcase, too. Did you tell him the truth? Did he ask you when I had the insemination? Well? Did you?"

"He didn't ask."

"You're lying to me, Willy."

"I'm not lying. All he told me was I should get to you quickly and get you calmed down. He's very concerned about your current mental state."

I laughed.

"Everyone's concerned about that. I've been thinking about Janet. What do you think really happened to her, Willy? Do you want to hear what I think really happened?"

"All right, I'll listen. What?"

"She wasn't strong enough for this, Willy, this accelerated pregnancy, and all the intimidation that came along with it. I'm sure she had plenty of phone calls and who knows what else. I guess we're supposed to believe they didn't know she had a heart issue. Maybe they didn't have sophisticated enough machinery to spot that problem or maybe they didn't care. They gambled. She was expendable. They must have dozens incubating out there, tossing the sperm dice all over the country. I imagine they have no lack of his sperm."

"His sperm? Whose sperm?"

I laughed.

"Like you don't know. Who makes the deals? Who makes the promises? Who tempts and tempts until we succumb?"

"You can't really believe all that, Kate."

"Of course, I was always an ideal candidate, wasn't I? Strong, perfect health, always taking good care of myself. A perfect candidate. How did you describe me to Dr. Aaron that time, Vitamin Kate? Remember? She eats right, exercises, uses all the best skin products . . ."

"You won't believe what you're saying yourself when you calm down."

"I told you. I am calm."

I backed out of the parking space.

"You're not. If you drive off, you'll only get into trouble, Kate. Be sensible. Wait for me. I'm minutes away."

"I'll see you later, Willy. Maybe. I have no idea about my future now," I said and closed the cell phone. It rang again almost immediately, but I ignored it, turned onto the street and headed east in the general direction of our home. I really didn't know where to go.

For a moment I thought about going home, being with my parents, but the incredulity I would find on my mother's and my father's faces dissuaded me. I didn't need any more of that. Where could I go, to whom could I go where I would be believed and taken seriously?

I stopped for a traffic light. The cell phone rang again.

And then I heard someone at the passenger's side door. He had his hand on the handle and was looking in at me, the man in black. I nodded and hit the button to unlock the door. He slipped into the seat.

"Thank you," he said. He nodded at the street in front of us. "Take your second right."

I did as he asked.

"Thank God you've been able to come to your senses," he said. "Few take control of their lives the way you are doing. Most feel so helpless. I'm sorry about all the phone calls, the threats. Follow the street out. We're going to take the 10 Freeway east," he added.

"What about Trinity? What about my security?" I looked into the rearview mirror but didn't see them.

"They've been detoured," he said smiling. "Don't worry about them."

"Who are you exactly?"

"I could tell you I'm part of a secret organization with its genesis back to the period soon after Jesus wandered the desert and was tempted. In one sense I suppose that's true. We're God's policemen. Some of us are refugees from the wars worldwide; some of us are truly the saved. You'll become one of us, perhaps. Everyone has a different reaction to it all. What's ever in your nature to be, you will be. No matter what it is, at least it will be your choice. No one will be using you anymore."

I checked my rearview mirror again.

"Someone's following us I think."

He turned to look. I could see the driver's face.

"It's Eve!" I cried. She drew closer, close enough for me to see the angry, determined expression on her face as she leaned over the steering wheel to peer ahead at us.

"Accelerate. Hurry!" he told me.

I did so.

We went through a red light, but Eve had to stop because of the cross traffic.

"Turn here, quickly," he screamed. "Pull over here. I have to drive," he said the moment I had done so.

I pulled over and we switched seats. He drove off, turning down a few different streets, the tires squealing with the sharpness and speed of his turns. I looked back, but didn't see Eve.

"Don't worry," he said. "We'll lose her."

Minutes later we pulled onto a main thoroughfare and headed toward the freeway entrance. When we got onto it, he accelerated until we were going nearly 100 miles an hour.

"I don't see her," I said, looking back.

"Good.

I turned around and snapped in my seat belt. A sharp pain made me shudder and moan.

"You look very uncomfortable. He's kicking away, right?"

"Yes."

"Sure. He knows it's almost over. This is one that won't be born. Tell me, describe it quickly. I need to know everything that's happening."

"I think I'm having . . . . I don't know for sure, but it feels like contractions. I think I'm going into labor."

I moaned and then I screamed again with the pain.

"Hold on," he said. "We're almost there. You'll be all right. We'll end it before it starts. Don't you worry about that."

When we took an exit, there was another car waiting for us. It followed us onto a side street.

A few minutes later, we pulled into the driveway of what looked like an office building.

"What is this place?" I asked him.

"It's our battlefield. We always win here," he said. "Don't worry."

The second car pulled in right behind us and two women in nurse's uniforms got out to rush to me. One opened the door and the other helped me emerge. They led me to the front entrance.

The tinted windows made it look like a deserted structure, but when we entered, I saw an immaculate light red tile floor. They hurried me down a hallway to what looked like a hospital operating room. The contractions grew stronger.

"What are you going to do?" I asked one of the nurses. She looked like a woman in her fifties. She was tall with firm hands.

"We're going to end it, terminate," she said. "Perform a dilation and extraction."

"It's what they call a late-term abortion," the other nurse added. "You'll be fine."

I looked from the one woman in a nurse's outfit to the other and thought they were sisters, perhaps even twins.

They guided me to the gurney and one began to help me undress, while the other set up an IV drip.

"This will help you relax," she said, reaching for a syringe on the table beside me.

"I'm afraid," I said.

"Don't be. Everything is under control now, thanks

to you," she said, smiling. She wiped my arm with the alcohol pad and then injected me. Almost immediately, I felt myself start to drift. I didn't pass out immediately. It was as if I were leaving my body, rising slowly above it all.

I could feel them adjusting my legs, getting my feet in the stirrups.

"It will be over soon, dear," the first nurse said.

I heard a door open and, looking through what seemed to be a cloud of fog, saw the man in black now dressed in a doctor's frock step up to the table.

"Not a moment too soon," he told the nurses. "Get thee behind me!" he cried.

I thought I heard laughter followed by a horrendous howl that echoed as I descended into the darkness.

18.

Willy was waiting for me at the house. I was still in what is described as the twilight zone, vaguely aware of my surroundings and people talking, but it was all still distant. I couldn't even say who helped me to my bed. I fell asleep quickly and when I woke, it was twilight. The shadows seemed to be seeping in through the windows, crawling slowly over the walls and the floor. I felt no pain, but I did feel a numbness. When I touched my stomach, I was surprised at how flat it felt. Then I turned to my left and saw Willy sitting there, crouched over, her elbows on her knees, her head in her hands.

"Willy," I whispered. "Willy."

She lifted her head slowly to look at me.

"How do you feel, Kate?"

"Like I'm floating, drifting."

"They told me you would. It's the sedatives they gave you."

"Who?" I asked, struggling to remember everything.

"The ones who have been calling, who came for you. The Guardians, as I heard them call themselves," she said. "I'm so sorry I wasn't there for you, Kate, but by the time I arrived at Dr. Malisoff's medical building, you were gone and I had no idea which direction you had taken. You didn't answer the cell phone. I thought that you might have gone home, so I headed here."

It all began to rush back to me.

"He was waiting for me, the man in black, the one who had tried to run down Eve in front of Dr. Aaron's office. Eve was then suddenly behind us," I said. "Her face looked distorted, especially around her eyes."

"She couldn't have been behind you, Kate," Willy said softly. "She was with me. I didn't leave her behind as I had promised. I thought I might need help with you."

I just stared at her for a moment.

"I saw her," I insisted.

"Okay."

"Stop humoring me, Willy. I saw her."

"All right, Kate. All right."

"Where is she now?"

"She's gone, Kate. We talked it over and we decided it would be better if she left. I gave her a generous settlement payment. She was disappointed, but she accepted it."

"I'm glad. She was part of it, one of them."

Willy shook her head and lowered it again to her hands.

"After all that has happened, are you still going to sit there and try to convince me otherwise?"

"No," she said. "I'll admit I don't know what she knew and what she didn't about all this. I just don't think it was what you think it was and what they, the so-called Guardians, think it was."

"Really? You want to go talk to Dr. Malisoff and ask him about the fantastic pregnancy, see what he has to say? Go ahead," I said, raising my voice as high as I could. I still felt very weak.

"It's not necessary. I'm not challenging any of that. Unfortunately, we got caught up in something that was other than you think, than they think, something not less bizarre, but something else nevertheless."

"Oh really. And what would that be, Willy?"

"It was experimental, but it wasn't Rosemary's Baby, Kate."

"Experimental?"

"They're perfecting a way to accelerate fetal development."

"What are you telling me?"

"I didn't know any more about it than you did up until very recently. I thought it was that pseudocyesis thing, too, but after your ultrasound, I got on the phone immediately with Dr. Aaron and that was when she told me about the process. They were hoping it would all be over before we realized it, you realized it."

"And you believed that?"

"Yes, Kate. They have obvious difficulty getting any woman to participate in such research. Women who go through the insemination process are easier to utilize."

I stared at her.

"But that would be horrible deception and maybe could even risk the woman's life."

"Let's just be grateful that it's over and you're all right."

"I can't believe you bought that story, Willy." I turned away from her. "Maybe you want to believe it. Maybe it makes you feel better."

"I didn't do anything to put you into this situation, Kate. No matter what fantasies you create, I didn't sell my soul to anyone. What good fortune we had was just what it was, a lucky break."

"Oh, is that right? All of it comes from my fantasies, huh? Tell me this then. Why did Eve lie about what happened to her brother?"

"She didn't lie. Those investigations take time. It wasn't black and white. She found out the results just about the time you did and she's been sick over it. It was another reason why it was so difficult to let her go.

"And I don't believe this Dr. Yan was part of any conspiracy either, Kate. She was used just as we were. She accepted the referral and conducted her analysis with the same assumptions. I had her checked out. Our attorney made the inquiries for me. You can go over and see her for yourself later on. I'm sure she is just as disturbed about all this as we are."

"What about these people, the group you call or you say call themselves, the Guardians?"

"They're just a bunch of kooks, if you ask me, but I suppose if a poll were taken, more people would reveal they believe in the existence of Satan than don't. The Catholic Church certainly does. I imagine most of these people in the group are Catholic, although I don't know for sure.

"Everything else we thought about them or we would told about them appears true. They're well organized. They're determined, driven, and believe anything they do in the name of their God is okay. What's new about that?

"Eve and I were talking about all this one day and she told me that Pope Urban II, the Pope that started the Crusades, changed the penance for killing and basically declared it was acceptable to kill another individual as long as that person was not a Christian. Killing Muslims became acceptable in the eleventh century."

"It doesn't surprise me that Eve would know about that."

"Oh and that makes her Satan?"

"She was trying to discredit them."

"Please. You've got to get hold of yourself. You've got to stop this."

I turned away. The tears were building under my eyelids, rising to stream over and down my cheeks. Willy came to me and took my hand.

"I know you have gone through hell, pardon my pun. I've been thinking about starting a lawsuit."

"I could never describe this in court," I said. "I'm sure without any hard proof, everyone would think I was crazy and I don't imagine the Guardians would make for credible witnesses. Maybe we'd make the front page of the Enquirer, but nothing else."

"Exactly and those are the reasons keeping me back from doing it. All that really matters now is you get stronger, get well. I've already contacted your gynecologist and made you an appointment for next Monday so we can be sure you have no other problems, no lasting effects."

She leaned over to kiss my cheek.

"I don't expect I'll be attempting another pregnancy, Willy," I said.

"Oh, you never know. In time . . ."

"I couldn't see myself doing it."

"But you wanted a baby so much."

The tears came now. I couldn't hold them back. Yes, I did, I thought. Yes, I did.

She crawled in beside me, cradled me in her arms and kissed my hair and cheek. I closed my eyes and in the comfort and security of her embrace, fell asleep.

But I didn't sleep well, and a dream I had became so vivid I woke with a start. Willy moaned and turned over on her side. I didn't want to wake her. I didn't want to tell her what I had dreamed anyway, but the visions, the sounds, and the feelings were still so strong, it was as if I were still in the midst of it. Maybe I was walking in my sleep, but I rose and quietly slipped my feet into a pair of sandals. I was only in my nightgown, but on the way out of the bedroom, I scooped up my light blue jacket and continued through the house.

I wasn't shaking and I didn't feel weak. Somewhere, somehow, I had reached deep down into my very soul, my essence, what and who I was to draw up the strength I needed to go forward. The visions were still streaming past me, images, voices. It was too real to be imagined. It was too real to be anything but memories.

As quietly as I could, I went into the garage and got into my car. The garage door made a lot of noise going up and I thought that it might bring Willy to the door to the garage, but I backed out quickly, didn't close it, and didn't put on the headlights until I was on the street. Then I accelerated into the night. I had a long drive ahead of me, but that didn't discourage me. I was bolstered by my surge of energy and my revitalized strength. The adrenaline was flowing, I thought. I would do wondrous things.

How I found my way, I did not know. Something invisible, something instinctive pulled me along. I was more like a wild beast captured by the primeval forces that governed a species rather than an individual. It was embedded in my nature, the nature I had almost denied.

I had no idea how fast I had been driving, but in what seemed to me almost like blinking my eyes, I was coasting down the street upon which Dr. Aaron's office and home were located. I saw a good half dozen or so cars parked in front. Although the office lights were off, the house we well lit up inside. I pulled into an empty space behind the first car on my right and shut off the engine.

I got out slowly and closed the car door softly. Then I stood there for a few moments to be sure there was no one outside, no one watching, waiting.

There was a small rise in the lawn as it ran toward the front of the house. I walked through the grass and kept out of the bright areas illuminated by the lawn lights and the lanterns around the door and front windows. I drew closer, my heart thumping harder and faster with every step I took.

Suddenly, I heard the sound of the front door being opened and I rushed to get to the side of the house and into the shadows. When the door was fully opened, I heard music and laughter. The voice of whoever was stepping out seemed familiar when I heard him say good night. I waited for him to close the door and continue down the front steps and sidewalk. As soon as I saw him, I gasped and nearly gave myself away.

It was Sterling Plunkett, alive and well. He paused for a moment to light a cigarette. I thought he gazed in my direction and I held my breath in anticipation of being discovered, but he put his lighter into his pocket and continued down to one of the cars. I watched him get in, start it up, and drive off.

Had I crossed into the Valley of Death or was there some other explanation?

Instead of walking toward the front, I turned to my right and headed for a lighted window. Carefully, I leaned forward and peered through the opened shutters. There, gathered around a bassinet, were Eve Stoner, Trinity, Kerry Barnes, Dr. Aaron, Dr. Matthews, and Eve's sister Bea. They were all looking down and smiling.

Other people came into the room, men in suits and ties, beautiful women, handsome young men, all dressed fashionably. Behind them came the man dressed in black. How could he be here? These people were supposed to be the enemy.

The group parted to let him draw closer to the bassinet. He reached in and lifted the baby out. He didn't cradle the infant in his arms, but instead raised him above his head. No one spoke. Then they all lowered their heads and began to chant what I knew to be the Lord's Prayer.

But backwards!

"Evil from us deliver but temptation into not us lead and us against trespass that them forgive we as . . ."

They broke into laughter, and then he passed the baby to Dr. Matthews, who kissed his face and passed him on to Dr. Aaron, who did the same. The baby was circulated among them all and never cried. Eve took him last, kissed him, and returned him to the bassinet.

They congratulated each other and slowly left the room, closing the door behind them.

My baby, I thought. He's my baby.

There was no dilation and extraction.

I was never being protected from evil, nor was the world. The Guardians belonged to Satan.

I started to turn away, when I heard the baby's cry. It drew me back to the window.

I waited to see who would return.

The baby cried on, but the music was louder and the laughter and celebration in the living room was in high swing. No one heard.

The baby wailed. Surely he's hungry, I thought. Why didn't they have a nurse, someone?

I pressed on the window and with ease it went up. Pushing away the shutters, I crawled into the room and went to the bassinet. The baby either saw me or sensed me and immediately stopped crying, its small arms swinging up and down. I felt this terrific circular warmth under my breasts, this longing for the baby's lips on my nipple. It was a drive, a force, a desire beyond anything I had ever felt or imagined feeling.

I pulled my right arm out of my jacket and lowered my nightgown. Then I carefully reached in and lifted him to me. Hungrily, he suckled at my breast, and the feeling that ran through me as he did so was overwhelming, sexual and ecstatic. It filled me with the greatest sense of completeness I could ever imagine.

It took me back to my dreams of birthing, the dreams that used to annoy Willy. It was truly as if a prophecy had come true and I could resist it no more than I could resist the urge to survive, to defy Death. I was like any other living creature struggling to live, to escape any threat, any predator. I had a revelation. With my baby beside me, part of me, I was invulnerable. Nothing could ever harm me; nothing could keep us apart.

The music grew even louder and the laughter longer and louder as well. It sounded like a raucous bacchanalia, and when I opened the door slightly to look out, I saw them, naked, coupling, drinking, passing each other around like hors d'oeuvres on a silver tray, breasts to lips, hips hugging and gyrating, bodies entwined on sofas, chairs, even on the floor. They were quite taken and occupied with each other. No one looked my way.

I closed the door softly.

My baby continued to feed.

With great care, I moved to the open window and slipped my legs over the sill. For a moment I sat there waiting to see if there was anyone outside. It was dark and quiet. I dropped gracefully to the ground, my baby never pausing in his feeding. I didn't run. I walked slowly down the lawn to my car. Finally, he pulled away from my nipple. I burped him and then opened the car door and set him softly on the seat beside me.

I started the engine and pulled away from the curb to turn into another driveway and then back out. As I drove past Dr. Aaron's office and house, I saw the front door opening. My heart skipped and fluttered. I accelerated, but looked back through the rearview mirror.

A group of them had stepped out, still naked, still holding each other.

They were looking my way.

I made a turn and they were gone from sight as was I was gone from theirs.

My baby slept all the way home.

The garage door was still open and Willy was still asleep when I arrived.

The baby nestled comfortably in my arms and huddled against me as I sprawled out beside Willy. She moaned as if in a dream of her own, but she didn't awaken.

The three of us slept together just as I had envisioned so many times.

Epilogue

"How can you be sure he is your baby?" Willy wanted to know.

It was a logical question, but it wasn't something easily explained to someone who had never been pregnant, never become a mother.

"Oh, I know," I said. "I'm sure. There is no question. I know with my very being, body and soul."

"Kate, you might very well have kidnaped another mother's child. You can't keep the baby."

"They saw me leave, Willy. They saw me drive away and by now they know the baby is missing, right? Why aren't there police knocking at our door?"

She couldn't answer, but I saw she was very nervous. Finally, she went into another room and called Dr. Aaron. She thought I wasn't listening but I was at the door, peering in at her.

"I don't understand, Dr. Aaron. These people told me the baby had been aborted."

She listened.

"How long did you know your security had someone on the inside?"

She listened and nodded.

"Yes, I can understand that, but when did you retrieve the infant?"

She shrugged as if Dr. Aaron could see her.

"So, why wouldn't they have come to us to tell us?"

She listened and said, "I see. Yes. But if the child is proof of the validity of your research . . .

"I understand. Of course. No, I doubt she would ever surrender the baby now. Whatever your reasons, Dr. Aaron, I have a good mind to sue you or expose you.

"Lucky for you," she added after Dr. Aaron's response. She hung up without saying goodbye. I saw her just sit there staring. The baby started to cry and I returned to him.

When Willy stepped into the bedroom, I looked up smiling and said, "We have so much shopping to do."

She nodded. It was Sunday. The plant was closed. I could see the fear in her face. Our roles had been reversed. I was filled with a sense of inner strength, a contentment and power, and she was the one trembling.

"Don't worry," I said. "It will be all right. Everything will be all right now."

She looked at me with surprise, but also with the realization that this was to be, that nothing would prevent it.

It wasn't difficult to create a plausible story. After all, no one but Dr. Matthews, Dr. Aaron, and Eve knew how long ago I had been inseminated. Dr. Malisoff accepted that I had been close to a mental breakdown and very confused. He could see no other possible explanation for the baby reaching term. Furthermore, when we took the baby in for him to examine, he found him to be in perfect health and as alert and developed as infants even somewhat older.

Right before we went to the doctor, Willy and I discussed what name we would give the baby. We ran through family names and went on the Internet to look at what was popular. We still couldn't decide. Finally, I said, "We should call him Adam for so many reasons. I'm sure it would please Eve."

Willy wasn't pleased, but in the end, she agreed. We also agreed to use my last name for him. I offered to use hers, but she thought mine sounded better with Adam. I was afraid she was trying to create some distance between herself and the baby, but even if that was so, in time that fear dissolved. She turned out to be more doting than I was and far more protective of him. No matter what he did, she found an excuse or a rationalization. Adam could do no wrong in her eyes.

Despite finding my pregnancy and birthing incredulous, my parents became doting grandparents as well. They flooded our home with gifts and sought any opportunity they could to visit or have us visit them. As I had been told, a child does bind a family, mend fences, and thicken the blood ties. My relationship with my brother and his family even warmed.

One late May day three years after I had brought

Adam home, Willy and I were relaxing at our pool and watching him explore the yard, challenging birds, hunting down different insects as he made his way over the grass. He was as firm and muscular as Willy had hoped he would be. I could see her envisioning all the athletic training she would give him. She had no fear about his being competitive or aggressive.

I had never told her exactly what I had seen at Dr. Aaron's home. All she knew was, I had found the baby there and brought him home. I was afraid that she would think I had even gone farther off the deep end, or she would believe every word and not want to go near Adam.

I knew she wondered if I still harbored what she called my fantastic beliefs.

"Tell me something, Kate," she said as a cloud passing over the sun dragged its shadow over Adam, following him on his journey toward the casita.

"What?"

"Are you ever afraid?"

"Of what?"

"Of him?"

I started to smile and then stopped.

"No," I said with as much confidence as I could muster.

"Why not? You don't think he's inherited evil?"

"Not any more than any of us," I replied, and she laughed.

"Seriously," she said. "No more of those nightmares, no more of those dreams?"

"It doesn't matter what comes. A mother's love is more powerful," I said. "It can defeat it all." She started to laugh at me and then stopped.

"You really believe that?"

"Of course I do."

"Not the power of the Almighty? Just the power of a mother's love?"

"Yes."

"Sounds pretty vain, Kate, pretty arrogant. Isn't pride Satan's favorite sin?"

"I'll risk it. For him," I said.

Willy laughed again, but it was a thinner, more nervous laugh.

And Adam, who had reached the casita, pulled himself up to look in the window. He stood there, gazing through the glass as if there was something truly wondrous inside.

Then he turned slowly to look our way.

And in his face I saw that I had truly gone too far to be saved.

Edge of your seat thrills from Pocket Books!

Choke Point
A Simon Leonidovich Novel
Jay MacLarty
The courier is back in the crosshairs—and the only way out
is getting smaller with each passing second…

Prisoner of Memory
An Eve Diamond Novel
Denise Hamilton
Reporter Eve Diamond is caught in the cross-fire between
old and new worlds when a Russian émigré's son is viciously
murdered.

Orbit
John J. Nance
Trapped miles above the earth, one man's once-in-lifetime
chance for adventure becomes a global fight for survival.

18 Seconds
George D. Shuman
One woman has the gift to see the last 18 seconds of a
person's life…but is it enough to catch a vicious killer?

Holy Terror
Richard Marcinko with Jim DeFelice
Only the Rogue Warrior® can stop a terrorist plot to turn
the Vatican into the world's largest Roman candle.

Available wherever books are
sold or at www.simonsays.com.

16283

Pulse-pounding excitement from Pocket Books!

Prayers for the Assassin
Robert Ferrigno

"I pledge allegiance to the flag…of the Islamic Republic
of America…."

Seven Deadly Wonders
Matthew Reilly

A lost ancient relic. A flight for ultimate power. The hunt is
on—and only the winner survives.

Deception Plan
Patrick A. Davis

Probing the wreckage of a U-2 spy plane, a military investigator
uncovers the shocking truth—about his own past.

The Wall
Jeff Long

A half-mile up the sunlit walls of Yosemite, a rope breaks,
a young woman plunges to her death…and the rescue
from hell begins.

The Triangle Conspiracy
David Kent

Faith Kelly's latest case leads her into a web of lies,
conspiracy…and murder.

POCKET BOOKS
A Division of Simon & Schuster
A CBS COMPANY

POCKET STAR BOOKS
A Division of Simon & Schuster
A CBS COMPANY

Available wherever books are
sold or at www.simonsays.com.

15608

Not sure what to read next?

Visit Pocket Books online at
www.simonsays.com

Reading suggestions for
you and your reading group
New release news
Author appearances
Online chats with your favorite writers
Special offers
Order books online
And much, much more!

13456

www.ingramcontent.com/pod-product-compliance
Lightning Source LLC
Chambersburg PA
CBHW011508100726

47900CB00009B/2643